Beth sat forward, clasping her hands before her on the desk. Her knuckles turned white. "How long were you watching my son?"

Oliver lowered himself to the edge of a chair. It creaked slightly and he determined it should be replaced. "The proper study of a subject can take a moment or a lifetime."

Elizabeth shook her head. "For all your brilliance you still cannot answer a direct question simply. I ask again, what brings you to here?"

He met her gaze, still struggling to see her as the mother of Turner's child. "The boy escaped my notice."

She licked her bottom lip and then splayed her bare fingers over the desk surface. Oliver noticed the absence of a wedding band on her left hand and wondered when and why she had stopped wearing it when she had proudly displayed one on her delicate fingers a dozen years before.

Her fingers tapped. "And how exactly did he come to your notice?"

Oliver would not admit how. To do so would confirm that he was, at times, unobservant. "Where did you walk to today?"

Her brows rose. "Were you watching us?"

Heather Boyd

BESTSELLING AUTHOR

Guarding the Spoils

Wild Randalls

3

WILD RANDALLS SERIES

BOOK 1: ENGAGING THE ENEMY (LEOPOLD AND MERCY)
BOOK 2: FORSAKING THE PRIZE (TOBIAS AND BLYTHE)
BOOK 3: GUARDING THE SPOILS (OLIVER AND ELIZABETH)
BOOK 4: HUNTING THE HERO (CONSTANTINE AND ROSEMARY)

Dedication

———◆———

For Dad
Thank you for trusting me to make my own decisions and only
stepping in when I need you most. You taught me so much
without saying a word. Love you dad!

Chapter One

---◆---

When Oliver Randall had been very young, he'd believed heaven could only be found in the thirty-feet-square library of Romsey Abbey. At seventeen and wrenched from his studies, he'd been assured he'd never see that library again and the long, lonely years after proved that heaven would be denied him. At eight and twenty, and thanks to his younger brother Tobias's daring rescue two weeks prior, he'd thought he would be granted his reward. Yet once he'd stood within Romsey library's hushed confines, filled with books of every sort and description, he'd acknowledged that this place was merely a stepping stone on the path to adventure.

"Have you taken leave of your senses?"

Oliver set the polished wood stepladder against the uppermost shelf edge and scaled the heights of literature, prose, and radical thought in search of entertainment. "They are all still there as far as I can tell, Leopold."

"Damn it, Oliver. Come down at once before you break your neck," his elder brother demanded.

Oliver ran his fingers over the spines of the books closest. So many bright minds had been granted the freedom to live and experience the world as they saw fit while he had been condemned to the never-ending repetition of days and years with only the wonders of nature's transitions outside his window to provide any sort of adventure. "Given the circumstances I've endured at the duke's hands these past years, I do not find your reference to my sanity particularly amusing. I'll come down when I'm ready and not a moment before."

Oliver had only recently returned to the family fold, to the Romsey Estate and the sweet freedom of personal liberty. Leopold did not understand that Oliver looked for adventure at every opportunity now, even if it was merely helping himself to a second corner of toast and strawberry jam at breakfast or exploring a new point of view. He was plotting his biggest escapade yet—a grand tour of the known world. A world far away from this library.

He plucked three volumes from the shelves at random—Greek, Italian, and French—and descended to the main floor. Just enough light reading to last him until morning. Unlike others in his family, he enjoyed reading at all hours of the day and night. He devoured books as quickly as his younger brother demolished a well-roasted leg of lamb at dinner. The years without such precious volumes were a gaping pit of boredom he needed to fill.

"Everyone is waiting on you to go into dinner. Whatever you are doing can wait at least two hours."

Oliver set two of the books beside the maps of the continent he'd appropriated for his preparations and settled in his favorite chair. "I'll eat later. A tray in my room, perhaps."

As he was about to open his first selection, Leopold snatched the book from his hands. "You will not return to the patterns of your youth. I will not indulge your obsessions as Mama did. We dine together each night and if I have to drag you there and strap you into a chair to accomplish that feat, I certainly will."

Oliver assessed his brother's mood. Not much had changed in Leopold's demeanor since they were young lads on the cusp of manhood. Bossy. Opinionated. Stubborn. Leopold would make a fuss and bluster until Oliver capitulated. He'd never enjoy one fresh new word these books offered in peace at this rate. He resigned himself to the inevitable. He would have to adjust his daily schedule to include this unnecessary interruption of his study until he departed England. Hopefully, word would come soon concerning a ship bound for his destination and save him from excessive sentimentality. "Very well. No need for threats of violence."

Leopold shook his head. "I never really understood how much trouble you must have been for Mama to manage when Father was away. Families eat together."

"If you insist." Oliver stood and drew on his tailcoat. "But I should point out that our definitions of family differ considerably. You're not even married to the duchess. Nor is Tobias married to Lady Venables. Hardly a family affair."

A quick grin crossed Leopold's usually serious face. "All in good time. The wedding date is set. Hurry up now."

Oliver couldn't quite decide why his brother's happiness bothered him so much. Lust and love were two concepts he had never been comfortable with. It was so very easy to confuse the former for the latter and he'd given up trying to tell them apart. Emotions muddled logical thought and made men act irrationally. His brothers claimed to love their future wives, but how did one prove it wasn't merely obsessive lust? Perhaps the source of his frustration was that Oliver had planned to leave England with his brothers and both of them were determined to remain behind. He hadn't allowed for their stubbornness. He hadn't even considered they'd be on the brink of marrying. But two more smitten fools couldn't be found in the county. It was impossible to reconcile the brothers he remembered with the men he spoke to now.

As they crossed the entrance hall, Eamon Murphy, his old friend and the new butler of Romsey Abbey, appeared before them, holding a little silver tray with a note on top. He grinned at Leopold. "Congratulations, Mr. Randall. I thought he'd give you so much more trouble tonight."

"Threats worked well in this instance," Leopold murmured as he took the note and read it.

"Good to see you up and around again, sir," Eamon said to Oliver.

Oliver's brow rose beyond his power to control it. "Sir?"

"Well, I'm the butler of Romsey now. Must observe the proprieties."

Oliver had known Eamon since they'd been young lads and considered him as much a part of his family as his brothers. Watching Eamon bow and scrape as if they were unequal sat ill with him. "Then you should leave off flirting with the upstairs maid and let her get on with her duties in a timely fashion instead of waylaying her on the stairs," he teased.

Eamon's face turned a fiery shade of red, but he did not fire back with the expected cocky retort. The lack of response disappointed Oliver immensely. He was fast losing his patience for this nonsense.

Leopold cleared his throat. "The duchess has no objections to her male servants flirting with the female ones provided there will be a marriage ceremony at the end."

At Eamon's panicked expression, Oliver raised a brow. "Someone must remind me what a proper courtship entails these days. I am sure I have a different understanding of how a man may behave around an unmarried woman."

"If you'll excuse me, sirs," Eamon said quickly. "I should be getting back to my duties."

He fled back the way he'd come without looking back.

Leopold gave Oliver a look that suggested he'd misbehaved. "That was cruel. Eamon will do the right thing in the end."

What was cruel was losing a friendship so completely that Eamon no longer replied to a ribbing as he once would have done. "I found it mildly enjoyable, actually. Consider it his punishment for insisting I stay abed so long."

"Those were my orders," Leopold said quietly. "You were very weak when you returned. You must rest in order to recover your full strength."

Oliver frowned. "You do like to throw your weight around, but if memory serves, Eamon never used to follow your orders so precisely in the past. He was my friend, not your lapdog."

Leopold shrugged. "Things are different now."

Things were *too* different for Oliver's taste. He glanced at the note. "News."

Leopold scowled and crumpled the paper. "Nothing yet."

For a small moment, Oliver had hoped for news of their sister, Rosemary, and her likely location. Her disappearance was an irritating puzzle he couldn't solve.

Reluctantly, he followed Leopold into the drawing room where the ladies and his younger brother, Tobias, waited. He bowed to the duchess but kept his distance. The habits of old were hard to break. In his mind, the Duchess of Romsey was a person to avoid. Her younger sister, however, was fast becoming one of his favorite people. One did not snub a woman such as Lady Venables. Blythe might be a stickler for the proprieties, but she was his younger brother's future wife and she had befriended him when his identity hadn't yet been revealed, which had forever elevated her status to that of an angel. He bowed. "My lady."

"Sir, I am sorry we dragged you from your studies." She spoke with a wry twist to her lips and he concluded she was not sorry to see him outside the library at all.

He smiled at the lie. "Think nothing of it."

Tobias jumped to his feet and set his arm around Blythe's waist. "Well, it's damn shoddy. A man could waste away to nothing at this rate."

When Tobias leaned down to press a quick, impudent kiss to her cheek, Oliver turned away. He didn't want to make Blythe uncomfortable by noticing the inevitable blush that would grace her cheeks in a few moments. His brother delighted in embarrassing his future wife. Or perhaps he sought to proclaim the lady as his. Tobias had no cause for concern in that regard. It was very clear to anyone who observed Blythe properly that her mind was turned in one direction only. She strove to make his brother a gentleman and the center of her world.

When Leopold's elbow connected with his arm, reminding Oliver that he had one more person to greet, he faced the last lady in the room and bowed.

Blythe's companion was a face from his past and an uncomfortable presence within the abbey. Miss Elizabeth Jennings, or rather Mrs. Turner now, had been his sister's interruptive, giggling conspirator once. Now a widow, she did not giggle as much but she was just as lovely to behold. She dipped a graceful curtsy that allowed Oliver a tantalizing glimpse of the top of her breasts before she rose again. "Mr. Randall."

As her greeting encouraged no further words on his part, Oliver stepped back. He never knew what to say to the widow, not even when she'd been young and paying social calls on his mother. The complexities of inane conversation still escaped him, but he was well aware that he always did or said something wrong. To avoid misunderstandings, he preferred to remain silent around women but that did not stop him wishing that those breasts could be explored and examined. From a distance he judged them a perfect fit for his hand.

"Dinner is served, Your Grace," Eamon Murphy intoned

importantly from the doorway.

"Very good." The duchess hooked her arm through his and steered Oliver toward the dining room. "No chance of escape," she murmured for his ears alone.

"I wouldn't dream of it, Your Grace." He paused at the doorway, noting that the table had shrunk considerably in size from yesterday. At least they wouldn't have to shout for this meal. "May I compliment you on the rearrangement of the room?"

"Yes, it is very snug and much more comfortable." She beamed. "But you must compliment Mrs. Turner. Such a treasure. She thought the family would be more content with a smaller setting and made sure to organize everything."

He nodded and considered what response to make. Elizabeth was likely at the end of the procession into dinner and wouldn't hear his response. He glanced over his shoulder as he held out a chair for the duchess and saw Elizabeth on Tobias's arm, laughing at something he said. When she noticed his interest, her eyes fell and her smile slipped from her face. It wasn't the first time his scrutiny had produced a similar effect and yet he was disappointed. Had his incarceration changed him so much that he couldn't be looked upon with ease?

The duchess laughed. "Oh, do stop looking so grim. It is just a conversation."

Self-conscious, Oliver smoothed his graying hair and strove to put it from his mind. He couldn't help that he looked a great deal older than his eight and twenty years. "Forgive me, Your Grace. I was unaware I was making any particular face. I'll stop immediately."

Gooseflesh swept his skin but he strove to ignore the uncomfortable sensation as he took his place, a seat beside Elizabeth. Talk resumed among the couples, leaving only Elizabeth and himself silent. After a moment, she leaned slightly in his direction. "I can see you would rather be elsewhere."

"I cannot deny it. They say the hot-springs baths of Bagno Vignoni can cure a man of anything."

Her eyes widened. "Are you unwell, sir? You've only to say so and return to rest."

"I am fine," he assured her, rather pleased by her concern. "I suppose it is impossible to regain my looks."

"Your looks are not in doubt." Her breath caught and when he met her gaze a blush was climbing her cheeks. She glanced down at her hands that were twisting in her lap. "Where is Bagno Vinoni?"

"Italy."

"Ah." Silence fell between them again and she did not ask another question about his travels. Everyone at Romsey was the same; no one cared where he might go, only expressing the hope that he would not. Couldn't they see the possibilities for adventure? There was so much more to the world than Romsey Abbey.

As he glanced around the table, the duchess caught his eye. "The fourth duchess of Romsey thought very highly of you, Oliver. Did you know that?"

Oliver blinked. "I wasn't aware that I had inspired such an opinion in Her Grace."

"I have her journal. You're mentioned several times. My husband never spoke of her, but I find her journal observations fascinating. What was she like?"

"Terrifying," Tobias chimed in.

"Stern," Leopold added. "I cannot remember if I ever saw her smile."

Oliver considered. "Her Grace was a formidable woman. After all, she was a distant cousin to the king and was, in my opinion, quite intelligent. It was she who encouraged the construction of the stables and other improvements to such a grand style."

"I thought the old duke did that," Leopold said, eyebrows rising.

"No, that was not the case." Oliver shook his head. "She was great friends with many of the notable architects of the time and consulted with them extensively prior to construction. In fact, the most remarkable features of Romsey Abbey were brought about in no small part by the influence of the past duchess."

Her Grace set her elbow to the table, chin resting in her palm in a manner that no prior duchess of Romsey would have dreamed to do and sighed heavily. "It seems I am quite a failure as a duchess. There are no stone edifices erected simply because I decreed it be so."

She laughed suddenly, merry, for no reason Oliver could detect. It was this very changeability that flummoxed him. If she would just remain the remote Duchess of Romsey as she was supposed to be then he would have a chance to understand her better. Yet she surprised him at every turn. It was a wonder that his stern elder brother remained under her spell.

Across the table, Leopold grinned. "There is still time for you to leave your mark, my love."

The pair continued to gaze at each other until Elizabeth cleared her throat. "The event may not be cast in stone, Your Grace, but from what I understand reuniting the Randalls under this roof is no small achievement."

"Well said, Beth." Tobias laughed. "Who'd imagine the disavowed sitting down to dine here together?"

"I only did what was right," Her Grace argued.

"And that is something the other duchess's could not accomplish," Oliver added. "There has been discord within the Randalls for centuries." He knew the family history quite well, thanks to his ability to remember everything he was told or saw with his own eyes.

"Well, that is certainly behind us now," the duchess insisted, laying her hand upon Leopold's. "We shall all be very happy together for many years to come, I'm sure."

A ripple of unease flooded Oliver. He wished she would not profess to know the future as it related to him. He would be gone soon. He could never be happy here. As he opened his mouth to say so, Elizabeth's hand slid sideways and pressed against his thigh, efficiently silencing his protest.

"How goes the improvements, Mr. Randall?" She asked her question firmly without sparing him a single glance. "Is everything working out with the new farmhands as you hoped?"

Oliver's leg remembered her touch far longer than was good for him. As the discussion progressed, he studied his dinner companion, impressed by her skill at steering conversation away from an emotional subject. Her pale blue eyes were fixed on Leopold, silently encouraging him to speak of estate matters, and did not veer once in his direction no matter how long he observed her.

While his brother spoke so expansively of crops and likely yields, Oliver resumed his meal in silence, listening with half an ear, discontent with the small, never-ending concerns that filled his brother's days yet aware of the woman at his left. She puzzled him immensely. If he didn't know better, he'd believe that she'd used her allure to tie his tongue on purpose.

"What do you think, Oliver?"

He raised his head and met Blythe's gaze. "Forgive me. I wasn't paying attention just then," he admitted honestly.

Her brows rose. "As I thought. You and I, sir, need to have a little chat very soon."

Tobias laughed. "Now you've done it, Ollie."

Oliver had respected Blythe's opinion from the moment they met, but he was in no way intimidated by her. "I cannot imagine what you hope to gain by such a candid discussion but if you feel compelled to lecture me, then by all means, you may do your worst at your earliest convenience."

"Oliver," Elizabeth hissed.

He slid his glance sideways, face warming at her rare use of his given name. He wanted to hear it again. "I beg your pardon."

A frown line formed on Elizabeth's brow. "Nothing."

When Oliver glanced back across the table, Blythe's lips had pressed together in a tight line. Blythe might not like it, but he wouldn't be taken to task over the dinner table. She said nothing, so Oliver returned his attention to the meal and stayed silent until the end.

Elizabeth stood as the other women rose; her hand brushed his coat sleeve lightly. "You hurt Lady Venables's feelings," she said softly, blue eyes flickering to his face, disappointment clear in her gaze. "Apologize to her."

He remained on his feet until the ladies had swept out in a rustle of silk and animated chatter and then sank into his chair again. Yet he couldn't work out what he should apologize for. *They* had disturbed him. He would have happily remained apart in the library but he'd been given no choice. And now he had to remain here for at least another half hour, drinking and discussing the estate yet again.

Leopold handed around glasses of port. "I am always amazed that someone with your intelligence, Oliver, could irritate almost every person they meet."

Tobias grinned. "Imagine the damage he will do on the continent."

"Please, I'm trying not to picture that." Leopold sat forward. "Are you sure you must go? We've only just got you back."

A brief rush of heat swept his skin again. Devil take it!

Perhaps he was not yet fully recovered from his ordeal. A light sweat broke out over his skin, and he pushed the port away untouched. He could not risk missing his ship because he had sickened. "Are you sure you shouldn't just come with me," he countered as he steadied himself against the table.

"I need to stay with Edwin," Leopold said immediately. "I would never be easy to leave him behind."

Oliver frowned. Leopold's strong feelings for the child baffled him. He'd only known the duke for a short time. What difference might another year or two make?

Tobias lifted his feet and set his heels to the edge of the table. "Blythe would never forgive me if I left her behind and I have no intention of exposing her to the dangers beyond England's borders. Honestly, I'm not keen on facing them again myself. Life is much better here than away."

When Leopold nodded his agreement, Oliver stood and stared around him, irritated beyond belief. They would never yield and he should stop expecting them to fall in with his plans. "Then I go alone and from now on you pair can keep your opinions to yourself."

Tobias, ever the peacemaker, leapt to his feet and laid a hand on Oliver's shoulder. "Do not be cross with us."

Oliver shrugged off the weight of Tobias's grasp and faced them. "I am not cross. Only disappointed. You are each determined to remain leashed to the estate and the past. I will not."

Tobias's smile dimmed. "Can you not wait for news of Rosemary? The advertisements have been published in the *Times* and she will want to see you."

Oliver shook his head, ignoring the hurt forming in his younger brother's eyes. "Rosemary will understand my restlessness and I am sure you can write to me of her triumphant return when I'm settled in Rome."

Rome, with her classical ruins and spluttering volcano, was his ultimate destination. The thought of seeing both had kept him alive. They didn't understand. Without those marvels to explore before him, he had no reason to exist.

Chapter Two

◆

"**I** swear that man is impossible!"

Beth Turner didn't have to raise her head from her embroidery to understand exactly which gentleman Lady Venables referred to. In her experience, Oliver Randall had a profoundly unsettling effect on everyone he met and he'd been in fine form during dinner. Perhaps it was how his deep brown eyes stared through a person or how he paused so long before making any response. Beth had become accustomed to the way Oliver judiciously weighed his answers before speaking long ago. He never said what was on his mind without due consideration and inner debate. But neither the duchess nor the countess had grown used to his ways yet.

"Do not distress yourself, my lady," Beth soothed. "At least Oliver is well enough to come down now."

The countess continued to pace, moving behind Beth's chair and occasionally tapping the carved wood. "Well, it is very annoying. Attending dinner and being agreeable enough to converse is hardly considered a chore in civilized circles. How does he imagine he'll get on? Does he plan to speak to no one, or just carelessly offend them all?"

Beth pressed her lips together to cover an unwise response. What went on within the Randall family was none of her concern. She shouldn't interfere even if she had an idea of how to head off future discord. But it would be best if they reconciled to the fact that Oliver Randall was incapable of doing exactly as he pleased and damn the consequences.

The duchess caught her sister's hand, forcing her to cease her pacing. "Blythe, dear, do stop fretting about him."

The calmly spoken words gave Beth hope that they would move on to another topic quickly. One more suited to her immediate needs.

The countess dropped into a chair and picked up a fan, idly waving it before her face. "Yes, well, I suppose you are correct. I shouldn't vex myself."

The duchess's eyes narrowed. "What was Oliver's disposition like before, Mrs. Turner? Did you know him well? Is he much changed by his time in Skepington?"

Pain caught Beth unaware. When she was young and unmarried, she'd thought she had known his character best of all the gentlemen she'd met. But she'd fooled herself quite thoroughly. She pulled her stitch tight before answering and smoothed out the shirt she was mending for her son. "Not well, but he is little changed from what I remember."

Lady Venables's fan snapped shut. "And Mrs. Randall put up with his rudeness without a word of protest?"

A smile pulled at Beth's lips at the memory of the late Mrs. Jane Randall, furious over a birthday dinner ruined because of Oliver's tardiness. Mrs. Randall had possessed quite the temper when pressed beyond endurance. "I don't think that statement is entirely accurate. They did each inherit more than a passing amount of her character."

The duchess sighed. "I do wish I could have met her. From all I hear she was an outstanding woman."

Beth's smiled dimmed as she returned to her needlework. "She was wonderful."

"Tobias says much the same," Lady Venables murmured. "Mercy, when will you send invitations for the wedding?"

Beth's attention was drawn to the mantel clock and she counted the minutes since their arrival. Although she strained to hear, she detected no sound of approaching servants. That could only be in her favor.

The duchess groaned. "Very soon. It all depends, of course, on securing a reliable and efficient housekeeper. I cannot invite anyone without filling the position."

The sisters exchanged a look full of understanding and Beth dropped her gaze to her work, stomach churning into knots. If all went well, she hoped she would be the housekeeper of Romsey when the wedding date came around.

The countess stood suddenly and jerked the bell repeatedly. "Have you had any likely candidates for the position yet?"

"A few." Her Grace let out an undignified huff and flopped back into her chair. "It seems finding just the right person on short notice was an impossible dream. Everyone we have interviewed has not suited my needs. If not for Mrs. Turner's assistance these past weeks, I am sure the abbey would have fallen into complete disarray."

Beth steadied her nerves. She shouldn't be ecstatic that the tea was so late in arriving, but that did work in her favor. This lapse could only strengthen the proposition she would make to the duchess about the housekeeper's role. The new servants were still finding their feet and required someone competent to guide them.

So far, Beth had enjoyed the challenges she'd met assisting the duchess in running the abbey. She would like to continue on a permanent basis. Beth set her needlework aside, heart beating faster. "Thank you, Your Grace. Perhaps I can offer a suggestion with regard to the vacant housekeeper position."

The duchess met her gaze directly, appearing eager to have all her problems solved with as little disruption to her life as possible. "You have my complete attention, my dear," she said.

"I should like to suggest myself as the new housekeeper of Romsey Abbey," Beth said boldly, hoping she was not about to be laughed at.

The duchess's mouth fell open. Silence held for a long, anxious moment. "Absolutely not," she cried out eventually.

"No. Never." Lady Venables agreed. "The situation is not so desperate as all that."

Beth clenched her hands together. "I have been giving the matter a good deal of thought and it seems the perfect solution to all our problems. The duchess requires a competent woman to run her house and servants and I need the security of a secure position for my son. Surely you can see the sense of it. Small matters, such as delivering tea after dinner, are a regular part of your routine and there is no reason for mistakes of that kind."

The duchess closed her eyes. "I see the sense in having a woman I trust run my house. However, if you were to assume such a position then your circumstances and status would change considerably."

Beth frowned, confused. "You are pleased with my assistance so far, yet you do not wish me to continue?"

Lady Venables moved to sit at Beth's side. "What my sister is trying, and failing, to delicately point out is that if you became housekeeper of Romsey you could not sit with us in the evenings."

"Or participate in outings with Edwin," the duchess added urgently, as if that loss was the ultimate horror. "You would have to stay behind when we go to London next season and could not enjoy the company of the guests invited for the wedding."

"Forgive me, Your Grace, but you forget that I have not lived in luxury my whole life. In fact, living here is as idle as I have ever been. It is true that the few outings with the young duke have been enjoyable treats. My son, George, has also relished the additional comforts afforded living here, particularly the library. But I'm sure you can understand my anxiety that my arrangement with Lady Venables is coming to an end." Beth smiled a little sadly. "I don't imagine Lady Venables will need my company once she becomes Mrs. Tobias Randall and moves to Harrowdale."

The one thing Beth wanted in particular was to be settled with the security of a stable position and roof over her son's head. She most certainly didn't want to be a burden or in the way of a pair of ardent newlyweds.

Her employer had the grace to appear a little guilty. "Mercy and I have been discussing what's best to do for you, too."

Panic threatened. Had they decided she was no longer needed already? Beth pressed her knees together and folded George's shirt over them, desperately trying to control her fear. Securing another position, particularly during the winter months, would be difficult in the extreme. She had not saved nearly enough funds to stand on her own two feet again and there was George to consider, too. She needed the housekeeper position to support her small family.

"If you feel the position is beyond my abilities, I assure you I would seek Mrs. Finch's advice when needed," she added quickly. Lady Venables housekeeper, Mrs. Finch, had been managing both Romsey Abbey and the smaller estate of Harrowdale without complaint since the previous housekeeper had fled into the night along with half the indoor staff last month.

But of late, Mrs. Finch had mentioned a growing tiredness and pain in her knees. She shouldn't be asked to continue for much longer at Romsey with its many stairs. The smaller house at Harrowdale suited her age and stamina far better. Beth was still young and the stairs didn't bother her. She would work hard to become worthy of the position, but she had to convince the duchess to let her try, first.

"I'll need to think about it," Her Grace murmured, "and discuss the matter with Leopold at length."

Beth gripped the shirt. "Of course."

The clock chimed the hour and Beth risked a quick glance at it again. It really was getting late for the tea to arrive. George would be already tucked up in bed, waiting for her to say goodnight, if he hadn't fallen asleep already. "If I may suggest, I should like to pay a visit to the kitchens to determine what the delay may be."

"Thank you, Mrs. Turner," Lady Venables agreed with a warmer smile. "That would be much appreciated. I cannot imagine what could be keeping them."

Beth stood on shaky legs and quickly dipped a curtsy. "I will be back in a moment."

The duchess held up her hand. "After you have sorted out the kitchen and staff, we will completely understand if you would prefer to retire so you may say goodnight to your son. Do not feel compelled to return if you would rather stay with him."

Beth glanced between the two ladies but could not determine if she was being shown a kindness or being sent away so they could talk about her when she was gone. In the end, she chose to believe it was from kindness. "If you no longer need me, I should like that very much."

Lady Venables waved her toward the door. "How many times must I mention that your duties were not so rigid that you could not slip upstairs without waiting for permission? Go and tuck George into bed. We'll see you at breakfast as usual, but remember tomorrow is your morning off."

"Thank you, my lady." Beth curtsied again. "Goodnight, Your Grace."

Lady Venables smiled fondly. "Goodnight, Mrs. Turner."

"Sleep well," Her Grace added.

Beth scurried for the doors and pulled them closed behind her. As they clicked shut, she clearly heard the duchess exclaim. "Well, how was I supposed to answer her? The discussion was completely intolerable."

Beth's heart sank. She'd overstepped with her offer but it was done now. If the duchess refused, she didn't know what the future would hold. She hurried for the kitchens, chastised a maid who had delayed the footman with her flirtations, and saw that the tea tray was properly prepared and sent up. Then, with no other demands on her time save her worries, she trudged up the long flights of stairs, through deserted corridors, and stepped into the pair of rooms she shared with her son.

The pretty bedchamber did nothing to ease her nerves. She'd known from the start that she was being granted a boon larger than she deserved when Lady Venables had employed her as a companion. Her duties to the countess had been hardly taxing on her abilities and she'd thought herself better suited to the housekeeper role. Clearly the duchess hadn't agreed with her assessment.

She slipped into the smaller adjoining chamber and leaned against the doorframe to observe her son. His dark head was bowed over yet another book from the Romsey library and he didn't notice her at first. A wave of sadness flooded her. Being in service of any kind at Romsey Abbey had proved a very good circumstance for him. The duchess and Leopold Randall treated him very kindly and encouraged him to borrow whatever books they agreed were appropriate reading material for his age. The promised tutor had not been found as yet, but Beth had never pinned her hopes on that extravagance. "Is it not too late to be reading, George?"

His head rose quickly, an expression of guilt crossing his face. "Is it bedtime already?"

Beth walked forward and tousled his hair. "It's one quarter after ten o'clock. You should have been asleep long ago."

He grinned. "The story was too exciting to stop."

"That is what you always say."

He marked his place with a scrap of parchment and closed the book. "What shall we do tomorrow?"

"I'm not sure." She picked up her son's hand and squeezed. "I had the opportunity to speak to the duchess about the position of housekeeper tonight."

George came up on his knees, his face keen with anticipation. "What did she say?"

"She said she'd think about it."

George nodded slowly. "She will choose you. I'm sure of it."

"Thank you, George. Let's hope you're right."

George fell back against the mattress. "She has to choose you. I never want to leave Romsey."

Beth laughed. "You only say that because you are young and easily impressed. When you're older, you'll want to have an adventure or two to brag about."

A frown clouded his features. "Do you think my Uncle Henry is happy on his adventure in America?"

"Goodness, why ever would you think of him now?" Beth placed the repaired shirt into a drawer and picked up George's soiled garments, which he'd tossed carelessly aside. "He's been gone such a long time now that I wonder if he'll ever return."

"Papa said Uncle Henry went to America to make his fortune. I hope we hear from him soon."

Her brother-in-law had traveled to the Americas quite a number of years ago, but she'd not heard from him since. She forced a hopeful smile to her face. "I do, too. Sadly we will never know unless he writes to tell us where he is."

"Will he be able to find us here by letter?"

Beth nodded. "Everyone in the village knows where we are. Someone will pass any news along."

"Good." He pulled the covers over his head and burrowed under their comforting weight. At least here they were at no risk of being cold. The countess had given them every comfort they could ever need. Beth pulled the covers back and straightened the bedding around him. It was so good to have enough blankets to wrap around her child on chilly nights.

George smiled up at her with drowsy, contented eyes. "Goodnight, Mama. Sleep well."

"I will. Sweet dreams, Georgie."

George made a face at the nickname and then closed his eyes. Beth extinguished the lamp and returned to her own chamber. Once there, she sat at the writing desk and withdrew a half-written piece of paper to make notes of chores she'd discovered needed attention soon. When she was housekeeper, her gift to the newlyweds for their kindness would be to see that every part of Romsey was made presentable for the wedding.

Chapter Three

———◆———

"There surely can be no finer view in all of England."

Oliver ignored his brother's ardent remark on the landscape as he trudged to the hilltop and surveyed the browning fields of the Romsey estate. A winter chill was nipping at his lungs as he caught his breath, making them burn with the effect of the climb. "It is the same view we had as boys, Leopold."

The first falls of snow were due any day. Time was running out to make his trip across the channel pleasant. He ran over the things he had to do before he could leave England behind. The most pressing was still regaining his health and the walk, culminating in a climb up the hill today, proved he still had a goodly way to go.

His brother grinned, wagging his finger to and fro. "Yes, but the difference is now we may walk anywhere we like without a word said against us. No more sneaking around to avoid detection."

Oliver brushed away the film of sweat from his upper lip and leaned against the support of a crumbling dry-stone wall. The exertion of the climb had left him quite breathless. "You are far too easy to please. Would that these were the hills above Napoli and I could be content to admire them forever."

"You'll get there soon enough," Leopold murmured. "Patience."

"I've been patient enough." Oliver looked out over the fields, reluctantly admiring the precision of the ducal estate. The procession of field, gate, and plotted tree reminded him of his brief venture into the study of garden landscapes during his youth. As much as he didn't find the day-to-day affairs of the estate interesting, there was a certain beauty in its artificial design. Even the workers, black dots from his vantage point, moved in a soothing rhythm. A pair of shepherds and a hound herded sheep, two figures of disproportionate size traveled along the abbey drive, making slow progress as the smaller one darted from the path constantly. Another group clustered around a fallen dry-stone wall like the one he leaned against, correcting the imperfection. Everyone and everything within his view had a place in the grand design.

Leopold joined him against the wall and folded his arms across his wide chest. "About you leaving: I dislike the idea of you traveling so far on your own."

Oliver returned his gaze to the slow-moving pair, hope making his heart beat faster. "Have you changed your mind about accompanying me?"

"No. However, I would feel better if you had someone I knew and trusted at your side. You've not spent enough time in the world to predict the dangers that you may face. A companion, someone with a similar taste for adventure and more worldly than yourself, would also give you someone to share the experiences with."

Oliver bristled at the suggestion he couldn't defend himself. He might be weak still, but at Skepington he had accurately assessed danger through an opponent's posture and expression and, when attack was unavoidable, had met each challenge efficiently. He did not need a nursemaid following him about.

The smaller figure darted toward a pond and poked at the water with a stick while the taller, a woman in long skirts he now decided, remained upon the road, hands perched on hips. "There is no one. Do not fret, Leopold. I have always been alone."

Leopold's sigh was heavy with disappointment. "It doesn't have to be that way."

Oliver glanced over his shoulder, searching for their tardy younger brother and Eamon Murphy so this discussion could be diverted to something else. Since the pair hadn't stopped chattering and bickering the whole of the walk, Oliver was confident that Leopold would join their conversation—if only to shut them up. "I did not mean to imply that I disliked solitude. It's just that I have reconciled myself to the idea that few share my interests."

"Part of that blame must fall on you," Leopold said with deadly seriousness. "You have taken little interest in anyone else's affairs since you were a boy. In general, people like to talk about themselves, too. But you will not take the time to listen."

Oliver faced him. "And you take enough interest in everyone's business for the pair of us."

Leopold stabbed a finger toward his brother's chest. "Stop avoiding the subject. At least I allow myself to care about the welfare of others and receive affection and companionship in return. I see what you're doing and you're going to be a bloody miserable old bastard one day. Far sooner than needs be. Do you never wish for more?"

Eamon Murphy, who'd lagged behind with Tobias, rushed up to them. "Here now. What's all this?"

Oliver shrugged. "My elder brother is lecturing me."

Leopold stalked to the precipice in a huff.

"Again. Devil take it! Can't you just make a bigger effort to fit in?"

Oliver raised a brow in surprise at Eamon's outburst. So far he'd been a simpering lapdog without a voice. Now, how to continue his transition into the semblance of his former friend? "Excuse me? Who are you to tell me what to do?"

"You never change," Eamon said, hands clenched at his sides. "You never try to make other people happy and yet you expect everyone to toe your line. Leopold has been taking the brunt of the consequences for your misbehavior all your life. I should know. I hear everything. Every snub. Every teary young woman you overlooked or spoke down to without thought. Enough is enough. You've got all the maids at the abbey utterly terrified of you."

"He's right," Tobias said quietly. "Even I made less of a ripple when I returned and we all know my failings as a gentleman. But you, you're like an iceberg that has to be navigated. Treacherous to get close to."

Oliver was relieved to finally have his friend and younger brother speak their minds; he was tired of people tiptoeing around him. He wasn't exactly enjoying their honesty, however. "Then it is a good thing that I will be leaving soon. You'll all be at ease then." He stood, brushed any dirt from his backside, and faced the path winding down the hillside toward the abbey. It didn't bother him that he was feared. He'd never consciously spoken harshly to anyone. If the servants were too dim-witted to understand that his mind was elsewhere when they interrupted him, then so be it. People couldn't be made to change.

The odd pair on the drive had drawn closer while he'd endured the scolding. The woman had dark hair, bonnet swinging from her fingers. The smaller figure was a child, a boy he decided, and they both appeared to be headed for the stables.

"For God's sake, Ollie, don't be a daft fool," Tobias said as he appeared before Oliver, halting his return to the abbey. "Leopold will only worry more when you go. We all will."

The woman embraced the child before he disappeared into the stables. Oliver squinted at her. There was something familiar in her movements. Her hand lifted, perhaps to brush her hair back from her eyes, and then she entered the kitchen gardens, stopping to speak with the gardener.

"What has captured your attention so completely?" Tobias spun on the spot and viewed the abbey, too. "Trouble?"

The woman had almost fully disappeared behind one wall of the garden and Oliver could only see her uncovered head. He took a pace forward.

"I should like to place an advertisement in the newspaper," Leopold called out. "Surely there is another academically minded fellow willing to risk his life to visit the continent as your companion. We can easily afford the additional expense of that."

Oliver nodded. "If you must. That might be agreeable if the person has some sort of decent sense about him."

"I thought you wanted him to be safe," Eamon argued. "You never know what kind of scoundrel could answer such an advertisement. They could promise anything. It ain't hard to procure false letters of recommendation. Believe me, I know. Oliver could be murdered on the road even before he left the country."

"Murphy, that does not make me feel easy," Leopold grumbled. "Speak only if you intend to offer up workable suggestions."

Silence fell behind him as the woman in the garden crouched low, bobbing out of sight, most likely to pick an herb.

After a moment, Tobias faced him. "Are you watching Beth?"

Oliver squinted as the woman stood again. Perhaps it was Elizabeth. But if so, then who was the boy she had embraced? He was too tall to be the young duke.

"Fine," Eamon said at last. "I'll travel with him. But if Oliver behaves like a donkey's hindquarters I get to say so, and loudly."

"Excellent," Oliver murmured. Eamon could be counted on to be a good companion. He was useful at bargaining in taverns and remarkably good with his fists. A period of time on the continent could broaden his horizons considerably.

"Oh, and if I'm murdered along the way then I will come back to haunt Tobias as recompense for the trouble he's caused me," Eamon warned.

"Here now," Tobias voiced in outrage. "There's no need to draw me into this."

"If you must," Oliver said absently, ignoring the growing squabble. He kept his eyes on the woman a bare moment and then returned his gaze to the stables. The boy sat atop a pony now, being tutored by the stable master, Charles Allen. Since Allen was family, his illegitimate cousin, Oliver was sure the boy was not his child. Allen's two sons were adult-sized and had no need for lessons in horsemanship. "Who is the boy on the pony?"

Tobias swiveled to look at where he indicated and then he swore. At the end of the tirade, Oliver concluded that Tobias had quite the vocabulary of unseemly words. Some of which he was familiar with and others that would bear further study to determine their exact meaning.

Tobias threw up his hands. "See, this is exactly what we are talking about. You never pay attention when you should. There is no reason to be so obtuse."

"What's going on?" Leopold asked as he joined them.

Tobias scowled. "Oliver wants to know who the boy is on horseback in the stable yard."

Leopold smiled. "That's George. Allen says he's becoming

quite comfortable on Zeus."

"Excellent." Tobias threw Oliver a dirty look. "However, our learned and yet dim-witted brother still appears puzzled. He has no idea who George is because he's had his head buried in his books and his own affairs so completely that he does not pay attention."

Leopold stared. "How could you not?"

Oliver blinked. What had he missed? "How could I not what?"

Tobias clapped a stunning blow to Oliver's back that threw him forward. When he straightened, Tobias had folded his arms in a perfect imitation of their elder brother. "There are times when I am ashamed to admit we have the same blood in our veins," Tobias said with some heat. "Excuse me. I think I'll return to the abbey and see if Blythe needs my company. At least I'm happy to listen to the people around me." He shook his head and stalked away.

After a moment, Leopold shook his head too. "Murphy, see what you can do with him."

Why should he have paid attention to the talk of small boys? Oliver did not spend time with the duke. He was too young to be interesting yet. If not for this George person learning to ride on the duke's pony and Elizabeth embracing him, he would be unremarkable.

Eamon patted his shoulder. "See, this is exactly the type of situation you could avoid if you lifted your head from study and paid attention."

Oliver frowned as the boy continued to circle the stable yard. "Who is George?"

Eamon's sigh was loud and prolonged. "George Turner. Age eleven and growing like a weed."

"Turner?" He focused on the boy but could discern little of his appearance beyond the dark hair from this distance.

"You really are an idiot, Ollie. That is Beth's son."

He stared at the kitchen garden where Beth tarried among the plants and then looked back at the boy. "No one mentioned his existence."

"I'm sure they did. Beth speaks of him at every opportunity."

Oliver slipped his fingers inside his waistcoat pocket and

fingered the ribbon hidden there. Elizabeth was a mother. The idea changed his perception of her considerably. Despite her having married his brother's ill-mannered friend, he'd not considered the possibility that she had a family of her own. The idea should have occurred to him prior to this. "He's not given liberty within the house? I've never seen him."

"Well, no. It wouldn't be proper for George to play in the public rooms. Beth is employed as Lady Venables's companion. A servant like me. He mostly spends his days outside or in the long gallery."

"Fascinating. I often hear Edwin at play, but never this child."

Eamon captured a handful of pebbles from near his feet. "He's not particularly rambunctious. At first, he was quite timid around Mr. Allen's sons but I'm sure he's settled in now. He's been at the abbey a bit longer than you."

A question that had bothered him from the first thickened his tongue. "Why is she in service?"

The air hissed as Eamon flung the handful of pebbles into the long grass before them. "You'd have to ask her."

When he turned to view the abbey again, Elizabeth was disappearing through the terrace doorway, a bunch of green sprigs in her hand. If he tried to ask her, he'd surely bungle it. "I'm asking you. You always know the gossip and the truth."

Eamon stood and pinned him with a look that probably was meant to convey something important. Something else that escaped Oliver at that moment. "Why does any woman go into service? She had no family left, was as poor as a church mouse, and had a boy to support. Lady Venables has been very generous."

Oliver frowned as he turned his mind to the past, a place he didn't care to linger overlong. "Didn't Turner have an older brother she could turn to? Surely he wouldn't abandon her or the boy."

Henry Turner might have been every bit as boorish as his brother but Oliver couldn't believe he'd abandon his nephew completely. He'd faced the Turners over ridiculous misunderstandings before and he still remembered their tactics. One did not ridicule the younger Turner for his shortcomings without expecting to face the elder later. It always surprised him that Leopold had been friends with them.

"Henry Turner's not been heard from since he left the district. He's supposed to have gone away to make his fortune but I've heard nothing of that." Eamon shrugged. "With William dead, the pair are better off here, even in service, than elsewhere on their own."

"I see your point." Oliver also saw that the lesson had ended abruptly and that George Turner was charging for the servants' entrance to the abbey.

He pondered the boy's likely nature. "I suppose he is as bad-tempered as his father."

"Not that I've seen. He's rather quiet." Eamon stood. "Why the sudden interest?"

Oliver stared at the servants' entrance. The pull of curiosity about the boy was greater than the current need to make preparations for Eamon to join him on his travels. An odd circumstance indeed, but he wanted to meet the boy. He faced Eamon. "Isn't that what you want me to do, pay attention to the people around me? Let's return."

Chapter Four

The speed with which a bright shining moment of carefree happiness could tarnish astonished Beth. She crouched low beside her son in his bedchamber, thankful she'd already changed into a practical gown that couldn't be ruined by any dust on the floor, and attempted to understand George's mumbled explanation of why he was upset. "I'm sure he did not mean to shout."

"He did," George insisted, angry emotion coloring his response. "I can't do anything right anymore."

The morning had been so glorious up until now. They'd strolled to see an acquaintance at the village, she'd bounced a new babe on her knee, and she'd had precious time alone with George without fear of anyone listening in on their conversation. When they'd parted near the stables, George had been in excellent spirits.

She smoothed his hair from his eyes. "It takes time to learn to ride, to feel comfortable on horseback. Mr. Allen knows that. He just wants you to try harder."

George wiped his nose with the back of his hand and then dropped his head onto his knees. His arms tightened around his bent legs, his fists clenched. "Don't want to learn to ride one of the duke's stupid horses. Don't want to stay here anymore."

Beth let a long moment lapse before she spoke her good news. "The duchess agreed to my proposal a moment ago. I'm the new housekeeper of Romsey."

George started crying in earnest. "Now I'll never get away from them."

Beth frowned. "Away from whom?"

George covered his head and didn't speak until Beth shook him gently. "George, explain yourself. Who do you want to get away from?"

He slowly lifted his head and stared at her sullenly. His face had mottled to an unbecoming shade of red. "Jacob and David Allen."

Beth frowned and smoothed her fingers over his hot cheeks. "Are they unkind to you? George, what's been going on?"

He took a deep breath. "I don't like it in the stables. They know it and push me around."

Beth drew her son against her chest and rocked him. "You should have said something to me long before this."

Something sharp stabbed her arm and when she investigated, she discovered straw, lots of straw, stuffed down the neck of his coat and under his waistcoat. Astonished, Beth pulled his coat off and gave it a quick shake. Dust, likely from a haystack in the stables, floated to the floor. She quickly removed his waistcoat too, and checked his best shirt was still decently clean. "Did they do this?"

He nodded, head hung low with embarrassment. Beth closed her eyes. She had not expected him to be bullied by the stable master's sons. She would speak to Charles Allen about it and demand he make sure it never happened again. Up until now, she'd thought kindly of the Allens, but it seemed her trust had been misplaced.

George cuddled against her. "Are you really the new housekeeper?" he asked, voice wavering with misery.

Beth pulled him close to her and kissed the top of his dark head. "Yes. But there are some conditions."

"What kind of conditions?"

"Nothing for you to worry about. I'll manage." She stared into his face, pained by the misery etched there. He hadn't been this unhappy since his father had died. "Listen, George. I know our life has changed for the worse since Papa's death, but bear with me just a little longer. I'll make sure Jacob and David do not trouble you again. The housekeeper of Romsey commands respect. Things will turn around for us soon. I promise."

"Yes, Mama."

Beth smiled. "We just need to stick together. I had intended to start today, but I don't want to leave you alone if you're unhappy. If you promise to be very quiet you can come with me to the housekeeper's rooms. Just this once, mind. There is much to be done."

He nodded and then wiped at his face, leaving dirty streaks behind.

She pushed him toward the washbasin. "You'd better clean your face and your hands if you want to be with me."

He hurried to do her bidding while Beth strayed to the window and peered outside. Allen was atop a gray mare trotting out of the stable yard, his two sons on similar mounts flanking him. Beth had trusted that George would be looked after while she'd been engaged with the countess. However, that didn't look to have been the case. She'd pushed George into the company of the stable master's older sons because she'd believed the fresh air and company would be good for him. However, George had been hiding his misery while she'd been sipping tea and luxuriating in the comforts of a proper lady. She'd failed to protect him.

George tugged on her sleeve. "Is this better?"

She turned, caught his face between her hands, and peered at him gravely. "Much better. As handsome as ever."

His cheeks pinked with a blush and his shoulders hunched a little. "Don't let anyone hear you say that out loud or I'll never hear the end of it."

She rubbed his back and he stood taller. "A mother is allowed to be proud of her son and I am so very proud of you. Your father would be too if he were still with us."

Beth helped him redress and then led him out of their chambers and down the main staircase. It was only when she reached the midpoint that she realized her error. She should have taken the servants' stairs. She hurried George along, glancing about anxiously until they reached the privacy of the housekeeper's sitting room.

Once inside, she closed the door and strove to relax. She couldn't afford to make a mistake like that again. She couldn't risk losing this chance for security. The duchess had insisted on a trial period and had hinted that she would continue to interview any candidates that presented themselves during the next month.

The housekeeper's sitting room was cozy and comfortable, but still far grander than her own sitting room had once been. Two well-cushioned chairs sat facing the hearth and a low table sat between. Room enough for two. Four in a pinch if she added the high-backed chairs currently placed around the small mahogany table pushed against the corner. A mahogany sideboard held a single bottle, sherry she assumed, and two glasses on a silver tray beside a set of china ornaments, seabirds of some description.

George glanced around curiously and then sat gingerly on the blue velvet chair closest to the hearth. "It's quiet in here."

Beth nodded and then advanced to the door set beside the hearth. With a deep breath she turned the handle and stepped into the housekeeper's workroom. Again, dark mahogany furniture filled the space: three chairs, a tall cupboard filled one wall across the room, and a large desk dominated the space. The walls held sketches of the estate grounds and floor plans of the abbey itself.

She ran her fingers over the smooth, polished wood of the desk as she walked about it. These rooms, unlike many in the abbey, had been kept in good order but were bare of papers or character. She drew the drapes back from the windows and peered out toward the stables, noticing the Allens had disappeared from view. She'd deal with them tomorrow.

"So this is where you disappeared to, Mrs. Turner," Lady Venables noted as she swept into the room.

Beth jerked around and dipped a quick, respectful curtsy. "My lady."

"Her Grace has informed me of the news."

Beth swallowed. Should she have formally handed her notice to Lady Venables? From her conversation with the duchess, she'd assumed the sisters had already talked the matter over in detail and agreed. "Her Grace has been very generous."

"Well, time will tell." She glanced around her. "I take it you're starting today."

Beth nodded. "I thought it prudent to get a head start. There is so much to do that it seemed unwise to delay."

Lady Venables glanced down and twisted an emerald ring gracing her finger; a frown line grew between her brows. Beth squinted at the ring. The piece was not one she was familiar with, but it suited Lady Venables's hand quite well. Beth's tongue thickened as she overrode the urge to compliment her on the piece. It was not her place to notice such things anymore.

Lady Venables glanced up, frown firmly in place. "Well, then. I see there is nothing I can do to change your mind."

"No, my lady. I am very happy to serve the Randalls in this capacity. I feel I can do a great deal more to repay the family for its kindness."

Her former employer sighed heavily. "A pity. I thought we were becoming great friends. I had a matter I wanted your advice on, but it is too late now." With one last look, Lady Venables turned on her heel and let herself out, shutting the door firmly behind her.

A pang of disappointment filled Beth. She had enjoyed her time with the countess. The lady was kind, often quite funny in her own quiet way, and had never made Beth feel inferior. They shared many of the same opinions, she'd discovered, and she could at times predict the lady's reaction to new situations quite accurately. However, becoming the housekeeper put an entirely different cast on their relationship. She had no reason to speak to the countess unless the matter pertained to Romsey Abbey. Whatever the countess had considered asking advice about would forever go unsaid.

Seeking relief from her disappointment, Beth sat at the desk and opened the drawers. Each one was completely empty. She would need to speak to the butler to discover what had become of the housekeeper's account book and other papers pertaining to the position before she could make an accurate assessment of their situation.

A knock sounded on the door.

"Come."

The door rattled and then the new first footman, John, came in, bearing a tea tray. "I thought you might require sustenance."

"Oh, thank you, John. That is very kind."

"Think nothing of it, Mrs. Turner."

He left, only to be replaced by the head maid carrying a small vase filled with aster. "Thought you might like something pretty on your desk. Mrs. Callinan always liked roses, but I noticed you pick these for your bedchamber."

Beth smiled at the tiny blonde. "Thank you, Annie. I do prefer them."

Annie would be the person she most relied upon in the coming months and years. She hoped they could work together well enough. She placed the vase on the corner of the empty table. "Is there anything else you might need, Mrs. Turner?"

"Nothing for the moment, thank you."

The new second footman came next before Beth had had a chance to pour a drop of tea, carrying a bucket full of coal. When he went out, Beth had to wonder who else might come trooping through her door. She should have considered that the servants reporting to her would attempt to curry favor with the new housekeeper.

Out of the corner of her eye she spotted George watching her from the other room. She tipped her head in the direction of the plate of biscuits and he snagged two before retreating.

Another footman arrived with a large desk blotter; an upstairs maid appeared, ink bottle in one hand, quill in the other. After an ongoing procession of servants bearing gifts, the first footman returned. "Cook is asking for the store cupboard to be opened."

Beth smiled. "I'll be there momentarily. You can take the tea tray away now."

She poked her head into the other room to see what George was doing and found him dozing in one of the chairs. He'd had a trying day so she eased the door closed and headed for the kitchens at a brisk, businesslike pace. The cavernous rooms were quiet, new servants sitting about the long table idly, waiting for work to do. Beth reached for the keys. "Good afternoon, Mrs. Roach. Are you settled in well enough?"

The older woman's glance dropped to the keys in her hands and a scowl crossed her features. "Well enough, but I'll never get used to having to ask for the store cupboard key. Never had to in my other positions."

Mrs. Roach had come on a recommendation from one of Her Grace's many friends. She seemed competent enough to keep the kitchen running smoothly and she'd already won Her Grace and the little duke over with her baking skills. Yet the duchess was hesitant to trust the new servants completely. The last ones, the servants that Beth and Mrs. Roach were replacing, had liberated quite a few precious commodities as they had made their escape on the night of Oliver's return. She didn't blame the duchess one bit for being cautious. "Well, I imagine it won't be for long."

Beth hurried to open the locked door and stood to one side as the cook and her assistants took out what they needed to make the evening meal into a feast. Even the servants, from what she'd observed, ate very well at Romsey. Later, she would dine in the upper servants' hall. Another disappointment with her new role was that George would spend his evening meal alone from now on. She wouldn't allow him to keep company with the stable master's sons anymore without being there to watch over him. She'd have a tray sent up to his bedchamber or he could dine in the housekeeper's sitting room and return to his studies as soon as he finished eating.

Since Cook was surly about the key issue and took more time than necessary, forcing Beth to cool her heels in the hot kitchens, she was delayed over half an hour. She wiped her brow with the back of her hand and hoped George hadn't woken during her absence. She should have left him a note to explain where she'd gone. Tonight, after dinner, they would work out a system and decide where he would spend his evenings and his days. She didn't like the idea of him prowling the estate alone.

Eventually, Mrs. Roach agreed she had everything she needed and Beth hurried to the sitting room and George.

Luckily, George was still asleep. But he had company. Oliver Randall sat in another armchair, staring into the hearth's flames.

Chapter Five

A floorboard creaked and Oliver immediately raised his head from his contemplation of the flames. "I did not wish to disturb him."

Elizabeth's wary gaze flowed over him like a hot touch on his bare skin.

She dipped a quick curtsy. "Good afternoon, Mr. Randall. Can I be of assistance?"

He stood and moved toward her, keeping his steps light so as not to disturb the sleeping boy. Elizabeth backed from the room quickly and when he passed her, she pulled the door to the sitting room until it was almost completely closed.

Unless they were at dinner, they had rarely been in close proximity and never alone like this. For a moment he was tongue-tied, so he focused on her appearance. Today Elizabeth was dressed in a somber style. Plain gown, hair confined tightly at the back of her head. She appeared almost as prim as Lady Venables, except in a gown of far lower quality. He frowned at it, wondering why she had retained such an inferior gown when he'd seen her wear far better.

She folded her arms over her chest, drawing his attention to the possibilities of the body beneath the gown. Elizabeth was still as slim as he remembered from a decade before. However, her breasts were fuller and pressed against the constricting fabric enticingly. He took a pace forward and her dark brows drew together over pale blue eyes framed by thick lashes. When she took her lip between her teeth, he broke out in a sweat. He took stock of his health, half afraid he was relapsing into illness again, and then dismissed his concerns. "I did not know you had a child."

A small smile tugged at her lips, her eyes grew unfocussed as if in thought. "George turned eleven last spring."

"The date."

Her gaze sharpened at his demand and her head tipped to the side as she told him the particulars.

Oliver stored the detail away for later consideration. "Do you have other children here?"

Elizabeth's mouth firmed. When she didn't answer, Oliver concluded he'd blundered into a delicate area. If they had died or been sent away to live with distant Turner relations he wasn't aware of, she might be upset over the loss. By her pained expression, there must have been more than just George at one time.

He glanced toward the door where the boy slept. "In appearance, he is more like you than *him*. That must please you. If I recall correctly, *he* had possessed a pair of unevenly matched ears. At least the boy will be saved from being teased about them."

Elizabeth sank into the chair behind the desk, eyes downcast as if she agreed with him but wouldn't speak of it.

Oliver continued his assessment. "The boy's face and build most resemble yours. He has none of the rude bulk of *him* either. To make an informed evaluation of his temperament would require him to be awake; however, he does appear in good health."

Beth sat forward, clasping her hands before her on the desk. Her knuckles turned white. "How long were you watching my son?"

Oliver lowered himself to the edge of a chair. It creaked slightly and he determined it should be replaced. "The proper study of a subject can take a moment or a lifetime."

Elizabeth shook her head. "For all your brilliance you still cannot answer a direct question simply. I ask again, what brings you to here?"

He met her gaze, still struggling to see her as the mother of Turner's child. "The boy escaped my notice."

She licked her bottom lip and then splayed her bare fingers over the desk surface. Oliver noticed the absence of a wedding band on her left hand and wondered when and why she had stopped wearing it when she had proudly displayed one on her delicate fingers a dozen years before.

Her fingers tapped. "And how exactly did he come to your notice?"

He would not admit how. To do so would confirm that he was, at times, unobservant. "Where did you walk to today?"

Her brows rose. "Were you watching us?"

Oliver nodded. "The existence of the boy surprised me. I dislike surprises."

Elizabeth's thick eyelashes fluttered as if she'd considered rolling her eyes and at the last minute thought better of it. Puzzled by her behavior, he settled into the creaking chair, resting one elbow on the chair arm as he studied her. Since many people had commented that they disliked his scrutiny, he accepted his behavior might make her uncomfortable. However, it wasn't in his nature to rest until a puzzle was solved. His curiosity about the boy would only grow if he did not satisfy it now.

Eventually, she drew in a breath, a jerky inhale, and shrugged. "I went to see Mrs. Clayton. She's become a friend."

Oliver sorted through his memory, brought Mrs. Clayton's image to the forefront, and then dismissed her. "She has a daughter."

Elizabeth looked up. "Mary Clayton married and moved away. Mrs. Clayton rarely sees her nowadays. I think she's rather lonely and likes to be visited."

Oliver nodded slowly. "That is the way of things. People's own concerns must take precedence over past emotional ties."

A muscle in Elizabeth's jaw clenched as she pressed her lips together. She shook her head. "Not for everyone, sir. Now, if there is nothing else, I have much work to do."

Oliver sat up. "I've angered you. How?"

This time, Elizabeth did roll her eyes. "Whatever could you say to upset a woman?" She stood, rounded the desk, and yanked the door open to the hall. The next moment, she yelped. "How long have you been standing there?"

Curious, Oliver turned his head slightly and spied Miles Colby, his brother's valet, standing at the door with his arms full of a tea tray. Oliver turned away, forcing his shoulders to relax. His discussion with Elizabeth was not going as well as he'd hoped. There should be a handbook written on how to deal with feminine creatures of her confusing nature.

"I was just about to knock and ask the new housekeeper if I can be of any assistance on her first official day," Colby said. "But I fear I may not be the first to come courting your good opinion."

Elizabeth's soft chuckle filled the room and Oliver's cheeks heated again. Perhaps he should retire before he sickened. He pressed his fingers to his wrist and counted the pulses until he was certain no significant change had overcome him.

"They have all been most kind," Elizabeth murmured to Colby. "This would be my second tea tray this afternoon."

China rattled. "Well, perhaps I can help you in other ways."

Hearing Colby's response, silky smooth with tones of imminent seduction, caused the hair at the back of his neck to rise. Colby was a single man and Elizabeth a widow. If she planned to take on the duties of Romsey's housekeeper, an idea he deemed foolish, she must ignore flirtations from the male members of staff. An alliance of a romantic nature between a valet and housekeeper was out of the question. The other servants would not appreciate any appearance of favoritism.

Oliver stood and faced Colby. "You may set the tea tray down and return to your usual duties."

Elizabeth's cheeks had pinked slightly. Was she flattered by Colby's rather obvious attempts to ingratiate himself into her company?

Colby smiled smoothly, and stepped into the room. "Excuse me, sir. I did not see you sitting there." He slid the tray onto the table, a sly smile twisting his lips. He wiped it away as he faced Elizabeth. "Will there be anything else, Mrs. Turner?"

"Not for now, Mr. Colby." She smiled, eyelashes fluttering a little. "Thank you for delivering the tea tray."

"My pleasure."

When Colby had gone, her smile dropped away. "I see you're

still as rude as ever."

Oliver shrugged. "People do not change."

She sighed. "Yes, I've heard you claim that before and in your case, I am sure you are correct. Did you apologize to Lady Venables for being so short with her at dinner last night?"

"No."

Her lips pursed as she poured a cup of tea, added milk, and handed it to him. "Can I offer you a biscuit, sir?"

Oliver declined and tipped his head toward the partially closed door. "The boy might like one, however."

Her head whipped around to the slowly opening door. "George?"

The boy timidly stepped up to the table, rubbing a hand over his face. "I didn't mean to fall asleep."

Elizabeth fussed over him, straightening his hair and coat. "Don't worry about it now. Are you hungry?"

"Famished."

The boy kept sneaking peeks at him from behind his over-long hair while he ate and answered Elizabeth's quiet questions. The more Oliver observed, the more certain he became that her child had untapped potential. There was a watchful intelligence gleaming from those pale blue eyes as he gobbled his biscuit, something that had been completely lacking in the boy's father at that age.

Intrigued by the surety he was being studied in return, Oliver shifted his attention to Elizabeth. "Will you introduce us?"

Her lips pursed but in the end she complied.

George appeared unmoved by his presence. "How do you do, sir?"

Oliver nodded. "Very well."

The boy lapsed into silence, but his scrutiny did not cease. His gaze raked him from head to toe. George had little of his father in him by way of appearance. Oliver had no sense the boy would erupt into energetic ramblings at any second. In fact, he appeared of a serious nature. Quite a rarity in Turner offspring.

Oliver was rather puzzled by the child. "How are you enjoying Romsey?"

"Very well, sir. There's always something to see and do here." His reply, voiced clearly and calmly, added to Oliver's opinion that George Turner possessed a balanced temperament.

Oliver took a sip from his cup of tea, noted it was made with the perfect ratio of milk, and then nodded. "The abbey is steeped in history and intriguing artifacts."

The boy bit his lip. He glanced at his mother swiftly and then back to Oliver. "Do you know if there is a book written about the abbey's history? I should like to read it if one exists."

Another biscuit disappeared from the plate as Oliver weighed the value of his answer with the boy's likely disappointment. However, disappointing the boy couldn't be helped. "There isn't one, to my knowledge. If there was, it is likely the former dukes destroyed it. They were intensely interested in preserving their privacy. Many things have been forgotten or hidden away."

George's face fell and Oliver was pleased to see he did not pout. He did lean against his mother's side and took comfort from her embrace. "Guess I'll never know who's in the painting or where it was painted now," he said to his mother.

Oliver frowned. "Is there one in particular that interests you?"

"The one in the other room."

Oliver stood and returned to the other chamber, George scrambling to follow. When he'd been here before, his attention had been focused on the sleeping boy rather than the contents. There was only one painting, hanging opposite the mantel, so he didn't have to ask for clarification. It was painted in the fashion of years gone by, a stable, lone horse, and a comely maid hugging a pail to her chest. Some might call it merely pretty. However, thanks to his unending memory, he knew the scene depicted a piece of Romsey history. "The stables of Romsey, as they were before the fourth duchess's expansion changed them."

George came to his side, staring up at the painting. "How can you tell?"

"There is a similar painting in the east wing. The rooms once belonged to my grandmother. Clearly she preferred the stables as they once were, too." He leaned closer to the boy. "Given the maid's appearance, I believe that could in fact be Her Grace dressed in disguise for the effect."

"Gawd, you've a good eye for detail."

Oliver smiled tightly. "I remember everything."

His gaze moved to Elizabeth where she stood at the doorway,

hands clenched at her waist as if she were uneasy. Her hands stretched toward her son. "George, that's enough now. Don't pester Mr. Randall with your chatter."

George tugged on his sleeve and Oliver glanced down again. "Will you tell me more about the abbey another day? It must be exciting to know everything."

Oliver considered the request. He did know quite a bit more about the abbey than most and he was happy to share his knowledge of some of the abbey's history. However, he should tell a member of the Randall family first rather than an unrelated boy. Yet curiosity burned in the boy's pale eyes and Oliver sympathized with George's thirst for knowledge. Without sufficient encouragement, he could soon lose all interest and become disillusioned with study. The idea of a fine mind going to waste disagreed with him.

"Perhaps I misspoke. I don't know everything," he corrected. "I simply remember well what I've seen with my own eyes and I shall be happy to answer your questions where I can. Shall we meet tomorrow at ten?"

George almost danced on the spot. "Yes, sir."

Elizabeth's brows rose, highlighting that his agreement had surprised her. "Thank Mr. Randall, George, and then would you mind fetching my shawl from my bedchamber? I am feeling a little chilled this afternoon."

"Yes, Mama." George nodded to Oliver. "Thank you, sir. Excuse me."

He skipped out, leaving them alone again.

Elizabeth closed the door, hands resting on the wood as if it held her up. "What game are you playing?"

He frowned. "I play no game."

Her hands curled into fists as she faced him. "I will speak plainly since I know you incapable of understanding subtlety. George is easily impressed and a man of your substantial intelligence, willing to converse with him about inconsequential matters, will go straight to his head. I will not have his affections toyed with by you, of all men. You don't even like people, so why pretend otherwise with my son."

Oliver moved until they stood inches apart. Elizabeth's display of temper did not concern him. In fact, he found her protectiveness of the boy quite reminiscent of his own mother's odd behavior. Both had fussed when there was no need for concern. He carefully placed his hand against Elizabeth's upper arm and gave her a pat that he hoped would prevent any unnecessary theatrics. "The boy has a curious mind and I have the time to answer his questions. What harm is there in that?"

Elizabeth jerked away. "Because you have made it plain that you are leaving, despite the urgings of your brothers to remain. I will not have him caught under your spell and then be discarded without a backward glance as you do with everything and everyone."

Oliver shook his head. "Boys are resilient and not so easily guided by their emotions that they see deeper relationships where none exist. He will understand and survive my leaving without any burden on his emotions. George has asked a question I can answer and I will continue to do so until my ship sails. Why do you deny him the opportunity to enrich his mind when the opportunity costs you nothing?"

"Only you cannot see the cost is far too high." She glared daggers at him.

The conversation and Elizabeth's ungrounded fears were quite absurd. The boy would view him as a tutor at the most with no harm coming to him at the end of their time together. Oliver had had many tutors, each one discarded without a backward glance when it became clear he'd exceeded their abilities. Eventually he'd pursued his own education without assistance. Those previous tutors were admired for their patience and willingness to guide him, but he'd cared little for them beyond that. However, convincing Elizabeth that George would be similarly unaffected would be impossible in her current agitated state. She was a creature ruled by her heart rather than her head.

He bowed to her, fully prepared to end the discussion. "I will see George in the library each day at ten o'clock."

Elizabeth shook her head stubbornly. "Do not expect him."

Oliver loomed over Elizabeth. She was being foolish in the extreme. Time would prove him correct, he was sure of that. He clasped her upper arms. Her scent and warm softness drew him closer. He breathed deep, holding her gaze steadily. The dark of her eyes widened; her hands touched his chest to hold him back.

"Since you understand my preference for honesty, I shall tell you straight that you are a fool to think your temperament suits the position of housekeeper," he informed her. "Why did you not stay as you were?"

"The reasons for my decisions could not remotely be of interest to you," she shot back instantly, scowling. She glanced toward the doorway. "Shouldn't you return to your plans to travel?"

He frowned. Elizabeth was trying her hardest to send him away, but he wasn't inclined to go. Not when he was enjoying their conversation so much. An odd yearning rose within him but he fought it back into the quiet, lonely corner of his mind and dropped his hands. "If George is not in the library by a quarter past the hour, then I shall come looking for him to ensure I keep my end of the bargain."

Chapter Six

———◆———

A week later…

"Mama," George groaned. "I'll be late again."

Beth set the heaped tray of silver on the table in the sitting room and handed over a cloth, ignoring her son's protests. "There, this is the last. Just polish those and then we can have luncheon together. Won't that be nice?"

George jumped up from his chair. "But what about Mr. Randall? He's been waiting for an hour already. We were going to explore the abbey today."

Regardless of George's protests, Beth could care less if Oliver Randall was kept waiting. As she had predicted, George had lapped up the man's attentions, stealing away to the library whenever her back was turned so that he might not miss a moment. He couldn't seem to understand that there was a line they could not cross. Beth was a servant now and by extension so was George. He should not be wandering so freely about the abbey, even when encouraged to do so at every turn. "The duchess's wedding will require much preparation and I have need of you," she insisted. "We can explore the abbey together after you've completed the chores I've already set you."

If Beth was lucky, that would be another hour yet and he might forget all about Oliver Randall and his never-ending stream of confidences and shared secrets.

"But I want to see it with Mr. Randall. He knows all about the abbey. Maybe you could come with us and he could help you learn the history too."

"You will do as you're told," she snapped, furious at yet another mention of Oliver Randall and how she should accompany him. Beth turned back to her office but then jumped. The Duchess of Romsey was sitting before her desk, her nose close to the open top of a canister. She appeared to be inhaling deeply. Her head lifted and she smiled a little sheepishly at Beth as she handed the canister over. "A gift to sweeten your day. They smell divine."

"Thank you." Beth pried the lid off and glanced at the contents. Caramels, straight from the new cook's talented hands. "You're very generous, but I fear these won't last long."

"Treats are for eating, especially by hungry boys." The duchess glanced into the adjoining chamber. Her smile slipped as she observed George furiously polishing a silver serving spoon. "I would have been here earlier, but Edwin wanted to play a bit longer today and Leopold was elsewhere. I had a hard time getting away."

"Of course, Your Grace." Beth cleared a space on her desk and drew a scrap of paper from the drawer in case notes were needed. "I quite understand."

Her Grace's frown deepened. "We must discuss the arrangements necessary for housing the wedding guests."

"Certainly." Beth dipped her quill in the inkpot and prepared to write.

"We will need the rooms prepared."

Beth made a note: *Bedchambers.* "How many?"

"I should think all of them. I must show my Leopold off properly and ensure any gossip is of the favorable variety. I'll provide you with a guest list shortly so we can decide who to put where, but there should be sufficient chambers. They'll just need a bit of cleaning."

Beth held in a groan at the work ahead and nodded. It was the duchess's prerogative to invite as many guests as she deemed suitable for her wedding. However, a great number of bedchambers within the abbey had fallen into disuse long ago. There would be much work to do to make them acceptable for guests.

"The public rooms will need to be reorganized to ensure appropriate seating arrangements are available. The pianoforte hasn't been used in some time and I'm uncertain if it still plays in tune." The duchess sat forward. "It is important that the wedding week goes off without a hitch. We will need to hire more staff, but we can of course count on those that come with their masters. My sister has some thoughts on the subject. She'll share them with you later."

"Yes, Your Grace."

Beth made a note to discover who could attend to the pianoforte properly and looked up. "Is there anything else?"

The duchess's expression grew serious. "I don't wish to interfere with the way you raise your son, Mrs. Turner, but George isn't required to do the work of servants. He's just a boy."

Beth put aside the quill carefully. "He must do something with his days."

The duchess leaned back in her chair and studied her. "It was my understanding that Oliver has offered to tutor the boy until he leaves Romsey."

"Mr. Randall has been far too generous with his time as it is," Beth said quickly.

"I was speaking to Leopold just last night about Oliver and from what I understand, he has never exhibited such a generous nature before. We believe tutoring George is good for him and the improvement of his social skills is promising."

Beth frowned. "Oh, how so?"

"For whatever reason, George's presence has had a positive impact. Oliver, as I'm sure you're aware, prefers his books to people. However, the last few days he's changed. I saw him smile yesterday for no reason at all."

Beth focused on a spot beyond the duchess's left ear. She'd known Oliver would cause her trouble, but encouragement from the duchess was not what she'd thought to hear. "Oliver rarely shows his emotions."

"Did his mother tell you that?"

"In a way." Beth forced a smile to hide the lie. "She was always concerned he would offend those he met. The man is incapable of pretending to feel one thing when he feels another. He would make a terrible diplomat."

"I knew you knew his temper better than you let on." The duchess crowed. "I agree. He's too honest by far. I do dread him meeting the wedding guests. Compared to him, some of them are quite frivolous in nature, but they do have feelings that can be crushed. I hope he will not be unreasonably cold if he does not like them."

"If I may be frank, Your Grace. It would be best to keep them apart from each other as much as possible and hope for the best."

The duchess tapped the arm of her chair. "That will be a difficulty as he is impossible to pry from the library. My guests, particularly the gentlemen, will congregate there."

Getting Oliver from the library would be next to impossible. When she'd surveyed the public rooms last night before bed she had noticed the disorder Oliver had begun in one corner of the library was spreading. In his search for information, he was casting the whole room into extreme disarray. Someone would have to clean up after him.

By rights, she should instruct the maids to do it. However, Annie was noticeably uncomfortable around Oliver and he would likely dismiss her before she could start. Only the strongest of temperaments succeeded in withstanding his arguments. The abbey couldn't afford to lose any servants this close to the wedding if he barked for them to get out. "Let me think on it a moment."

She cast her mind back to the time before her wedding when she'd been on intimate terms with those living at Harrowdale. The only way the late Mrs. Randall had contained Oliver was to restrict him to one particular room in the house. The book room at Harrowdale had been for his exclusive use, even casting the senior Mr. Randall's possessions to another lesser chamber.

She bit her lip, thinking hard. Oliver, and particularly the objects of his study, had to be moved away from the public areas of Romsey Abbey well before the wedding. But how to get him out of the library and achieve that goal? And more importantly, where to put him?

She stood to survey the abbey floor plans that adorned the walls of the room. There was a chamber off another, overlooking the west gardens, that was easily accessible from the main staircase but still relatively private. The room boasted a fine set of windows to provide good reading light and it would be quiet there. That covered two of the things Oliver was known to demand. He would disturb no one there and the only problem she could foresee was that he would be closer to the housekeeper's sitting room and George. She looked again at the plan, hoping to spy an alternative that would place him farther away. Unfortunately, there wasn't another empty chamber with similar features in good enough repair.

She tapped the map. "Here. We can put him here."

The duchess rose and studied the drawing, her head nodding as she considered. "That will do nicely."

George dropped a silver implement on the floor, drawing her attention. He'd made a very good dent in the polishing but as she studied his sullen expression, she decided he had a better use. "Would you agree that it is your wish to have Mr. Randall and his books removed to another part of the abbey as soon as possible, Your Grace?"

The duchess nodded. "He will be difficult."

If the duchess agreed to her plan, she could have George distract Oliver long enough so that she could move his possessions today. "Don't be concerned about Mr. Randall." She glanced at her son. "I believe I can concoct the perfect distraction."

The duchess grinned impishly. "I wondered if you might. Shall I take George with me? Edwin would love to see him."

Beth shook her head, puzzled by the duchess's offer. "I will need George. He will be the one to distract Mr. Randall, as I am told they were to explore the abbey again today. I can tidy up while he's busy elsewhere without hearing any arguments. Later, he may not be so pleased, but it will be far too late by that point."

"Oh." Her Grace winced. "I thought you were suggesting that you and he might…"

Beth stared, nonplussed. "Might what?"

The duchess resettled in her chair, her hand waving about as if she searched for the right words. After a moment, she squared her shoulders and met Beth's gaze directly. "Well, you are very lovely and Oliver does stare at you so much. I just assumed the two of you had become more than friends."

Beth's cheeks heated at the idea. "I am not so foolish as that. It is simply his way. We are but specimens beneath his magnifying glass, forgotten the moment his attention is diverted elsewhere. Oliver stares at everything."

"But at you more than others."

Was it possible to die from humiliation? Since she'd survived it once before, she doubted she couldn't again. To succumb to anyone's seductions would endanger her position as housekeeper. To consider a dalliance with Oliver Randall would prove her without good sense. Beth had mistakenly believed him interested once, when she'd been younger, and had the door to happiness slammed in her face when she'd overheard his views on his future. She couldn't afford to lose the security she'd fought so hard to gain. The duchess must never have any doubts about her character. "Regardless of your assumption, incorrect I must stress, I do know my place, my lady. I shall never do anything to bring dishonor on your family or my place here."

"Mrs. Turner, before Leopold returned I had convinced myself that I was perfectly happy with my life. I was alone and completely in control, or at least as much as I could be under the circumstances. Do you know the one thing I missed most when I became a widow? The lack of contact. Touching another person and having them touch me in return, for whatever reason, I've found is essential to my happiness."

Astonished by the candid confession, Beth strove to keep her expression neutral. "I have George for affection. He has not grown so large that he shuns my embraces."

"I was not talking about a mother's love for her child, but a man's ardent return of affection. There is nothing quite like it." The duchess grinned again. "I don't expect you to hide an attachment or affection should romance develop. A little dishonor can be very soothing to one's nerves."

Beth shrugged to hide her discomfort. "I do not agree with you."

The duchess's expression grew thoughtful, her stare quite similar to Oliver's wordless study. "Then I fear you never really loved or were loved in return. How sad. I think there is much to admire about you, Beth. You deserve to be adored and have a man make a fool of himself on your behalf. I believe Oliver has the beginnings of real feelings for you."

Beth glanced down at her hands and squeezed her fingers until her knuckles turned white. She willed them apart and strove to appear unaffected by the duchess's words. There was much truth in the first part. She had never loved her husband enough. It was a constant pain in her heart that she'd cared for him but never fully loved him. She had tried with all her will but when he had died, a little part of her had been relieved because she wouldn't have to pretend any longer.

But to hint that Oliver could be a man in love enough to be foolish showed how little the Duchess of Romsey understood him. Oliver Randall was oblivious to anything of an affectionate or even romantic nature. He didn't require anything from anyone in order to be content.

"Have I made you uncomfortable?" The duchess's soft question forced her out of her introspection.

Beth rubbed her brow. "No, of course not. But there is really nothing to say. I have no feelings, one way or the other, for him or anyone. If I may be candid, Your Grace, I would prefer it if you did not turn your matchmaking inclinations in my direction."

The duchess scowled. "I was successful with my sister and Tobias. What makes you think I cannot do it again?"

Beth might be in danger of overstepping on her first day in her new position, but she had to stop the duchess from pursing this line of foolishness any further. "I respect Lady Venables more than words can say, but two more opposite creatures you could never hope to match again. The difference, and why your success was assured, is that both she and Tobias were willing to change to make each other happier."

The duchess's brow rose. "And you resist change. You do not believe in love?"

"Far from it, Your Grace." Beth shook her head. "I have never backed away from a challenge presented by new circumstances. My life has been full and quite uncertain at times. A woman must learn and adapt if she is to survive and thrive again."

The duchess wrung her hands. "Then you believe Oliver incapable of change, even for love?"

"Yes, Your Grace." A lump formed in her throat and she swallowed to continue speaking. "There is no room for love in his life. Once he decides on a path he will stick to it until the bitter end. I have no doubt of that. You are wasting your energy and will only be disappointed by him."

Chapter Seven

———◆———

The profound silence of the east wing of Romsey Abbey soothed Oliver in a way he couldn't understand. This wasn't his first visit to the derelict chambers and likely not the last. He left the door ajar and glanced around the bright rooms that had once been his paternal grandmother's private apartment. He could easily imagine her outrage at their sorry state. The old woman had been meticulously neat.

He stepped farther into the room, brushed his fingers over a small gilt-edged tabletop, and then rubbed the dust from them. When he looked across the space, he noticed tracks crossing the dusty floor from the door to the center of the room. One man-sized. One smaller.

Beside him, George Turner crowded closer. "Are you sure this room is safe?"

"Of course." To prove his point, he jumped up and down a few times. "Romsey may be dusty but she is quite sound. All she needs is attention."

The boy shrugged. "I suppose."

Curtains had rotted and fallen into suspicious heaps on the floor by the windows, giving the room breathtaking views as far as the eye could see. "Can you not see the potential of the room? The space, the light, the aspect."

"All I see is work." George shrugged. "The duchess and Mama were talking this morning. Many rooms have to be prepared for the wedding."

Oliver frowned. "Not these ones."

"Why not?" The boy picked up a cushion with two fingers and when he dropped it a cloud of dust erupted around him. He backed away, coughing. "It's big enough for a whole family."

George wandered off to peer into the adjoining chambers. Oliver's grandmother's apartment was dirty but spacious, neglected but opulent, and would be fit for even the king to sleep in. Given a few days of care and attention it would be quite comfortable. Yet the idea filled him with unease.

"George?"

George's reply was muffled, as if from a long distance away. Oliver followed the sound and found him seated on the floor in one of the smaller bedchambers before a tall replica model of the abbey. George had opened the front face, revealing the interior rooms and was carefully examining the contents.

Oliver knelt down at his side and peered in. After a moment, he grunted. "It's remarkably accurate."

"That's what I thought, too." George set a tiny chair back in place. "I can almost see my mother taking tea in the drawing room with the duchess, but she says she will never do that again."

Oliver frowned. In his opinion, Elizabeth had made a mistake in becoming the housekeeper. A life of leisure and comfort had been assured if only she'd taken advantage of the opportunities afforded her. She might have traveled in the duchess's company to places far away from here. She may have danced and dined in elegance and discovered more wonders than she'd ever dreamed possible. Accepting the housekeeper's role, although a well-respected position, offered nothing but hard work and long hours away from her son.

He glanced at the dark head beside him, noticing how the dust had dulled the shine. On impulse, he brushed his hand over the boy's head to remove it. "You'll look as old as I if you are not careful."

George scrubbed at his head but immediately returned his attention to the model-sized abbey. "May I ask your age, sir?"

"Eight and twenty last January."

"Mama is almost the same age." George pulled on a cord hanging down a wall and a small bell tinkled inside the model.

He wriggled around until he was flat on his stomach and peered into the lower levels. "There's the housekeeper's sitting room door."

"Yes."

The boy turned over and looked up at him. "They say you knew my mother when she was younger. What was she like?"

Oliver climbed to his feet. "I knew her, but not well."

The boy frowned. "Oh."

"She was on good terms with my mother and sister."

George scowled. "That's all you remember? I thought you'd have funny stories to share like Tobias does."

"I should warn you that my younger brother does occasionally add fiction to his retelling." Oliver cast his mind back, picturing Elizabeth on one of her many visits to Harrowdale. "Your mother laughed quite often. I could always tell when she was at Harrowdale because my mother became merry too and my sister, Rosemary, ceased her scowls and complaints."

"So she was happy then?"

The boy's questions puzzled him. Elizabeth was almost always happy as far as he could tell. "Yes. I do not believe her to have been at odds with anyone in the district."

"And you knew my father." George pulled his knees to his chest. "What was the wedding like?"

Oliver stilled. There were certain moments in his life that he worked to forget, although some were hard to cast aside. He had not particularly cared for that day. He had not attended the wedding ceremony at her home, but his mother and sister had attended with Leopold as their escort. When they'd returned, Rosemary had been theatrically cross about the affair. She'd prattled on about love and marriage until his ears had ached. He shook his head. "It was a long time ago. I don't recall the exact details. You should speak to Leopold. He may remember."

George nodded and then continued his study of the model.

There was so much of Elizabeth in George that he could easily overlook the influence of the father. But George was a boy William Turner should have been proud to call his son. If Turner had been capable of pride in a son as bookish as George Turner appeared to be. What Oliver most clearly remembered was that William Turner had imagined other uses for books and none of them was for study.

"Mama cries at night sometimes," George said suddenly. "She thinks me asleep but I've crept to her doorway and I've seen her miserable. She pretends nothing is the matter and won't tell me why. Do all mothers do that?"

"Some." The idea that Elizabeth had been unhappy enough to cry irritated him. "I imagine she misses your father a good deal. In time she will be happy again."

"I suppose." George shrugged. "May I stay here to examine the model?"

Oliver nodded, although George could likely not see. "Do not remain too long. The air is still very thick with dust. It will be better once the room has been attended to. I'll see you tomorrow."

"Thank you, sir. I'll be all right on my own now."

Oliver hesitated to leave. By rights he should see that the boy returned to his mother's care before he resumed his preparations for travel. Yet, for whatever reason, he felt compelled to stay and answer the boy's next question. George had an agile mind that drew in knowledge quicker than Oliver could supply. There was still plenty of time for his plans.

He glanced around the chamber uneasily. There was a great deal to do in this room to bring it to a livable condition for wedding guests, but he did not like the idea of others living in this space. He surprised himself with the idea that *he* could be comfortable here. He could wake up each day in pleasant isolation, admire the view, and study until hunger called to him. He could claim the space before he departed and then he could return to it once he'd seen enough of the world.

But not before the rooms were made presentable.

"I'll return shortly," Oliver advised.

The boy appeared surprised, but he smiled as if the idea of his company was pleasant. Oliver hurried out, keen to venture to the lower levels and secure a footman and maid to do his bidding. If there were none to be had, he's make a start himself. It would be nice to get away from the duchess's incessant chatter.

On the stairs he passed a servant, arms full of books and papers. He slowed when two more passed him, carrying the large globe that should be in the library. "What's going on here?"

The servants' gazes lowered. "Just doing as we're told, sir."

Another servant appeared, arms full of rolled maps. Oliver's maps. "On whose order are you doing this?"

"Mrs. Turner's, sir. She said we're to clear the library."

Oliver hurried down the stairs and burst into the library in time to see the final stack of books lifted from the floor and removed via another doorway. He followed the footman, furious with this interference. He took the servants' stairs and Oliver remained close on his heels, determined not to lose sight of his research material.

When he gained the upper floor the man headed for an open doorway. The footman disappeared inside and Oliver stopped on the threshold to survey the room. Two tall windows, fireplace already blazing with heat, and a long, wide chaise lounge positioned opposite a sturdy desk. Every comfort he could possibly want.

Elizabeth directed the man to the far side of the desk and had him place his pile of books on the floor. She stared at her handiwork, a pleased smile gracing her lips.

"Proud of yourself?" Oliver asked.

She turned, her face flushing a deep shade of red. "Yes, as a matter of fact I am. I've followed Her Grace's instructions to the letter and brought everything here exactly as it was below."

"That remains to be seen." He glanced at the footman lingering at Elizabeth's elbow. "You can go," he told him.

The servant glanced at Elizabeth for confirmation and when she nodded, he hurried out.

She set her hands to her hips. "There is no need to be surly."

Oliver slammed the door shut. "Haven't I a right to be?" He scowled. "I distinctly recall mentioning that you should not be housekeeper of Romsey. I do not meddle with your possessions and do not wish you to meddle with mine."

Elizabeth rubbed her arms, a sure sign he'd made her nervous. Good. She deserved it after this act of treachery. "On the contrary, you've done specifically what I asked you not to do."

He knew what she meant, but teaching the boy the history contained in the house and improving his grasp of Latin could hardly be termed meddling. The boy was gaining something of value, after all. "George?"

Her smile grew brittle. "Enjoy your new accommodations. Her Grace has granted you this room to use as your own. You will only be disturbed here for the fire and on Friday mornings when a servant will come in to clean."

When she made to move past him, he caught her arm and held her steady. "We are not finished. What have you done?"

"Nothing. Everything is how you left it below, only crowded a little closer together on account of the smaller table."

Oliver dragged her, surprisingly pliant, toward the table and surveyed her handiwork. Everything was indeed the same, but knowing his papers had been rifled through set his teeth on edge. He made a conscious effort to ease his grip so as not to damage her, but he couldn't let go of the soft flesh in his hand.

She shifted her weight from foot to foot. "Where is my son now?"

Oliver studied her face. No matter what he did, he couldn't seem to unravel the reason why she fascinated him so. Perhaps because he saw she had two sides. The happy one she shared with others, and the one he saw most often. "He's playing in a deserted room in the east wing. We stumbled on a replica model of the abbey. The boy finds it fascinating and wished to remain to study it."

A frown creased her brow. "He has other chores to do today."

"Yes, he did mention them but I wondered if you might spare him for work in the east wing. My grandmother's apartment is large but uninhabitable as yet. I thought we might work together to clean it up."

"You're proposing to spend even more time with my son?"

Oliver snorted. "Outside of the servants, quite possibly it will be my paltry efforts that set the rooms to order rather than his. I imagine the model will claim his attention for a good long while yet."

A frown line appeared between her dark brows. "Why would you do this?"

"I like the room."

Elizabeth shook her head suddenly. "No. Return him to me. You can play at being interested in the abbey with someone else. I knew this was a mistake."

The anguish in her tone made his pulse increase. Oliver

tightened his grip. "The boy says you cry at night. Why?"

She struggled to get away from him and he let her go reluctantly. She backed toward the door as if afraid of him. "Nothing in my life is of concern to you. Go away, Oliver. Go off on your adventures and leave us alone."

Confused by her words, Oliver followed as she tugged on the door handle. She turned when she discovered the door wouldn't open and he kept her against the door. He touched her arms and then bent his knees so he could see her face. "Why are you always so upset with me?"

She met his gaze and scowled. "Indifference is better than turning into a bully. Release me."

But Oliver couldn't seem to do that, nor ignore the way her eyes had grown glassy-bright when she spoke. "There is no reason to cry."

"No, of course. None at all." Her voice cracked on the last and he cupped her jaw. When her face turned up to his, tears slid down her cheeks unabated.

He searched her expression for clues, but could see no sign of why she was upset. He was only trying to help the boy become a wiser man. He'd never understood her disapproval. He doubted he ever would. But right now he couldn't bear to see tears streaming down her face. He cupped her face with both hands and wiped them away with the pads of his thumbs.

Elizabeth closed her eyes. Shutting him out.

The warm body against him shook and he moved closer to offer comfort. But Elizabeth's hands thumped against his waistcoat and held him back when all he wanted was to hold her against him. Her teeth clamped on her lower lip, heightening his confusion. The action reminded him that it had been a very, very long time since he'd lain with a pretty woman, and the one in his arms fit that description perfectly.

When Elizabeth opened her eyes again, Oliver dipped his head and kissed her.

Chapter Eight

Elizabeth froze, stunned to be in Oliver's arms like this. Her heart rejoiced but her mind screamed. Wrong. Wrong. Wrong. This was not supposed to happen. He did not care for her at all. Yet Oliver's lips played over hers in a soft, compelling dance, making her vow to forget him impossible. Making her need him. His fingers cupped her skull, sliding into her hair and battering her defenses. His touch was gentle, almost reverent, but his lips were sinfully skilled.

They shattered every belief she held that this man could never feel passion.

He moved closer, pulling her deeper into his embrace and his warmth burned through her gown as if she were naked. The touch of his hands against her upper back grew firmer and he teased the seam of her lips with his tongue until she let him in. A soft moan escaped her at the first stroke of his tongue across hers and she curled her hands about his neck, knowing she was making the second biggest mistake of her life.

She should not succumb to this madness but her body had other plans. She tightened her grip around his neck, curved her body to lie against his, seeking more as she kissed him back hungrily. His hands slid to the small of her back and eventually curled over her bottom. With a deep groan, Oliver jerked her hard against him, lifting her feet from the floor while pressing her against the door. His legs wedged between her skirts, their hips aligned. Beth broke the kiss and turned her face away.

She struggled for breath as Oliver's mouth seared the skin of her throat. He nibbled and nipped, sending her senses soaring. But this was not what she wanted. She was not the kind of woman to seek pleasure in a cold man's arms. When it was over, she'd have even more reasons to cry herself to sleep at night.

After a few moments, Beth pushed against his shoulders. Eventually, Oliver ceased kissing her skin and allowed her to regain her feet.

When she faced him, he wasn't smiling. "Is that better?"

Beth gaped. His eyes were dark pools that stripped her down to bare skin, his lips were flushed but pressed firmly together. To think he'd had his tongue in her mouth and still couldn't appear happy took her breath away. She shoved hard against his chest to regain perspective. Even at a distance, he appeared dispassionate. "I think I preferred it when you ignored me."

His brow creased with a frown and before he could offer more cold words to follow such a devastating kiss, she blindly reached for the doorknob, turned the key this time, and threw the door open.

Lady Venables was waiting on the other side. "The duchess requests your presence in the drawing room, Mrs. Turner."

Beth scrambled to gather her scattered wits. She quickly bobbed a curtsy. "Of course, I'll be there momentarily," she agreed self-consciously. Her lips still tingled with the remnants of that kiss. Her body pulsed in places it should not. She pressed her hand to her stomach as panic overwhelmed her. The disapproving look in the countess's eye hinted she knew exactly what had been going on behind the closed door. Beth didn't dare glance over her shoulder at Oliver. She wasn't sure whether she could be trusted not to hit him for destroying her peace and reputation or throw herself at him to ensure her downfall was complete. She had worked so hard to earn a place here and Oliver had ruined everything. "Excuse me."

Lady Venables eyed her gown, glanced behind to where Oliver stood quietly, and looked back. "Her Grace suggested that you may wish to wear something a little finer for this meeting and I do believe I agree with her. You have a visitor and must look your best."

Beth frowned. "Who would come to call on me here?"

A look of distaste crossed the countess's face. "A Mr. Henry Turner presented himself to Her Grace a short time ago, demanding to see his family."

"Henry is back?" Beth swayed, overcome with hope. "That's my husband's elder brother. I'll change and come down as quickly as I can. Good grief, so he is alive? George will be so pleased to hear it."

"He is alive, indeed." Lady Venables caught her arm and hurried her down the hall. "The duchess requested Annie attend you. She should be waiting there now."

"Thank you." Beth impulsively squeezed her hand and then fled down the hallway, up the stairs, and along to her bedchamber.

Annie was waiting beside the fire. "The duchess asked me to come."

"Thank you, Annie. I'm sure I shall need it."

She threw open her wardrobe doors and considered her options.

Annie stepped up to her side. "Her Grace was very clear that you were to wear the pink muslin and cream shawl."

"Is that so?"

Annie nodded and placed the gown on the bed. "She also asked me to restyle your hair. I see it was a timely suggestion. Whatever happened to you?"

Beth turned to the mirror and then closed her eyes. Oliver had quite deftly destroyed her efforts to appear serious and neat. Her hair was in danger of complete collapse. "Your help would be very much appreciated, Annie."

With Annie's cheerful assistance, her gown was changed and her hair restyled into elegance rather than practicality.

While the maid fussed, Beth twisted her fingers together in her lap and tried to still her racing heart. Being kissed by Oliver was unexpected, but that feat paled in comparison to the return of her husband's brother. A thousand questions flooded her mind. Had Henry made his fortune in America and returned now to set up his own household? She hoped so. Was he married? When he learned of their situation here would they be welcomed guests or invited to live there with them forever? Would George have the cousins he'd always longed for?

"There you are. Pretty as a picture." Annie added one last pin to her hair and stood back so Beth could see her handiwork. She looked nothing like a housekeeper and that bothered her. She appeared to be a lady of leisure again. Beth fiddled with the borrowed bracelet Annie had pressed her to wear and then removed it.

She peered at her hair and was impressed by what she saw. "Thank you, Annie. You've done a splendid job."

She took a deep breath, then gathered up her shawl, wrapped it around her shoulders, and hurried downstairs.

Eamon Murphy was waiting for her at the base of the stairs and his appreciative smile hinted she looked very fine. "Mr. Randall has joined Her Grace for the meeting."

"Oliver?"

Murphy's lips twitched and a wry smile slowly spread. "No. Oliver and the Turners never got along. Leopold is inside. Tobias is elsewhere today."

At the drawing room doorway she took a deep breath and nodded to Murphy before he announced her. "You wished to see me, Your Grace."

The duchess's smile was sincere but her eyes showed no joy. "You have a visitor my dear. I'm sure you remember Mr. Henry Turner."

When the duchess gestured toward the window, she spied Leopold Randall in conversation with another man. She took a few paces in that direction, puzzled for a moment by the rotund fellow. It took her a long moment to recognize her brother-in-law's face amid the wreckage confronting her. Henry was so changed from the man she knew that she was almost afraid. His skin was pitted by pockmarks, his cheeks full to bursting, though his clothing was quite fine. He had a pale scar that ran from cheekbone to jaw and stretched unnervingly as his smile grew.

She dipped a curtsy to hide her shock. "Henry."

"Beth, my dear." He rushed forward and caught her hands. "It's been too long."

The hands holding hers were rough, hard, and covered with small nicks and scars. She jerked her gaze upward to his eyes. "It has indeed. It's been many years since we've had a letter. We were beginning to fear the worst for you."

"I'm not much for writing." He laughed suddenly and released her. "And the worst could never stop me. Where is the boy? Fetch him to me."

She swallowed, suddenly nervous. "He's upstairs."

"Working as a pot boy in the great house?" His voice hardened with a tinge of anger and Beth drew her shawl closer around her shoulders. She hoped he assumed she was simply chilled.

Her Grace laughed suddenly, breaking the tension. "Of course not. He's become quite a favorite with the young duke. The best of friends, in fact."

"Ah," Henry said, his smile returned in a split second. "That's all the better. Cannot bear the idea of my brother's son, my heir, slaving away when there is no need. He shall never toil in service. Not when he can have servants of his own in America to do his bidding."

The mention of George being Henry's heir blindsided her. "You are going back?"

Henry sat forward, a superior gleam in his eye. "My interests in America are vast and it's fitting that young George sees firsthand what will be his one day."

Never for a moment had she imagined Henry returning to take George away. She felt a little faint at the idea.

"Shall we sit?" Leopold caught her elbow before she toppled over and steered her toward a spot beside the duchess. When Her Grace caught her hand, Beth gripped her tightly until her panic settled. Her brother-in-law beamed as if she should be happy about his news, but she was utterly terrified of this new development.

Leopold faced Henry. "Tell us more about America, Turner. I've heard such conflicting stories."

Henry spread his hands before him. "Business is booming. Profits are up and expenses are low. It's a prime time to be in business and we are doing well."

"So, you've family in America?"

Henry laughed rudely. "No. No. My partners and I are confirmed bachelors, every last one. That's why young George is so important to me."

Beth licked her lips. "You never married?"

Henry sat back in his chair and looked about him with a speculative gleam in his eye. "Never found the time. It was a hard life to begin with and I've not the time to dance attendance on females. As you can imagine, you don't get far with a woman in tow."

She and the duchess exchanged a horrified glance. Henry Turner was not an enlightened man. Her Grace squeezed her hand in a silent gesture of support.

When Beth caught a glimpse of Leopold's face, he'd turned an unhealthy shade of red. "Come now," Leopold chided. "There is as much to be gained from a woman's point of view as any man's." He spoke with a distinct growl to his tone and Beth silently cheered his good sense. No wonder the duchess loved Leopold Randall so much. Not many men she'd met in her life would voice support for the fairer sex's usefulness. He'd been such a stalwart friend when he could have abandoned them without looking back. But he'd ensured she and George were comfortable in their own cottage and had eventually brought them into the abbey on the pretext they were filling a need.

She had seen through his plans at the time, but she'd been so moved by his determination to help that she'd agreed. She hadn't regretted her decision to act as Lady Venables's paid companion and when it was clear the countess would marry Tobias Randall, she'd found a way to repay his kindness by entering the duchess's service.

Henry shrugged aside Leopold's comment as if it were of no significance. "George will see that things are different in the colony and learn to act accordingly."

A tiny gasp left the duchess's lips and Beth feared she'd cut her brother-in-law down to size. However, for a change, Her Grace did not flay the man. She regarded him coolly and played with the band of diamonds around her wrist. "Where does your estate lie, Mr. Turner?"

"Augusta." The location meant nothing to Beth.

"And what do you grow there?" The duchess managed the question with so much disdain that Beth would have laughed if not for her need to appease her brother-in-law.

"Cotton."

"I've heard you need a good many field hands to do well. Do you have trouble finding reliable workers? Do you own slaves?"

Proper land management required plentiful hands and here at Romsey, Leopold had been striving to increase their numbers. Slave ownership in England was against the law but the practice still thrived elsewhere. Henry's glance flickered around the room. His eyes narrowed. "I've a few darkies about the place but they are free to come and go as they choose."

Beth didn't believe him. He was up to his neck in slaves but wouldn't admit it to the Duchess of Romsey.

Chapter Nine

———•———

Oliver took a pace back from the door and from Blythe. She followed, a frown marring her features, and shook her head at him. "I had no idea it ran in the family. I thought you at least would be spared."

"It?"

She scowled. "Impulsiveness. A careless disregard for the rules and a lady's reputation. What were you thinking?"

"Elizabeth is—" he began, but she cut him off with an impatient swipe of her hand.

"Is a servant in this household now," Blythe reminded him unnecessarily.

"I have already voiced my views to Elizabeth on her unsuitability of being housekeeper at Romsey." Her refusal to provide a sufficient answer as to why she would take the lower position still vexed him. One day the woman would just tell him what he wanted to know without making him wait forever. Unfortunately, he had no idea how long it would take her to reach that understanding. He shrugged. "She was about to cry."

Blythe's brow rose. "And why was that?"

"She wouldn't tell me."

Blythe settled on the chaise and patted the cushion beside her. "So she was upset and you locked the door, refusing to allow her to leave this room?"

Against his better judgment, he sat where she indicated,

considering how best to answer. Blythe at least appeared to want him to be honest, whereas most people did not appreciate it.

"No. Yes." He frowned. "I was angry. As you can see, I've been moved without so much as a word of warning as to the duchess's decision. It is intolerable and I told Elizabeth so."

"Mrs. Turner was following her new employer's instructions," she pointed out and then her eyes widened suddenly. "Just how far did you go in your anger?"

The question caught him off guard. Perhaps he had allowed his emotions to cloud his behavior somewhat. That could be one explanation for why the kiss had begun. Under normal circumstances he did not kiss crying women. However, Elizabeth's stubbornness had made it impossible to act sensibly. Her scent had clouded his mind, the taste of her lips had made him abandon all gentlemanly instincts. He had crowded her and pawed at her. He had not achieved exactly what he'd set out to do. He had made her angry again, but at least she had no longer been tearful when she'd departed. He counted that a small victory.

"I never hurt her. I would not." He took a deep breath, irritation with himself growing. As if he could ever harm Elizabeth. "I held her. I didn't want her to cry."

"You were concerned?"

"The boy says she cries at night. I thought I could discover whatever bothered her and inform him."

"You really do not understand people or women, do you?" Blythe shook her head. "Most people strive to hide their disappointments from those around them, especially from the ones they love."

Elizabeth appeared to love her son. She was very protective of him and sought to spare him from any disturbance. "So that is why she will not confide in George?"

Blythe's smile returned. "That and the fact that he may be too young to understand what has upset her."

Oliver nodded. Elizabeth's reluctance to explain made better sense now. "He will have to wait until he is older to become her confidant. I will remember that for future reference."

"What you should also remember is that Mrs. Turner is a proud woman and would only confide in someone she trusts completely. I've yet to meet that person and I hope one day to earn that right. I suggest you do the same." She sighed. "Until then, take care of her reputation. She has enough on her plate as it is with her brother-in-law visiting."

Elizabeth didn't trust him? The idea that she didn't have faith in him set his teeth on edge. "Why?"

"Because Henry Turner has the look of a man prepared to do battle and take what he wants without thought to the consequences. I don't know him but I've seen a man wear that same determined expression before. Your younger brother wore that expression on the day we met. He frightened me half to death."

That wasn't the answer he was looking for but Blythe's answer was intriguing on its own. "Why would you marry a man who frightens you?"

"Because in the end he proved himself to be different from that terrifying first glance. He's not afraid to show kindness and was willing to sacrifice his needs, even his very life, for the sake of another's happiness."

Tobias had almost died saving Oliver from the blaze at Skepington Hall. No matter how much his younger brother tried to make light of his rescue, his selfless bravery had made him so proud. Despite the years apart, he had not changed. "Tobias always did try to make everyone happy when he was young."

A dreamy smile passed over Blythe's face before she recovered and remembered their topic of conversation. "I may prove to be wrong in the end but in the short time I was with Henry Turner I'm convinced he possesses not one shred of human kindness."

"That may be true." Oliver shrugged. "However, Leopold will know how to deal with Turner."

"Deal with him?" Blythe shook her head. "There is nothing to be done when George is Henry Turner's heir. Without a husband to lend his support and protection, I'm sure Henry Turner will pressure her to take him to that dreadful place." When he frowned, she added, "To America."

"Ah." Oliver considered the likelihood. She could be correct about Turner's immediate plans, but he didn't believe Elizabeth would enjoy relocating. She had friends here that she liked to call upon. He could not imagine her living happily anywhere else. No, she and the boy belonged here. Turner would see that eventually.

Blythe stood. "Now, if you will excuse me, I must find George and return below to offer my support. I'm sure Beth will want George presented to his uncle shortly and in his best clothes, too."

Oliver stood. "I'll fetch him and bring him here to await the summons."

Blythe's expression grew puzzled. "That is unexpectedly kind of you."

He nodded and, although puzzled by her comment, he hurried back to the east wing. The fewer people visiting his new apartment until he had fully moved in, the better.

The boy was exactly where Oliver had left him and very dusty. "Mr. Randall, come see this."

"No time for that now."

"But wait, I have to show you before I forget."

When Oliver crouched low beside the boy and looked at the model, his blood ran cold. "Interesting," he managed to choke out.

"I was poking the study furniture with my finger and a section of the wall swung open. There are stairs going down from the study. Of course, it's only a model and stairs are painted in, but how clever it is. I wonder if the stairs are really there."

Oliver closed his eyes. George had found the location of another hidden passageway in the abbey. This could be a problem. He had done his best to assure the abbey's inhabitants that the Duke's Sanctuary was lost so they might be safe from further villainy. However, he had not known the existence of this model or that it was so accurate. There were three secret passageways built into the design of Romsey, which he'd discovered in his youth. One was blocked. This one led nowhere. A trap for the unwary. The last led to the Duke's Sanctuary, and if George continued to poke and pry, he might very well stumble onto its location, too.

He grabbed George's arm and lifted him to his feet.

"Ouch," George complained as he was released.

"Your mother needs you."

"I cannot wait to tell her about what I found in the model."

Oliver rubbed dust from the boy's shoulders and chest. "You

must wait."

"But why? She'll be curious too and she is the housekeeper of Romsey."

If he said no, would George listen or grow stubborn and tell her anyway? Would he run off alone to explore the abbey and draw attention to what he found? Oliver had to take a chance that the boy possessed sense. In this, George must learn to hide the truth from everyone, especially his mother. He leaned down to the boy's level. "The abbey holds many secrets. Some of them are quite dangerous and it's best that no one learns all the secrets of Romsey. You must promise me you will mind what I say on this."

"I already told Mama about the model." His eyes widened. "Should I not have?"

Oliver winced. "I mentioned it too. Perhaps she will forget in time. It is in her best interest that she does so."

George's expression grew thoughtful. "Will you show me someday?"

Against his better judgment, Oliver nodded. "When your uncle has gone we will explore the abbey together, but you must not make the attempt on your own. Promise me."

George's eyes widened. "Uncle Henry has come?"

Oliver nodded again, disturbed by the happy light in the boy's eyes. "You're to change and wait with me until summoned."

George grabbed his hand and pulled him in the direction of the doorway, practically running. "Mama said Uncle Henry went to America to make his fortune. Is he very grand, do you think?"

"I have not seen him to be able to say."

"Papa spoke very highly of my uncle, too. He said America was filled with wonders. Do you think they have many grand buildings there that could be studied the way you like to do?"

The boy prattled on without pause until they reached his bedchamber. Oliver breathed Elizabeth's scent as soon as he stepped through the doorway and that odd sensation that had possessed him when Elizabeth had been in his arms returned. It was a pleasant sensation.

The boy rushed to the cupboard and Oliver followed. He'd never assisted a child in dressing and wondered what exactly was required. In the end, he need not have fretted. George selected suitable clothes, changed himself into them, and when he was done the only thing required was for Oliver to suggest George run a comb through his hair. They strolled back to his new chamber and sat down.

As they waited, Oliver recalled their previous conversation had not been completed to his satisfaction. "You didn't promise," he said quietly.

"Oh, I promise, sir." George nodded emphatically. "I won't poke or pry or say a word without your permission."

George fidgeted then and poked into the corners of the room while Oliver strove to describe what he was feeling. There was little in his life to compare with the emotions the boy stirred in him, but he thought he might be proud of George Turner. That thought made no sense at all. He'd had nothing to do with the boy's life or in forming his character except for these short weeks. Yet he could not wait to see what the boy would do or say next.

Footsteps approached and he stood expectantly. Elizabeth came to a stop just outside the doorway. She'd changed from her drab housekeeper's gown and looked so lovely that he took a pace toward her before he considered her likely reaction. She scowled and then held out her hands to George. The boy hurried to her side and she hugged him tightly. "Your uncle is here and wants to see you."

"Is he rich?"

Elizabeth smoothed her son's hair and the gesture reminded Oliver of her hands threading through his own locks while they kissed. He'd liked the sensation very much. He moved to the doorway to hear her answer.

"He says he is."

The touch of doubt in her voice propelled him out the door and into the hall.

Elizabeth glanced at him. "Excuse us."

She caught George's hand and towed him toward the main staircase. Just before they reached the top of the stairs the boy dug his heels in and faced Oliver again. "Are you not coming to meet my uncle?"

Oliver considered and, seeing the expectation in the boy's eyes, he closed the door to his new chamber and moved to join them. "It's been many years, but I would be happy to."

Beth appeared dubious of his company, but she was silent as

they descended. She allowed him to open the door for them and he followed. The next instant, George stepped back onto his right foot. He winced and caught the boy by the shoulder. "Steady there," he warned.

"My word, he's grown," a deep voice rasped. "I hardly recognize him."

Oliver faced the sound and determined Henry Turner's pockmarked face as the cause of his bruised toes. He forgave the boy immediately, squeezed his shoulder, and then stepped around him to thrust out his hand in greeting to the newcomer. "Turner."

Henry Turner squinted at him and then began to chuckle. "Good Lord, Oliver Randall, as I live and breathe. Now, I would never have recognized you if we were not standing here inside Romsey Abbey itself. By the devil, you look positively decrepit."

In Oliver's opinion, Henry Turner lacked the intelligence to imagine very much of anything. He studied him as he would an unstable element. The meaty paw pumping his hand lacked any kindness, the eyes darting about the room only to return to stare at George set his teeth on edge. Oliver increased his grip, only satisfied when the man's smile disappeared. "Some things change and some do not," he murmured as he studied Turner. He let the man's hand go and returned to his position behind George.

Beth nudged her son forward. "Are you not going to greet your uncle?"

"Of course. Sorry, sir. How do you do?"

When George stuck out his hand as Oliver had, Turner looked at it and then pulled the boy into a rough embrace. Elizabeth's breath hitched and Oliver could see the boy struggling to get away from the man holding him. After a moment, George was released and Turner made a show of wiping at his eyes. "My own flesh and blood. I never thought it would take so long to see you again. You were just a wee babe when I left. I suspect you don't remember me."

Beth slid her hands over George's shoulders and pulled him closer to her. The boy appeared to prefer it. "His father spoke of you often and George asked after you just the other day."

Henry Turner beamed and there was suddenly no trace of tears in his eyes. Intrigued, Oliver moved away to stand at the sidelines to better view proceedings. His brother's face was set in grim lines as he conversed with Turner. In the past, Leopold and Turner had been close acquaintances, but Oliver had a feeling that something bothered his brother about this visit.

Turner spoke of a grand house and the even grander society he moved in. Henry Turner professed himself a pillar of the community and that made Oliver doubt his stories. People did not change, no matter how fine the suit they wore. Turner had been a bully as a boy and he doubted he was any different now. His face and rough, scarred hands gave away his lifestyle.

When Turner took his leave with a promise to return tomorrow, Oliver followed him to the door, ensuring he heard every single word he spoke. George trailed after, his face eager for stories of how wonderful his uncle's life was, and Turner was happy to embellish quite liberally.

When Henry Turner's horse disappeared from view, George tugged his sleeve. "May I return upstairs again?"

Oliver took a moment to consider where the boy should be. If he knew anything about Elizabeth and her moods, she was upset again. If George was here she might not speak her mind. Perhaps the boy did not need to be present. "Off you go."

George sprinted up the main staircase as if the devil chased him.

"He looks to you for advice," Eamon murmured at his side.

Oliver shrugged. "Take the afternoon off, Eamon. I'm sure you deserve a pint or two at the tavern."

His friend hesitated. "Won't I be needed here?"

"No, Eamon," Oliver said as he cast one final glance outside before the door closed. "Your gift for ferreting out the heart of important gossip will serve us better. Find out everything you can about Turner and particularly his business interests in America."

"Do you believe he's lying?"

Oliver shook his head as Elizabeth was led to a chair and comforted by Blythe and the duchess. His disquiet grew. "I cannot determine that until I have more than just his word. I need facts and you're the man to furnish them."

Chapter Ten

Beth stared into the flames as panic clawed her throat. She'd done her best to hide her emotions while her brother-in-law had been present, but she had no desire to comply with his wishes and travel to America. How could she take her son away from everything he'd known?

A soft, comforting arm curled around her shoulders and drew her back to the chairs. She was pushed into a well-padded seat, fussed over, and then a teacup appeared before her. The tea was black, the way she liked it. "Drink this. I'm sure you'll feel better soon," the duchess murmured.

She lifted her arm to take it and when she did, the cup rattled on the saucer. The duchess swiftly took it back and drew her into her arms. "Shh, my dear. We'll muddle through this."

Her embrace was firm and comforting and for a moment Beth needed that. "I do not see how. He threatened to take George whether I like it or not. I did not imagine that, did I?"

She dropped her face to her hands to hide her distress, but Lady Venables settled on her other side and rubbed her back. "I'm sure it will not come to that," the lady murmured soothingly.

"It may," Oliver interjected abruptly.

Beth jumped. She thought he'd returned to his studies, but she could see his boots at the edge of her vision. She wished he would go away. He was not one to hold back an opinion to spare her feelings. When she lifted her head to look at him, he'd taken a chair opposite. His expression was full of speculation, but he kept any further thoughts to himself.

She sat up straight again, determined not to appear weak and emotional. "Thank you for your assistance in this, Your Grace, but I should return below."

"You'll do nothing of the sort. You've too much on your mind now to bother with your duties. Why don't you spend what is left of the day with George? I'm sure he'd enjoy that very much."

"I'd much rather be gainfully employed, given the circumstances. I don't want to leave you in the lurch with the wedding so close at hand. I'd like to do what I can before I leave."

"Leave?" several voices said at once, Oliver's the loudest.

Beth nodded but wondered why he cared enough to comment. It wasn't as if he would be here to miss her or George. It wasn't as if he missed anyone. She wiped away the tears pooling in her eyes. "I'll not let Henry take George away without a fight, and if he will not relent then I will accompany my son. I haven't any choice."

Oliver stood abruptly. He took a pace away and then turned back. "Excuse me." His footsteps were loud and hurried as he departed.

"Now he remembers his manners. Usually he just leaves the room without a word," the duchess grumbled under her breath. "The wedding preparations can be managed by others. In light of your decision, I'm afraid I must insist that you give up the position now. I was never easy about you taking on so much."

Beth gulped and clenched her hands together to still the tremble. If she did not have the position at Romsey then she did not have a reason to remain and couldn't claim to even have a roof over their heads. She'd have no choice but to comply with Henry's demands and leave England. "As you wish. I'll leave immediately."

The duchess patted her hand. "You'll do no such thing. I'm not letting you or George out of our sight for another moment."

She stared at the duchess, puzzled by her remark. "What? Why?"

She squeezed Beth's hand again. "Did you really believe I would give in to such a bully? I consider you a friend and you have far better bargaining power as a guest in my home than as a mere servant in my employ. You were far too good for that position anyway. Desperation is my only excuse for allowing it."

Beth held her hands to her face. "Are you still not in such dire straits, Your Grace?"

"My name is Mercy and I will not answer to anything else from you from this moment forward."

Beth swallowed the lump in her throat and tears sprang to her eyes at the kindness she was being offered. It might not be for long, but she would take any help she could get in this matter and later revert to formality. The duchess nudged her. "Go and see George. Spend the day with him and do not think about your brother-in-law again. Despicable suggestion. I'm certain there is a way around the problem and we will find it together."

"Thank you," Beth said and then remembered, "Mercy."

The duchess released her with a delighted smile and Beth tottered from the room on unsteady feet. The move to Romsey and giving up her independence had been a painful choice. Leaving her home, a failure in her mind. Although life had not always been easy she had never considered striking out to find a better situation. That she could one day be on first-name terms with the Duchess of Romsey had never occurred to her.

At the first landing on the staircase, she passed Oliver. She did not meet his gaze and he offered no greeting. But he fell in step beside her as she continued upstairs. When she turned in the direction of her bedchamber, where she hoped to find George, he called her back. "George is this way."

Startled by the softness of his voice, she blinked and then turned around. He gestured toward the deserted east wing.

Beth hurried forward, eager to know why George was in this part of the abbey again. To her knowledge it was deserted, with only dust and possibly mice as occupants. The door at the end of the hall was ajar and she hurried to it, conscious of the man following close on her heels.

She stepped through and blinked in the bright light. When she looked around, the space took her breath away.

"My thoughts exactly," Oliver murmured as he moved farther into the chamber and left her standing alone.

At some time in the past, the whole end of this wing had clearly been a beautiful apartment but the state of it was terrible disrepair. What a waste. It would have looked so much prettier years ago. Any guest coming for the duchess's wedding would be happy to stay here once it was made livable.

Oliver stopped at a distant doorway, spoke a few mumbled words, and then the next moment George's head popped out of that same door. "Can't I stay?"

Beth rubbed her arms. George did not know his uncle wanted to take him away to America yet and his question caused gooseflesh to rise on her arms. She had a little time to work out how to break the news. "For a little while. But only if you are not disturbing Mr. Randall."

George squinted up at Oliver and, after a small smile had flittered over the man's usually impassive face, he grinned and disappeared again.

"The boy does no harm," Oliver assured her.

Rather than meet his eyes, Beth moved to a window and tried to slow her chaotic thoughts. Outside, the season was turning toward winter with a slow and steady march. This was the time of year she loved, curled up beneath a warm blanket with the cold as her excuse to be idle.

Oliver moved about restlessly behind her and left her with little peace. He embraced the idea of experiencing new places— she'd heard nothing but his grand plans to travel since his return. Yet the idea filled her with unease. She knew nothing of America, in truth very little beyond the district. Her brother-in-law was a virtual stranger to her as well, which did not help allay her fears.

What could she do to prevent Henry from taking George away? She had limited knowledge of the law, but Leopold had more extensive experience and he appeared worried and also not as friendly toward Henry Turner as he'd once been. She'd have to appeal to Leopold for help, although the idea did not sit well with her. Leopold had done too much already. More than she deserved.

Morose thoughts would not help her out of this situation. Work had always been a good distraction, but she'd none to do now that the duchess had dismissed her. In the end, Beth faced Oliver to see what on earth he was doing. He'd stripped himself of his coat and was striding about in his fine fitted waistcoat and breeches, gathering small objects from around the room and placing them together on one round table. Next, he forced a sash window open, letting a cold breeze flood the room. One by one, he threw dusty puddles of faded drapes through the gap and then several cushions with their stuffing falling out followed. "What are you doing?"

"Clearing some space," he replied without breaking his stride.

He prowled around and when he found nothing else to toss out with the trash he lowered the window again, leaving only a narrow gap to stir the air. He dusted himself off and scrubbed a hand through his short hair, the epitome of energy and optimism.

She was glad he had recovered his health. The first time she'd laid eyes on him again had made her weep into her pillow that night after George had fallen asleep. She'd always wondered what had become of the Randalls, but she'd never imagined Oliver would return so changed. He'd always been lean of build, but his face was now gaunt, although not as bad as the first day. Late at night, his eyes were dark, sunken pools of weariness and occasionally she detected traces of that same fatigue in the mornings when he'd remained up very late reading. It had taken days before she'd been able to look upon him without her fears for his survival surfacing. But he'd recovered and resumed his usual style of living. Remote and self-sufficient for everything he might want.

"May I ask why you are doing the maid's work?"

He moved a chair and began rolling a floor rug into a log, but it was just too long to do on his own. He glanced up and a rueful smile twisted his lips. "I will need your assistance to begin."

Caught staring, a blush heated her cheeks as she remembered his kiss from an hour earlier. The foolish moment had fled her mind once she'd learned of Henry's plan for George and it seemed Oliver had forgotten the kiss as well. There was no hint he'd even thought of it again. She moved to the other end of the rug and together they completed the task. She stood and quickly dusted off the hem of her skirts. Oliver moved off into another chamber without offering thanks of any kind. He seemed as indifferent to her presence or her help as he had ever been.

Irritation seized her and she hurried toward the room George had disappeared inside. She caught a glimpse of Oliver standing beside a large canopied bed in the other room, removing the faded curtains from the bed poles and balling them up at his feet. She blushed self-consciously as her gaze snagged on the wide expanse of his shoulders. She'd always admired tall, broad-shouldered men, even indifferent ones.

She sighed and turned away, afraid, she was backsliding rather badly. She wasn't a young girl anymore and she couldn't spend her time wishing for what she couldn't have.

The small chamber her son had disappeared into lacked drapes and dazzled her eyes momentarily with its brightness. George sat on a hardwood chair he'd dragged to the window and stared out at the scene below, a book lying neglected in his hands. He turned and smiled suddenly. "I like it here."

She set her hands to his shoulders and kissed the top of his head, admiring the scene outside the window. "It's a pretty view."

Outside, there was nothing but fields and forest. No one moved on the great estate that she could see. It was as if the world did not exist beyond the dirty panes of glass.

Beth glanced at the book George held. "Are you enjoying that?"

He shrugged. "I found it beneath the cupboard, but I cannot understand it."

She took the slim volume from him and flipped a few pages. She squinted. "It's in French, I believe."

George took the book and stared at the pages with a glum expression on his face. He'd never learned the language, and Beth's understanding was rudimentary at best so she'd not taught him. He looked so frustrated by it that Beth took the book back and set it aside. "We should go now."

He slowly got to his feet. "I like this room better than mine."

She tapped his nose. "The rooms we have are fine enough for the two of us. Come along. The duchess has given me leave for the afternoon. We can do anything you want."

She wouldn't tell George about her sudden change in circumstances yet. If she did, she'd have to tell him why and that could only lead to questions she wasn't prepared to answer yet.

"Can we stay here instead of going out?"

Beth looked at her son carefully and grimaced. His best clothes were covered in dust. "I'd rather not."

George shrank into the chair in an act of silent defiance. Beth sighed. George's growing reluctance to leave the abbey preyed on her mind. Had the stable masters sons become that big a nuisance?

When Oliver stopped in the doorway as if to speak with them, Beth pulled George up from the chair.

"Ouch," he complained. "That's twice today."

Beth pushed him to the door, past Oliver, and into the sitting area. "Enough. You've monopolized Mr. Randall's time sufficiently for today."

Although Oliver's brow rose at her comment, he let them leave without a word and when she was far enough away she let out a relieved breath. George turned back. "Good night, sir."

Beth quickly glanced over her shoulder and was surprised to find Oliver had followed them as far as the doorway. He nodded and Beth pulled George all the way down the hall until they reached their rooms. "There will be no more sneaking off to the east wing. Is that understood?"

"But I'm not in the way there," George protested. "I'm always in the way belowstairs and you don't want me in the public rooms like the library."

Beth pinched the bridge of her nose. "You cannot play in any part of the abbey you choose. It isn't fair, but that is the way of things."

"He doesn't mind."

"Who doesn't mind? Oliver Randall?" Beth choked on a laugh. "How can you tell if he's happy to see you or not?"

George grinned. "He's happy to see me. Happy to see you, too. He just doesn't talk as much as everyone else, but I figured him out."

Beth folded her hands over her chest. "Assuming Oliver Randall cares for anyone is always the first mistake. Try not to be too disappointed when you discover he doesn't. It can be a painful lesson to learn. Trust me on this."

Chapter Eleven

"**Y**ou're getting in the habit of absconding with my servants," the duchess grumbled to Oliver as she stepped into the chaos of his new apartments. Maids and footmen worked together to give the room a thorough cleaning and the mice had all been chased into hiding. He probably should have asked Elizabeth to assign the servants, but she'd appeared much distracted by the arrival of Henry Turner and it was far quicker to just arrange it himself.

"They were needed," he said, glancing about him at the improvements made so far to the room. One chimney had been cleaned and a nice fire burned in the hearth, casting a fine glow over the polished wood and chairs placed before it. The rugs were still out being beaten, but he anticipated their return by the end of the day along with fresh linen for the bed.

"So I hear. I would have preferred to have heard your plans from your own lips. If it's not too much trouble, that is." The duchess's sarcasm was palpable in her last statement and Oliver tried to hide a smile as he worked. The woman did not like to be ignored. She must always be at the center of everything. An attitude that he resisted pandering to.

Oliver stacked another full trunk against the wall. Now that he had the space, he had also made an impressive beginning to his departure. The items that Beth had moved yesterday had already been transferred here and as he looked about him, a feeling of contentment trickled through him. Everything was coming together as he'd hoped.

A housemaid hurried past, bobbed an unsteady curtsy to the duchess, and fled into a bedchamber. His new bedchamber where he would sleep tonight in blessed isolation. Since his return to Romsey his family had hovered, surreptitiously checking in on him when they thought him asleep. His time at Skepington had taught him to sleep lightly. Tonight he would lock the east-wing doors, wander the rooms for as long as he cared to and sleep well past the rising hour if he felt like it.

The duchess cleared her throat. "I also understand that you gave Eamon Murphy leave to be absent from his duties yesterday."

Oliver nodded. "Eamon has a knack for ferreting out fact and fiction."

"About what?" Her Grace's hand punched one hip. "Must I wring that information from your lips, too?"

Oliver frowned. Even gossip took time to spread. "There is nothing to tell yet and to speculate without further enquiry would be unwise. Eamon will return shortly."

"So you are investigating Henry Turner?"

Oliver shrugged. "Perhaps I am. I am curious about him."

"Why? Do you not believe him truthful about his life in America?"

Oliver paused. He had no concrete notion of why Henry Turner's answers bothered him so much, but the more he reviewed them, the more practiced they appeared to be. "He's a skilled conversationalist."

The duchess moved a pile of papers and settled herself on the chair. "So are many people of my acquaintance, but that doesn't mean I distrust them because of it."

"He wasn't when I knew him before and he leaves out specifics in his answers. Who are these great friends of his in America? He's yet to say one fellow's name."

The duchess tapped her fingers on the table impatiently. "So you are doing this out of idle curiosity alone?"

"Of course." He frowned, baffled by her question. "Why else engage in the study of another person and their affairs?"

She sat forward in her chair. "I thought perhaps you were concerned about Mrs. Turner going so far away," she said softly, casting a swift glance at the servants around them to see if her voice had carried. "You did seem a little startled when she said she would go, so I imagine you will be pleased that she is no longer the housekeeper of Romsey. I thought it best to free her time from the responsibilities of the position so she might have time to reconsider her decision to leave. Perhaps you could exert some of that Randall charm and convince her of the advantages of staying."

He blinked. No one had ever suggested he was charming, not once in his life. Annoying, exacting and self-absorbed were the most frequent charges. How could he convince Elizabeth to stay if she wouldn't listen to him? "She was far too good for the position, in my opinion, but I doubt she will listen to me."

A sly smile crossed the duchess's face. "Perhaps if you ask her the right way, ask the right question, she would have a reason to remain."

Oliver raised a brow. "Elizabeth may come and go as she chooses. It is Henry Turner who perplexes me. It is a long way to come simply collect his heir. I have prior experience of the man and he does nothing without the promise of potential gain."

The duchess clenched her hands together. "Leopold has nothing against him personally, only also wonders why he came back."

Oliver scowled. "Leopold trusts too easily."

He placed a compass into the knapsack he would carry and dismissed the matter. Elizabeth would stay or go. He had no ability to influence her decisions. She would remain with George no matter where the boy went. But like it or not, before she departed England, she would have the facts of Henry Turner in her possession. Better to go into a new life prepared than blunder about with blinders on.

The duchess stood suddenly. "You know, this will be a lovely room. Big enough even for a small family to live comfortably in for many years."

"My paternal grandmother lived here with a companion," he murmured. The companion's room had been cleaned, but the bedding had not been salvageable. He would keep the room empty and when he returned he'd make it his study. The room George had said he preferred, the one containing the model of the abbey, would be locked on his departure, nailed shut if he had to, and never opened again. No one must discover the other passageways.

When the duchess remained silent, Oliver looked up. Her eyes had narrowed. "I am sorry that you are going away from us so soon. I find I enjoy having Leopold's family and acquaintances around me immensely. Tobias has brought much happiness to my life by his devotion to my sister. Eamon Murphy and Beth Turner are two people I trust. I would like one day for the young duke to get to know you, too. There is much you could teach him about his inheritance, I think. I wish you would reconsider and stay a bit longer."

Oliver tossed a coin he held into an open trunk. "And how long shall I remain at Romsey Abbey, Your Grace, until you are satisfied?" he demanded angrily. "Another year? Five? A decade? Until the duke reaches his majority? How much more of life shall slip past me while I merely read about events in the world?"

A servant on the periphery of his vision gasped, quickly folded what she held, and decamped the room.

Her Grace swallowed but stood her ground. "Forgive me. I did not consider how my request might sound from your perspective. You are right to want more from your life."

"I apologize for raising my voice, Your Grace." Oliver scrubbed his hand through his hair. "You merely echo what my brothers have said since the day we were reunited. It is no one's fault that they are content here and I am not. But there is nothing to hold me to this place."

He turned away and collected another bundle of books, debating whether they were necessary or superfluous to his needs. He'd already read them from cover to cover. Perhaps they were unneeded. He set them aside, considering whether they could be useful for George Turner's study.

The duchess cleared her throat behind him. "Oliver, I know you have been some time away from society, but feel I should reacquaint you with the proprieties. Are you aware that you refer to Mrs. Turner by her given name? Always. I don't believe you have ever addressed her correctly within my hearing."

Oliver lowered the books to the desk, surprise and chagrin flooding him. He hadn't realized, yet he simply couldn't think of

Elizabeth as William Turner's wife. It seemed wrong somehow to say that name aloud. Oliver did not know quite how to respond, so he chose not to. He would make a greater effort the next time he had to address her. That decided, he continued assessing and discarding the things he'd gathered.

The duchess huffed. "It appears Mrs. Turner understands you far better than I, sir, but I am not so forgiving of your rudeness. You will turn around, sir, and finish this conversation."

Oliver pivoted slowly, rather surprised that Her Grace was suddenly behaving as she should. He bowed to her. "I was not aware that you were Elizabeth's confidant."

"Beth says little yet reveals a great deal. There is something between you, I am sure of it. You two are very good at keeping secrets."

The duchess saw more than she should, but he managed to shrug off the sensation that she might be correct. "On the contrary, Elizabeth is transparent in most things."

The duchess's eyes narrowed dangerously. "Forgive me for being blunt, sir, but I don't believe that for a minute. There might be one thing that could hold you to Romsey if you were brave enough to open your eyes and take the risk. You didn't listen carefully enough to what I said before and I shall let you deduce what that might be on your own. Until the dinner hour, sir."

Her Grace bustled out and the sounds of servants at work around him intruded on his mind. He shook himself. He had no ties to Romsey and Her Grace saying so did not make any connection real. It was just a kiss. A long overdue distraction. Once tasted, Elizabeth could return to the proper place in his memories. A path he had chosen not to take. He fingered the ribbon in his pocket.

Elizabeth would not have spoken of the kiss to the duchess. If she had, Oliver would have already have been pressured to make Elizabeth his wife, ending his plans to leave soon. He shuddered at that prospect. He could not live the rest of his life without seeing any of the world. He must strike out on his own and undertake the grand adventure of his life.

Yes, it was time to forget the past and focus on the future. He took the ribbon from his pocket and strolled into his new bedchamber, admiring the crisp new sheets on his bed as he passed. He opened the top drawer of the bureau, laid the ribbon in the empty space, and left it there. A reminder of the path he'd almost taken.

The tapping of boots alerted him to company. He strolled out to the sitting room and found his brother waiting.

"There you are."

"Here I am," Oliver replied, puzzled by his visit. "You're back again?"

He shrugged. "Cannot get enough of your company."

The patently ridiculous statement brought a smile to his lips. Even older, his brother had not changed. When Tobias's gaze narrowed on a bottle of whiskey across the room, Oliver quickly poured him a drink.

As he passed it over, he noticed his brother's complexion was pale and now he thought further on the matter, he had been pale at breakfast, too. "What's the matter?"

A hard shudder flowed through his brother's shoulders. "I can still hear them sometimes. The screams as they burned."

Oliver led his brother to a chair and eased him into it. He waited while he consumed the liquid and then took the empty glass from him. "There were many times when I thought death would be better for those sharing my incarceration. I saw the worst and best of humanity while confined and I can understand your fears. Skepington housed murderers, thieves, people so deranged that they were a danger even to themselves. The wardens were either cruel or tenderhearted. It just depended on the day."

"Were there any there as sane as you?"

Oliver saw fear in his brother's eyes and pulled him close as he would have done when his brother was smaller and injured. At his age, he'd have thought such measures unnecessary but his brother was greatly troubled by the past and couldn't let it go. Yet he had to. "No. I believed myself the lone voice of reason in that house of the damned."

He released Tobias quickly, ignoring him as he wiped at his eyes.

"How did you survive it?" he whispered. "How did you not go mad?"

Oliver reached for his pocket and discovered too late that he'd put aside his talisman. His hope. He squared his shoulders, determined to ignore the impulse to hurry for the other room and retrieve it. He could be at peace without a single scrap of ribbon. "The name I was forced to use by the duke, Seventeen, stirred much interest from visitors to Skepington. I always seemed to have company of some sort who wanted to study me and I, in turn, studied them."

His brother looked at him curiously. "It never bothered you that they thought you mad?"

"No." He sat back in his chair. "I knew the truth and trusted that those who knew me, should we meet again, would dismiss the claim as fiction. From time to time, I would playact that I was insane just to see what new reaction I'd get from a returning visitor. The difference was quite astonishing really."

"I thought you touched in the head when we met. You spoke so strangely to me and I couldn't understand why you didn't flee since you had the key to your room."

"Your lives were at stake." His fingers fell to his pocket again and the emptiness troubled him. "Or so I was led to believe at the time."

"The duke and his lies."

Oliver stood and poured a drink for himself and refilled Tobias's glass as well. When he passed it over, he raised his in a toast. "May he rot forevermore in his own juices."

Tobias drank with him. "I feel making toasts of that nature will never get old."

Oliver smiled at the quick change in his brother's demeanor. Tobias was the most emotional of his siblings, but his hatred of the duke surpassed anything he'd ever witnessed. Pleased that he'd turned his mind from regret and doubt, he sat down to sip his drink.

"How are you getting on at Harrowdale?"

"Making good progress on the house and grounds. Without Blythe there I can trim the ivy myself and not have her faint as I scale the walls. She doesn't like me to climb anymore."

A laugh built in Oliver's chest at the memory of Blythe's concern as she'd hovered over Tobias after the fire. "That would be because you almost burned off your eyebrows the last time. I clearly remember you saying you valued your looks and didn't want to spoil them for a lady you hoped to impress."

Tobias's smile hinted that the memories of the fire were banished by the thoughts of his future wife. They sat in companionable silence for a time, listening to the flames crackle. When Oliver finished his glass he stood and excused himself for a moment. He slipped into his new bedchamber, slid the drawer open and removed the length of ribbon. As he returned it to his pocket he realized two things. One was that bad memories are more easily banished by good, and Elizabeth was one memory from his past that he'd chosen to cling to. And second, it was good to know his family was safe and well. When Oliver left on his journey he would always know his brothers would be here at Romsey, waiting for his eventual return. There was only Rosemary to worry about now.

Chapter Twelve

---◆---

The trouble with eleven-year-old boys was that they possessed far too much curiosity and an inability to not demand it be satisfied immediately. Beth sent the ball spinning toward the ninepins, narrowly missing her target.

"Why are you so sad today, Mama?"

"It's nothing serious." She forced a smile to her face, willing herself to believe that this unexpected adventure would be good for them. "But come over here and sit with me. I want to talk to you about something important."

George placed the ball at his feet and hurried across to sit at her side. "What is it?"

"How would you like to undertake a long journey?"

It took two seconds for his face to change from concern to utter joy. He jumped to his feet quickly. "Oh, that would be smashing. I was so hoping we could go with him. Thank you, Mama." He threw his arms about her neck and squeezed so tightly she feared he would choke her. "Mr. Randall will show us the most fascinating places."

Beth winced and set her son apart. "We are not to travel with Mr. Randall. Your uncle has invited us to live with him in America, George. That will be even better."

George's face fell. "But what about Mr. Randall? We could go with him instead."

Beth smiled sadly. "Even if he invited you, I could not travel alone with him without causing a scandal. People would talk and a lady's reputation is very important."

A puzzled frown crossed his face. "If you married him there'd be nothing to say. Papa always said you made a good wife."

Beth's stomach dropped away and she quickly looked around to make sure they were still alone. When she was sure they were, she shook her son's arm. "Never say that out loud again, do you hear me?"

"Yes, Mama." George dropped his eyes to the parquetry floor, clearly disappointed that she didn't agree with him. She'd known he'd become enthralled by Oliver's intelligence and would grasp at any chance to satisfy his curiosity. But to suggest she marry to keep Oliver in his life was far too much to bear. George looked up at her curiously. "But why not marry him? He doesn't have a wife and he's kind. He likes me."

Beth pulled her son against her as tears stung her eyes. "How could he not like you? But as to the other, what you suggest is not simple or ever likely. I do not care for him that way."

She released him and faced the window, working to bury her emotions. It wasn't George's fault. He didn't know of her feelings or past disappointments.

A throat cleared not far away. "May we join you?"

Beth turned swiftly on hearing Tobias Randall's hesitant question. He stood at the door, half in, half out, his expression hopeful. Beth nodded quickly. "Of course."

He stepped through the doorway and then Oliver followed. Beth's heart stopped beating. Had they been overheard?

Oliver nodded a greeting and swiftly strode away down the room, halting at George's side to help set up another game.

"I've managed to lure Ollie from his packing," Tobias said quietly as he joined her. "Is it true that you're leaving us?"

"You heard?"

Tobias nodded. "Blythe's not too happy about it. She's talked of nothing else."

Relief coursed through her. So Tobias hadn't heard George's ridiculous suggestion that she marry Oliver just so they could travel with him. She could be at ease again. "I'm still hoping the trip will be unnecessary, but George knows now if you want to talk to him about your experiences in the Americas."

Play recommenced and Oliver proved more of a challenge for George than Beth had been. His accuracy was quite surprising. In his youth, Oliver had never been one to play games. However, now he seemed completely content to toss balls down the room and even ruffled George's hair when her son knocked them all over.

"What I know of America is not for the boy to hear. Where I went doesn't bear repeating. Better to let Oliver answer his questions." Tobias gestured at the pair engrossed in the game. "Ollie missed his true calling. He'd have made a good father, I think."

Beth stiffened and ignored the whispered comment.

"Heard what the boy said as we arrived," Tobias continued quietly. "George is disappointed, isn't he?"

"I'm sure once we're on our way his disappointment will fade."

"I wasn't talking about the trip." Tobias leaned against the wall at her side. "You are both good for Oliver."

Beth scowled. "Nonsense."

"Perhaps not. Don't forget I know the truth. You loved him once. He's changing, I swear. Not much, I grant you, but he's a little warmer each time I return. Who knows what another month will bring?"

"Oliver does not change." Beth shook her head. "Excuse me. I've no patience for fantasy today."

"I didn't mean to dredge up the past Beth, but Blythe mentioned she discovered you alone with Oliver in a locked room." Tobias caught her arm when she would have left him. "You could have a choice in this if you spoke to Leopold about it. Oliver may act in ignorance at times but he does know the proprieties must be observed with a lady."

A hot wave of shame flooded her face as she shook off Tobias's grip. "I hope I misunderstand your meaning, sir. What you suggest, trapping him into a marriage with a blatant lie, is the act of a despicable woman."

Tobias glanced at his brother, his expression thoughtful, and Beth took the opportunity to bolt from the room. She hurried to a small alcove she'd stumbled on one day and hid herself amid the folds of heavy curtains. When she'd been young, only a few had known the state of her heart. She'd loved Oliver with a girl's blind passion. Blind to his faults, blind to his indifference, blind to the fact he would never consider her for his wife. It had taken one painful afternoon to learn why her hopes would never be. He considered a wife and family a millstone about his neck and an end to his dreams. She hadn't meant to eavesdrop on the private conversation, but from that moment on her hopes had been doomed.

So when William Turner had come calling, she'd encouraged him. And when he spoke to her father about a marriage she had not said no. Oliver had no response either way to her wedding plans and so she'd become Mrs. Turner rather than Mrs. Randall. Her dreams had died that day.

She pressed her back against the wall and held her breath as footsteps hurried past. Three, she suspected. Tobias, George, and Oliver?

They continued without pause and Beth covered her face to stifle a sob. Misery had never been too far away and it appeared there was more coming. She wiped at her eyes, brooding on her future. What was she to do in America? She knew nothing of the place save that it was populated by savages that took scalps. She shuddered. How could Henry suggest they face such a danger?

The curtains brushed her arm and she looked up. Oliver stood three feet away. She hadn't even heard him coming.

"Come with me." He held out his hand. "Please."

The courtesy tumbled from his lips awkwardly as she shook her head. He caught her hand and tugged her into the open, hands shifting to touch her spine and propel her down the hall. "I've something to show you that may help you make your decision."

She stopped resisting and moved forward, curious about his insistence. It wasn't like him to involve himself in other people's affairs, but he'd become rather obnoxious with his questions of late. When servants appeared before them, going about their tasks, his touch dropped away but he remained close to her side, shoulder brushing hers occasionally. He led her to the library and to the far corner where a small spiral staircase stood. "The duke has an extensive collection. The section concerning America is up one level."

"Where's George?"

"Tobias was restless and they've gone out for a long walk. They promised to return at four for tea."

Beth had never spent much time in the library because of Oliver's constant presence and had never ventured up the stairs. She shouldn't be alone with Oliver. She had a reputation to maintain, but the lure of information convinced her the risk to her reputation was worth it.

Oliver gave her a little push, nudging her toward the spiral staircase. The stairs were steep and she had to raise her skirts high with one hand to manage them. Halfway up, he drew closer and gathered the rest of her skirts in his hands. "You won't fall, I promise."

Beth hurried up as quickly as she could manage and when she made the top she spun around, keeping her back pressed against the bookshelves. Did he deliberately ignore the rules of how proper people should behave? Yet Oliver made no further move to touch her. He scanned the shelves instead, long fingers running over the spines and plucking volumes from their perches. He thrust three books toward her. "These will do to start. I'll also peruse the newssheets and see what recent events are reported."

Then he returned below, pulling papers from a pile on a far table without a backward glance. He spread them out one by one, fingers running over the pages so swiftly that she was sure he could not possibly be reading them. Some he kept, some he discarded, never looking up to see if she needed assistance with the climb down. Since Beth didn't believe she could manage the stairs, her skirts, and the books on her own, so she sank onto the carpeted rug that covered the walkway floors and opened the first book.

An hour must have flown while she read in her private bird's-nest perch. There was so much to learn and she was grateful for Oliver's assistance. He'd given her two slim volumes containing travelers' recounting and a much-needed book of maps so she might understand the geography. The world intruded and she glanced down at the library floor as another voice joined with Oliver's in conversation. He and Eamon strolled the room, talking quietly.

Oliver wore another frown. "And you're sure?"

"Oh, yes. No doubt about it," Murphy replied. "He's not

staying at the Vulture, but he's been there toasting the locals and spreading his blunt thickly every night. He's quite taken with discussing the past and the changes he's missed."

They paused right beneath her. "And his servants? What do they say about their employer?"

"Not much. Got the feeling Turner took them on after he arrived back in England. He's got rather odd views about women. Expects them to act prim, but I heard he likes it rough between the sheets."

Beth's eyes widened and she quickly covered her lips with her hand to prevent a sound leaving her mouth. Murphy mustn't know she was in the room or he would never have spoken so carelessly about another man's bedding habits. She slid the book to the floor at her side and crawled forward to catch anything else that might help her deal with her brother-in-law.

"He's got one man with him, Fielding, who's calling the shots most of the time," Murphy continued. "Fielding's not a man you'd want to cross. He's got a fighter's stance and remarkably light fingers, too."

"Are you sure?"

"Saw him lift a pocket watch from Brown with my own eyes."

Oliver stared at Murphy, a wide smile lifting the corners of his mouth so he looked far younger and far more devilish than she knew him to be. "Did you retrieve it?"

Murphy brushed lint from his sleeve. "Of course. Might be a touch out of practice, but I remember everything you taught me. The ribbon trick never fails to impress the ladies by the way. Thank you for that."

Beth shifted closer to the railing and a floorboard creaked beneath her. She flattened herself on the floor, hoping the intricate metal railings still hid her from view. What might she miss if she gave herself away? Did Oliver really know how to pick pockets? And why would he take ladies' ribbons? He barely noticed women.

Oliver coughed suddenly. "Interesting."

"'Ere now, you're not getting ill are you? I only agreed to go if you were well," Murphy said, concern ringing in his tone.

"It's just the dust." Oliver slapped a hand to Murphy's shoulder and steered him across the room toward the door, pulling a paper from his coat pocket. "I'm improving every day. I thought this list might help you prepare for the journey."

Murphy studied the paper, brows drawn together as he read. Eventually he nodded. "Thank you. Wasn't sure what to take but now I know."

Oliver smiled. "Can't have you leaving without your smalls."

"I'm sure the ladies we might meet won't mind that at all," Murphy grinned. "What should I do now?"

Oliver glanced up, catching her eye briefly before he looked away again. But that look told her he was dissatisfied with what he'd heard. "Nothing. But keep your ears open and keep me informed of any new information."

When Murphy hurried away, Oliver slowly returned and climbed up the stairs. Beth sat up and smoothed her skirts to neatness again, only a little ashamed that she'd been eavesdropping on another of Oliver's conversations. The last time her heart had broken and she'd rushed away. This time, she had the courage to stay and demand an explanation. "Why would Murphy spy on Henry?"

"Because I asked him to follow your brother-in-law and report any discrepancies in his behavior or the stories he tells." He sat on the top step, very close to her feet, and Beth's heart tumbled over.

She clasped her sweaty hands together. "Why would you want to know more about Henry?"

His brow creased into a frown and he dropped his gaze to her fingers. She forced herself to still her fidgeting as he shifted closer. "I don't trust him," he murmured.

She sighed. "I understand that you might find it difficult to trust after everything that has been done to yourself and your family. It's quite understandable, really. But Henry is exactly as he presents himself. A little coarse, I concede. I understand that you want to keep your family safe from opportunists, but Henry has asked for nothing from the Randalls."

He tilted his head. "He's asked for you and for George."

Beth laughed to break the mood. "I'm a servant, not a possession of the Randalls."

"No. You are more than that," he murmured softly. "You're a friend."

Beth shook her head. Oliver was the last person she expected to express sentimentality over her leaving. Very soon he would be going away and she would never see him again. She would never see if some other lady managed to capture his attention in a way she never could. Beth swallowed past the lump in her throat. "Rosemary's friend," she whispered.

His gaze burned into her and set her body aflame. "More than that."

He didn't move, only continued to watch her silently. Beth struggled for a reply that could turn this discussion to more impersonal subjects. She couldn't bear to hear Oliver spell out in exact terms where she fitted into his definition of friendship. She didn't want what was left of her heart broken again.

After a time, he gestured to the discarded book. "Enlightening?"

"Worrying," she answered honestly.

Oliver reached over her lap for the book, fingers brushing her thigh in the process. The caress jolted her back to the present and her proximity to a man who couldn't love her.

"Adventure does not have to be frightening," he argued. "The more you know of a situation the better you will fare."

He flipped a few pages and began to read aloud. As Oliver spoke, Beth relaxed a bit and shifted until she was comfortable, legs stretched out before her. He had an excellent speaking voice and warmed to his subject easily. Perhaps it was not fatherhood that Oliver would have excelled at, but teaching. That was definitely a profession he could have undertaken with ease.

She closed her eyes, listening with rapt enjoyment and, when Oliver fell silent, she reluctantly opened her eyes again. He watched her, studying her in his own direct way. For a change, she was not unnerved by his unwavering perusal. Not even when his hand covered her ankle quite improperly did she look away. She did stiffen when he caressed her calf, hand disappearing beneath the hem of her gown. She fell into his gaze as he continued the soft touch, only waking from her daze at a sound below. A maid laid a tea tray on a table and then quickly hurried out as if the devil lurked in the library.

Oliver shrugged, but he did not remove his hand. "I'm told I terrify them."

His warmth seeped into her soul in a way she'd never

imagined. Beth wasn't in the mood for subtlety or lies. "It's the way you stare at people for so long. We're not only for your inspection."

A brief smile twisted his lips. "There are many ways to learn about people."

His hand slid up her calf again, his touch firm and warm as he traced the band of the garter tied beneath her knee. He reached as far as bare skin before she came to her senses and prevented further access. "You could always try simply talking to people," she said quickly.

"This is more enjoyable, yes?" The teasing light that lit his eyes took her by surprise. Oliver was flirting? Who would have thought him capable? Not Beth, certainly. "Or is love essential for you to accept pleasure?"

She knocked his hand away and stood, making sure she kept out of range of his wandering hands this time. "What do you know about love?"

"Nothing." He shook his head. "However, it did occur to me that your problems with Henry might disappear or be lessened if you remarried."

"I wouldn't marry anyone for that reason." Beth swallowed the hard lump forming in her throat. "But I am fond of talking."

He sighed. "Talking is not my strong suit."

He stood too, collected her books, and swiftly descended the spiral. When he returned, without the books, he was even smiling. "Would you care to come down for tea?"

She nodded, uncertain of the man before her. Maybe he was changing, but why now when they were both going in different directions? When she arrived at the top of the stairs, he held out his hand and assisted her down to the library floor without another word, just in time for George's return.

Before George, Beth could pretend that those kisses and caresses had never happened. He hurried to stand before the fireplace, rubbing his hands together vigorously. "There are kittens in the stables that you can pet, Mama. One is so new she's barely able to walk."

Beth ruffled his hair. "Before you ask, no, you may not have one."

"Because we're going to America."

"Maybe your uncle will allow one there."

George turned his gaze on Oliver. "Do *you* like kittens?"

"Only the busy ones that catch mice," he remarked as he poured tea for everyone, getting their preferences correct even without asking—milk and sugar for George, black for Beth.

Beth arranged herself on the settee, expecting George to sit at her side and tell her about his walk, but he fell on the food, munching without a word. When Oliver took his place at her side, she tried to ignore the sudden flip of her heart. It wouldn't do to appear too friendly with Oliver while around George. She did not want to add to her son's mistaken belief that a marriage between herself and Oliver was possible, even for the benefit of travel. She shifted as subtly as she could until they were not so closely situated. Oliver foiled that by reclining and laying his arm across the back of the sofa.

"The papers on the desk, George, might interest you," Oliver said. "I've found a selection that includes events from America that are worth reading."

George crammed one last piece of cake into his mouth and almost ran to where Oliver sent him, essentially leaving them alone again.

"He's a bright boy," Oliver said gently. "I hope he has access to good teachers in your new place."

"I'm sure Henry will see to his education."

"That's what I'm afraid of." Oliver touched her shoulder, a fleeting brush against her skin that made her far too aware of him. "If you have no objection I should like to send a selection of books from Romsey with you to further his studies until he is settled. I'd also like to provide you with a list of books for later consideration, should you be able to afford them."

"There is no need to exert yourself on our behalf." She swiveled to face him. "Do you doubt Henry is as rich as he claims?"

Oliver raked his hand through his hair suddenly, a gesture that was quite unlike him. "No one is ever honest when it comes to money and he has a temper. Be wary of him, Elizabeth. I should not like any harm to befall you."

Chapter Thirteen

———◆———

Oliver frowned in frustration at the growing pile of discarded goods cluttering his room. Each time he checked his lists and assessed what he would take with him on the journey, the discarded pile grew higher. A spare pocket watch had seemed a useful addition. There was always the likelihood one might be dropped and the other that Eamon would carry stolen. Thievery among travelers was rife and it was a wise precaution to be prepared.

And why not pack one more journal to write his adventures into? He could miss recording an important event if he had to search high and low for paper in some far-flung little town that boasted no market or shops. He tossed the thick book onto the desk and slouched into his chair, disgusted by his procrastination. He'd planned this adventure in his mind a thousand times, but he was still plagued by the nagging feeling that he was missing something. Something vital.

With a growl, he got to his feet. Restlessness had sunk its claws into him since he'd awakened. He should have gone on his adventure the moment he was freed from Skepington. He should not have given way to his brother's demands to stay at Romsey Abbey beyond a fortnight. But he had succumbed to curiosity about how his siblings might have changed during their separation and had spent many an hour studying them and the women they would marry. From what he could tell, they were smitten creatures with no will left to make decisions on their own.

He strode to the window and stared out at nothing. His mind and body craved excitement. Unfortunately, it was not the activity he'd wanted for the past dozen years. He should not have carried on with Elizabeth in the library or kissed her yesterday. The sense that he'd begun down a path he was unfamiliar with resurfaced, troubling him.

He did not normally importune unwilling women. They either responded to his advances or turned away. Elizabeth had frozen when he'd touched her but when they had kissed, she responded with satisfying enthusiasm. There could be more between them. She was a widow, not a virginal young girl. He could have her warm his bed until he left on his journey, but there were risks involved in that. She could lose favor with the duchess and be turned out. She could end up carrying his child.

He tapped the window frame with the tip of his finger. The risks Elizabeth could face alone if an affair was begun were not small burdens, easily forgotten. When they parted company, her to America, him to parts unknown, he would have no opportunity to learn if there had been consequences after sleeping together.

Perhaps that was the problem. Oliver did not like loose ends left behind.

Elizabeth remained at the edge of his mind, a reminder that once he might have chosen a different path for his life. A path that would likely have been short and abruptly ended given the old duke's fiendish plans to disperse his family. He was lucky not to have married her when the idea had been voiced by his parents. But he'd stuck to his principles and ignored their rather unsubtle hints, quite possibly sparing Elizabeth from a dangerous connection.

There was no doubt he found Elizabeth attractive and certainly pleasing to touch. Her soft body stirred him beyond normal bounds. But even he knew not to become entangled with certain women. Women who preferred marriage over easy, uncomplicated pleasure should be avoided for their own good. When he looked into Elizabeth's eyes he saw forever after, not the ruins of Pompeii, before him.

No, Oliver wanted adventure. He wanted to be free to choose his own path.

A timid knock sounded at the door and he swung around, grateful for the disturbance. "Come."

The small head of George Turner appeared, followed by his fast-growing body. George, too, held a peculiar fascination. Oliver kept making plans for the boy and discarding them the next moment. He would never learn how the boy got on in his life once he left for the New World. And that emptiness stirred his restlessness yet again.

The boy fidgeted with the edge of his sleeve. "Am I disturbing you?"

Oliver shook his head. "Come in. The place is almost livable."

George looked around curiously and mumbled something so softly that Oliver couldn't hear. That would never do. "Always speak your mind, lad. I prefer it."

A wash of color flooded the boy's cheeks, but he squared his shoulders and looked Oliver in the eye. "This room is bigger than our entire cottage was before we came to live here."

Oliver winced. He'd not considered overmuch the life Elizabeth and George had lived before. He should not have made his remark sound like a complaint when he had access to so much. Romsey Abbey, with its vast rooms and rich furnishings, must appear excessive when you were unused to such finery always lying within arm's reach. Everything around him, although Oliver might use them temporarily, belonged to the boy duke playing down the hall, so blissfully ignorant of the hardships of life and the responsibilities that would soon be his.

Like young Edwin, Oliver never paid much attention to his surroundings so long as there were not small creatures sharing the space with him and he was warm and dry. The room was now free of vermin, and the drapes almost entirely replaced to keep out the most persistent of the cold drafts. He'd begun to think the room rather cozy, but a boy used to far less wouldn't share that view.

"Your uncle might have a large house in America," Oliver suggested, intending to light the fire of George's curiosity about the faraway land.

The boy's brow creased as he considered, adding another

unsettling thought to Oliver's mind. He might miss the boy when he was gone. Already he'd begun to delight in the moments of revelation as they appeared across George's face. He was expressive and had an agile mind and thought rather than talked his way through a problem, which made for some fascinating viewing.

"How odd. Uncle George never mentioned a house, or any specifics that I remember."

Oliver silently agreed. Henry Turner had been expansively vague in his description of his life in America. "Well, if he did not then you must ask him about his property and his life over there. I'm sure he'll be happy to furnish you with the particulars since you are to live with him."

Oliver turned away as a slight ache formed in his chest. He rubbed at it, puzzled by the odd sensation.

George tugged on his sleeve suddenly. "Can I help you with your packing, sir?"

Oliver smiled at George's earnest expression, and the ache remained. "I suppose you might. Why don't you move that pile to the far table? I shall not need those after all."

George picked each object up one by one, his fingers flying over the items as he inspected them. "Will you or Mr. Murphy not need a compass on your travels, sir?"

"We have two already. The third is excessive."

George moved across the room at a snail's pace and lingered beside the table holding the discarded items longer than necessary to place them down. As Oliver studied him, he considered what the boy's future might bring. He would be tall most likely and broad of shoulder, too. Already, his arms appeared to be growing out of his shirtsleeves and his trousers were a touch too short. But how would his character change under Henry Turner's influence? The ache in his chest intensified and he sat down quickly in the hope it would pass soon.

Would George become as much a bully as his uncle or would he resist and suffer punishments for any rebellion? Oliver liked neither path and after a long moment's contemplation he decided that George should not go to America with his uncle at all. George had unlimited possibilities for his life here in England. He could study every book in the young duke's library—the duchess would likely not mind as long as he was careful. He could attend Harrow or some other worthy school on the duchess's recommendation and live in greater comfort and security. Leopold, because of his friendship with the late William Turner, would keep the boy safe and pay for everything without complaint until he came of age.

And Elizabeth? Elizabeth would be happier here than anywhere else. He had detected a warmth of approval from Blythe and the Duchess of Romsey toward her in the past weeks, despite her temporary position of housekeeper. A deepening of friendship and affection evident in their concern about her leaving the abbey so soon. They would likely shelter her should she refuse to go to America with her brother-in-law.

She would also be here when Oliver returned from his travels and they could talk again sometimes. Or rather she could talk and Oliver could listen. Yes, that was a splendid plan. Much better than the one to go away.

He looked across the room. George still fiddled with his discarded possessions and the yearning on the boy's face triggered the return of a memory, long faded from neglect. Even as a child, Oliver had enjoyed giving presents to others. It had been many years since he'd had occasion to do so, but seeing pleasure on the face of a recipient of his gift was something he longed to do now.

On an impulse he didn't care to contemplate too deeply, he crossed the room and selected three of the best and most useful items from the pile: a pocket watch, a box containing more pencils than could be used in a year, and the empty journal. He held them out to the boy. "For you. An early Christmas gift, if you will. I imagine we will not see each other again for some time."

The boy stared at his outstretched hand and didn't move. Oliver leaned down so he could better see the expressions on the boy's face. "Now you may write the thoughts swirling around inside your head and use the pocket watch to show you just how late you are for dinner because of them."

The boy gulped, hands fisting at his sides. "Is that what you did? Ran late for dinner a lot?"

Oliver lifted one of George's hands and placed the stack upon his palm. George captured the pocket watch with his free hand

and he drew the bundle to his chest, hugging them tightly.

He rubbed his hand over the boy's head, well pleased that his gift would be treasured and used as he'd intended. "Frequently, but my mother was a determined woman and refused to let me wallow in my thoughts for long. She accused me of driving her to distraction over my tardiness at mealtimes. I never meant any harm to her plans or the soufflé served at dinner. I never thought about the time. Try to be better for your own mother, lad."

The next instant, George wrapped himself around Oliver's waist, the book and pencil box squashed between them. The boy held on a long time and only released him at Oliver's urging. When he caught sight of the boy's face, he reached for his handkerchief and handed it over without a word.

"Thank you, sir." George sniffed and turned away to wipe his eyes.

In truth, Oliver was rather glad he did because the sight of the boy's emotions did strange things to him. He was not used to being ruled by feelings instead of facts. He'd rather discuss a topic rationally than be stirred to passion over it.

He returned to his packing, or rather repacking, for his trip, his thoughts whirling with arguments and contingency plans. He had to convince Henry Turner to leave the boy and his mother here at Romsey, and if he couldn't be persuaded by rational argument, then he would consider what incentive would be sufficient to sway him.

He dug down to a small pouch at the bottom of the trunk and calculated the sum contained there and in the other cases strewn about the room. Likely not enough to convince Henry Turner to go away, but there was always the Duke's Sanctuary below should he need additional funds quickly without raising eyebrows at his actions. People seldom went along with his plans until he explained them fully.

He returned his money to its resting place as he considered how to get into the sanctuary without being seen. That could prove a problem. There was a constant stream of servants traversing the corridor beyond and the long hall was in frequent use. But how to get back out without detection was the biggest worry. He'd likely need help. He'd need someone he could trust not to ask to see the room or covet the contents held there or speak of it to anyone else for the rest of their lives.

Even Eamon couldn't be trusted to that extent. The lure of that much untended wealth would be too great a temptation to avoid speaking of.

Perhaps he could sneak there at night.

George eventually drifted into the room he liked best, leaving Oliver alone with his thoughts. But he wasn't really alone, for now he had Elizabeth and George's happiness foremost in his mind. Now there were two people whose futures he thought of beside his own. The discovery disturbed him.

He sat down at a table and drew paper toward him. His reaction to Elizabeth and George were far from rational and he didn't trust his thinking to be clear. By recording his thoughts exactly as they occurred to him, he filled up a page with cramped script. The fors and againsts of interfering in Elizabeth's life.

When he was done, he poured a glass of port and strolled about the room, considering each item on his list. Firstly, there might not be sufficient funds to even buy the boy's freedom from his uncle's plans. Two, to become involved would arouse suspicion of Elizabeth's character and spark rumors of a relationship existing between them that might in turn give rise to a false expectation of marriage. Three, who was he to determine the course of another person's life? He valued his freedom and should extend the same courtesy to others.

He skimmed the remaining items and paused on the last. Elizabeth might not even want his help. When she had been faced with the news, it had not been him she had turned to for direction.

He tossed back the contents of the glass and refilled it, contemplating the frustrating woman. She was as headstrong and protective as she was pretty and intelligent, but likely to ignore sound advice when presented, no matter how thoroughly. Elizabeth wouldn't ask for his help at all and if he offered, she likely wouldn't listen.

He crushed the paper and threw it into the flames. There was no point involving himself too deeply if he was leaving. Elizabeth had made it very clear she didn't need him.

Chapter Fourteen

Getting to know her brother-in-law again was a slow and troubling task for Beth. Henry simply could not focus on answering the whole of her questions. Before he'd granted her an answer she wanted, he'd veer off onto another topic entirely and it could take almost half an hour to realize that fact.

Since Henry had insisted that it was too warm outside to be comfortable, she'd agreed to his suggestion to give him a tour of the abbey. She kept her eyes on him as they strolled through the library, but he wasn't very interested in books. They stopped often to admire the paintings hung on the walls, vases, and the views revealed at different locations.

Henry leaned close to the glass in the drawing room, peering out into the gardens beyond. "I've not missed England, let me assure you." His fingers skimmed the glass, leaving yet another careless finger mark that one of the overworked maids would have to polish away, and moved to shift aside the heavy red drapes that impeded his view on the next window.

Beth moved a few paces away, hoping to lure him toward the center of the room where there were fewer items he could touch. "Are there any dangers we should be prepared for?"

Henry dropped the drape, his expression thoughtful as he gazed about him. "A few. Nothing for you to be concerned about. I'll be there and you'll always have my servants about you at the plantation house. I gather this room is used most often?"

"It is. The duchess greets all her guests here," she said quickly before returning to her questions about his situation. "Is it named? The house at the plantation, I mean."

Henry studied the clock on the marble mantelpiece, his fingers gliding over the gilding. He tapped it with his finger. "Yes, I believe it has one."

Beth frowned at his answer. Every question answered left her wanting more. And if he did not stop handling the duchess's possessions she would have to ask him his intentions. His attentions to the small but expensive items in the house were making her extremely nervous about his character. "Will you not tell me what the house is called?"

"Lillyvale. I don't much care for it," he added with a shrug. He walked away from the clock and peered out another window.

"It sounds very pretty to me," she murmured.

"Pretty," he exclaimed with enough contempt dripping from his voice to make her shiver. "Now there is a word that could never apply to the place. "

During the course of his visit, Henry had given her the impression that softness or grace had no place in his life. Given what he'd told her so far, it seemed he'd worked very hard to get where he was today. He may be dressed as well as any gentleman she had encountered, but he wore it with such disdain. Dark brocade waistcoat above dark pantaloons, gold fob chain glittering in the sunlight, it all appeared the picture of propriety. The fit of his coat was perhaps a little snug, but that hardly mattered. Her gaze lingered on his hands too often, though. They were not a gentleman's hands.

She led him toward the long gallery where George had scampered ahead. "Do you act as host often to your neighbors and friends?"

"No," he said somewhat gruffly, pausing to peer at one of the Randall's less illustrious-looking ancestors. "There's little time for play in the New World."

"Are there no gatherings or even balls from time to time?" Beth quizzed, determined to learn what type of society she would join.

"Some, but I've no patience for that nonsense. I'm too busy with the estate business." He called to George and demanded her son wait for them to catch up.

Meandering from room to room as Henry was doing was not of interest to her energetic offspring. She could tell George would rather be elsewhere—the library, hanging on Oliver's every word, or pestering cook for biscuits—than spending the morning in this boring fashion. Henry still had some way to go in his manner before he could be considered a *beloved* uncle.

She wasn't especially surprised by her son's reticence to form a closer bond with the man. Henry rebuffed all attempts at kindness, and it was no wonder he had no family of his own. Perhaps all he needed was the right woman to soften his rough edges. Perhaps, when she'd come to know his character better, she could help him find a wife. As sister-in-law she'd be perfectly placed to honestly promote his good qualities to another lady.

With this new plan in mind she joined the pair, but their conversation stuttered to a halt at her approach.

George tugged her sleeve. "Can I go to the library now?"

"Perhaps later," Beth murmured quickly to stave off any arguments. The library was one of George's favorite places in the abbey. He could happily spend hours there and not be at a loose end. But his uncle was here now and shouldn't be abandoned simply because he was bored.

"But, Mama, please," George began. "I was reading about..."

Henry placed his hand on George's shoulder and must have squeezed hard because George wriggled out from under it and whirled around to stare at his uncle. "Ouch. What did you do that for?"

Instead of apologizing, Henry shrugged. "Where I come from that's mild. You don't get ahead in this world by reading from books. You think fast and do what you're told. Living here has weakened you, son."

"I'm not your son," George bit out hotly. "Stop saying that. I'm only your nephew."

"Don't talk back to your betters," Henry growled out, hand rising a horrifying fraction.

Afraid her son would provoke him, Beth drew George against her and kept her gaze fixed on her brother-in-law. When she took in Henry's reddening face, she became all too aware of Oliver's warning. Henry had a temper and George's harmless request had triggered it far too easily.

She caught her son's gaze. "I think perhaps you should return to our rooms instead of the library. We can go out for some exercise shortly. I should like to speak with your uncle alone."

George appeared unhappy about it, but he nodded. "Yes, Mama."

He rushed off, leaving Beth to face Henry. She wiped her suddenly sweaty palms on her skirts, troubled by Henry's aggression and what it might signify. "I would appreciate it if you would not chastise my son again. You are not his father to mete out a punishment. That is for me to decide."

"If you'd raised him right I wouldn't have to intercede. Children should do as they're told the first time and not complain about it."

"You've experience with children?" When Henry muttered "some," she continued. "George has always had an inquisitive mind, but we could never afford enough books to satisfy him. Being here has filled that lack. He was likely wishing to return to the library to continue his research on America, since we are to live there soon."

Henry pointed a finger at Beth. "Don't you speak ill of my brother. Do not dishonor your husband in such a fashion again."

Beth frowned. "I wasn't. William often lamented that he couldn't do more for George and his siblings. Each loss was painful to us both."

"They said you had another son."

"A daughter, too. They died suddenly of a fever that wouldn't abate." She stepped back from her brother-in-law. "Who spoke of my children? Who told you we were living here?"

"I've got ears." Henry looked around them, his eyes narrowing to slits. "But my sources also hinted you were doing more than that."

She understood his implied meaning immediately and did her best not to react. She had often feared Leopold's concern and charity would be misunderstood by others. The gossip about her moving to the abbey must be very thick if Henry had come here fully informed with groundless suspicions exactly one month since she'd improved her living conditions. "The things people gossip about," she said offhand, hoping to break the tension between them. "Not a grain of truth in any of it."

"They say Leopold Randall charged in to save the day. Quite the romantic story if one believes it."

The idea that Leopold Randall could have had romantic intentions toward her, or any woman after meeting the duchess, was ludicrous. She struggled not to laugh aloud because she suspected Henry wouldn't appreciate any levity. "My husband once said that Leopold would feed a starving field mouse if he could. He hadn't learned until his return that William had passed. When he saw how bad it was for us after William's death, he wanted to honor that friendship by supporting us."

Henry's expression grew scornful. "He brought more than just food. They say he brought you here to warm his bed."

"That's a lie." Beth's head snapped up, heat flooding her face at his vulgar suggestion. That he'd voice a suspicion aloud so determinedly proved he was not the kind man she remembered or thought she'd known. She struggled not to clench her fists. "I came to be employed as Lady Venables's companion. There is no impropriety in that."

He stepped closer, eyes hard as flint. "You've got a guilty look about you."

Beth lifted her chin. "I've done nothing wrong."

Henry's face grew skeptical. "Not yet, but women are all the same. Don't think I won't be watching you. You'll not be bringing disgrace on the Turner name if you know what's good for you and your son."

With that he took his leave, but Beth was shaken to her core. She leaned against the wall as she strove to slow the fast beating of her heart. It was clear Henry believed the rumors that she had *earned* her way into the abbey on her back. She covered her face as the memory of Oliver's hands and lips upon her body taunted her. If Henry learned the truth about Oliver then he might have cause for his anger.

But it had only been one kiss and not repeated. She would make sure it was not and that she was never alone with Oliver any more than she absolutely had to be.

She pushed off the wall and made her way upstairs to her bedchamber, expecting to find George there waiting. The peace inside the chamber gave her pause and she looked about. Instead of George, she found a note on her pillow. She rushed to pick it up. Notes were never good news. *Out walking in the east garden with Mr. Randall.*

Beth snatched up her warmest pelisse, hat, and gloves and quickly left the abbey. She trudged through the long grass and less populated area of the estate but saw no sign of her son. She kept walking until she reached a stream and the charming footbridge that crossed it. Downstream a little way, George stood knee-deep in water, a fishing pole poised in one hand. Beside him, Oliver Randall fished too.

So much for avoiding Oliver Randall.

Chapter Fifteen

———◆———

The cold of the slow-moving stream caressing Oliver's bare ankles as he secured the fishing line to the pole reminded him of happier times spent not far from here before his captivity. Then he'd been struggling to master angling with his brothers farther downstream. Trying and failing most often to catch even one trout to lie beside his brother's impressive efforts. Fishing was not a skill he excelled at, but when he'd seen the insect activity in the air outside the abbey's lower windows, he'd rushed outside, dragging Elizabeth's son with him for the adventure of the unseasonably warm autumn day.

The boy's brow was furrowed in concentration, as it had been from the moment the stream had come into view. He cast his line close to a fallen log some distance away. Even now, an hour after landing his first catch, he didn't appear bored by the activity. The boy's skill and persistence impressed him. He had more patience for the activity than Oliver had ever had.

A steady noise, audible over the slow rush of water, interrupted his musings—twigs snapping under the pressure of soft footfalls. He glanced over his shoulder at the closest bank, mildly annoyed by the interruption. His eyes widened and his pulse danced in excitement when his gaze locked on Elizabeth striding toward them. He held his finger to his lips. "Quiet, he has a knack for this."

As the boy's mother drew closer, he discovered his error in

thinking her an eager participant in the fishing adventure. Elizabeth's face twisted furiously. She waded out into the shallow water at the edge of the stream, wetting her footwear and skirts in the process, to grab her son by the arm. "I said to wait in your bedchamber. How dare you disobey me?"

The boy yelped and dropped the rod, guilt writ large on his face. "But Mr. Randall said we had to go now as the mayflies were out. I thought you would still be with Uncle Henry. He said you had things to discuss in private and I had to make myself scarce."

Oliver quickly retrieved the rod before it floated downstream, turning over the boy's words in his mind. At no time had the boy hinted he couldn't come when Oliver had invited him. He hadn't known about Elizabeth's instructions. He'd not meant to undermine her wishes. He cursed under his breath as her gaze turned on him, blue eyes hardening to ice chips.

"It's my fault," he said quickly, taking full responsibility for getting swept up in his own concerns with no thought to what she might have expected. It wasn't in his nature to think of others first, but when it came to the boy he had to remember to do that.

"Of course it is." Her grip on the boy eased and eventually she released him. "You listen to me and no other."

"Yes, ma'am." George retrieved his pole from Oliver and stood tall. "May I continue fishing or do I have to go back with you now? We haven't caught enough for Cook yet."

Elizabeth glanced at the bank where George's efforts, three sizeable trout, lay waiting to be delivered to the kitchens. "I suppose you may as well, but do not disobey me again," she said eventually.

George crowed with happiness and quickly cast his lure into the slow eddy he had been methodically working.

When Elizabeth struggled with her heavy wet dress to regain the bank, Oliver tossed his rod ahead of him before scooping her up in his arms. He carried her to shore, water streaming from her skirts, and deposited her gently on her feet on the grassy slope.

He knelt and caught the bottom edge of her gown and squeezed as much water from the material as he could. Her footwear was likely ruined, however.

He stood to tell her so and her expression caught him off

guard. To his eye, her agitation was too great for George merely slipping from the house without her permission or the inconvenience of a wet dress. Had something occurred with Turner when the boy had left her side?

Determined to find out, he called to George. "Keep at them, lad. I'm sure you'll catch another soon."

George waved and then happily resumed his preoccupation with the water and the lurking fish.

Oliver pointed to a spot downstream. "There's a charming spot further along where you might sit in comfort to remove your footwear. Can I assist you there?"

Elizabeth stared at him as if he'd grown two heads, but eventually she made her way to a rough bench set beside a large stone, big enough for two to sit in comfort. Her skirts slapped wetly against her legs with each struggling step. As she sat, her breath huffed in a telling confirmation that had nothing to do with being damp.

He knelt and set her foot in his lap to remove her footwear. "What happened with Turner?"

"Nothing."

She tried to remove her foot from his grip but he curled his fingers around her delicate ankle and held on. The soft kid boot was soaked completely, the strings tightly drawn and difficult to unlace. "Elizabeth." Her name came out as a soft growl, full of exasperation that had only a little to do with the difficultly of unlacing the boot. He might not completely understand her emotions, but he was certain they were heightened for another reason.

The first boot came free with a wet squelch and he upended it, watching the water trickle out onto the ground. Elizabeth drew her foot back and discreetly slipped her stocking from her own leg, leaving her bare, reddened toes to dangle beneath her above the ground.

Oliver reached for the next boot and it came free more easily. Before she could stop him, he ran his hands up her calf and slipped her stocking from her leg himself. When he handed the soggy length of fabric to her, she snatched it back, her face reddening to an interesting shade.

Oliver took a place beside her on the bench, rather stirred by undressing Elizabeth. He'd quite like to continue in a more private venue and without her son standing a short distance away.

She turned away as she squeezed the water from her stockings and laid them beside her to dry in the weak sunlight where he couldn't see them. He smiled with understanding at what her timidity revealed. His actions had affected her composure. She wasn't quite as disinterested as he had first supposed.

She licked her lips before she spoke. "There are rumors circulating about my purpose in being at Romsey."

"There is nothing unusual in that. Servants spread gossip about their employers every day. Even Skepington's reputation was largely made up. For instance, they had not mounted heads on the staircase walls." He nudged her shoulder with his. "But I digress. Do go on," he urged.

"Heads?" She pressed her fingers to her brow. "Before I came to Romsey, Leopold had done much to help us. He saved us, I am certain of that, but it wasn't hard to miss the speculation in my neighbors' eyes. When I became Lady Venables's companion, I thought having a position would prove them untrue. I was in an honest position and paid a wage. George and I needed the security of a roof over our heads."

"I am glad you were looked after so well," he said, because he thought he must say something to keep her talking to him. Eventually, she'd come to the heart of the problem.

"Because of Leopold's extravagant generosity in coming so quickly after his return and my move into the abbey as a paid companion, it seems my brother-in-law is all too willing to believe the worst of the gossip and has expressed doubts about my character."

"There is nothing to doubt in your character," he replied immediately. "The fault lies with Turner. He wouldn't lift a finger to help anyone when I knew him before and I doubt he's changed."

Elizabeth faced him and her expression hardened. "There are whispers that Leopold's generosity came with a scandalous price that I gladly paid. My character has been tarnished by false accusation I cannot refute to the teller because it's just gossip."

"He thinks you my brother's lover?" Oliver couldn't help the chuckle that escaped him. "Turner is a fool. My brother would never do something so dishonest with a friend's wife. He's far too virtuous for any villainy concerning you."

She huffed and faced the stream. "It's easy for you to laugh. Nothing ever bothers you. You've never cared how people regard you."

He sobered quickly at the pain in her voice. Elizabeth had the same fears as any woman he'd known. Their reputations were all the value they had. He understood now why her emotions were so stirred. The worst she had done was return his kisses. He tried not to smile at the memory and sought a way to ease her discomfort. "Were you supposed to have enjoyed my brother's phantom attentions? I imagine with the duchess in the picture too it must have been quite a wild romp."

Her mouth dropped open and then her hands covered her face. "Oh my. The duchess will be furious when she hears the tale."

He eased closer until their shoulder's touched enough that she could lean against him if she wished. "I'd say she is already aware of any gossip and has dismissed it. She's in a unique position to know the truth and has quite rightly ignored the wild rumor. Leopold wouldn't be anywhere but in her bed."

Elizabeth straightened, her cheeks flaming. "How can you possibly say such a thing to me and not expect me be shocked? You must think me a woman of low morals, too."

"If you had no morals, you would have assumed I was offering to marry you yesterday." He drew in a deep breath as disappointment filled him. For a moment, he had actually considered it a good idea, but she had dismissed it as impossible.

Elizabeth stiffened. After a moment, her blue eyes slid to the side to stare at him. "I knew you could not be serious. Why discuss an absurdity?"

"Absurdity or not, I made an offer, which you rejected out of hand. I doubt many women faced with similar circumstances and desperate for a way out would allow such an opportunity to slip from their grasp so easily." He shrugged. Her indifference to his suggestion hadn't bothered him at the time but discomfort filled him now. "I suppose I would make a terrible husband. However, there are other things I'm quite good at in private. Pleasures that you have not been indifferent to so far."

Her lips clamped together and she did not offer a response to his discreetly made suggestion that she'd enjoyed kissing him. Oliver leaned back against the rock behind them and studied her profile. For a woman who liked chatter and expected a response to her words, he would be a terrible husband. But there were other aspects of life he could easily take up without burdening her with his constant presence. One of them he knew Elizabeth already liked. Touch. He set his hand flat against her back, out of sight so her son could not see should he glance away from the swirling waters.

She gasped as he caressed her spine, curving his fingers to the contours of her body, studying, memorizing while he could. She softened a touch, leaning into his hand, and turned her head to look over her shoulder at him. "You should stop. You're leaving."

"You're leaving, too." His hand curved around her waist and her eyes widened at his daring. His lips lifted as desire filled him with impatience. "And this is far too pleasant to halt just yet, isn't it?"

The speed of her breathing increased; her eyes grew slumberous and soft. "What do you think you're doing, Oliver? This is madness."

He squeezed her bottom. "You said no to my proposal with absolute assurance, but you're not asking me to end this with any confidence now. What do you really want, Elizabeth? More of this, or none at all?"

He slid his hand farther around her back, fingers following the curve of her waist and up until the fullness of her breasts began. Just an inch more and her breast would fit his hand. He'd gauged the size as a perfect fit for his palm before and he longed for proof now. Her breath caught, but she didn't move out of reach. Her eyes were wide, her breathing hastened.

The look in her eyes confirmed his suspicions. She desired more of his touch and kisses, but wouldn't say so out loud. Reluctantly, he removed his hand from her body, sat forward to rest his forearms on his thighs, and stared at the water until his desire for the woman beside him ebbed. Upstream, George peered at the water in blissful ignorance of Oliver's behavior. Soon, they'd need to return to him and perhaps he should be ashamed of tempting the widow. But for now he and Elizabeth had a moment's more privacy to be completely honest with each other.

"I want you in my bed, Elizabeth. I want to run my hands over every inch of you and commit you to my memory." The truth tumbled from his lips with more blunt force than he'd like but he preferred to be honest with Elizabeth about the desire she stirred in him. "If you're willing, my door will be unlocked tonight and every night until I leave if you'd care to continue our intimate discussion in more privacy than this. There is no need to say anything now. Think on it and come to me if your answer is yes."

Silence stretched as he listened to Elizabeth breathe. Her breath churned, her hands twisted in her lap. The long wait for any form of response drove him to look at her. She stood immediately and their eyes met. "George caught a fish."

When she snatched up her stockings and shoes, caught her skirts in her hands, and fled back to her son without a backward glance, Oliver trailed after slowly, watching the pair's merriment over George's success while he buried his disappointment. He had insufficient information to judge his success or failure, but he suspected she might never come to him. She would deny her impulses for the sake of her reputation and propriety. She would cling to her morals and let the pleasure of a new adventure slip away.

When the boy displayed his catch proudly, Oliver smiled and said all the right things to make him happy. But he was very well aware that Beth kept George firmly between them for the rest of their time together. On the path back to the abbey, she refused the support of his arm as she struggled to walk with her wet skirts hindering her progress. Oliver feared it was a metaphor for their relationship.

Chapter Sixteen

---◆---

Beth pushed open the door of the east wing and quietly closed it behind her, heart racing. It was a relief to have traversed the abbey without coming across anyone, servant or master. Her planned explanation for roaming the halls of the abbey because of a nagging hunger was a thin excuse at best. Access to the kitchens was in the opposite direction to Oliver's bedchamber, after all, and so her excuse would not have stood prolonged questioning.

The corridor before her was dim and silent. Beth rubbed her damp palms over the day gown she'd slipped on and squared her shoulders. She was not going to wonder about Oliver Randall for the rest of her life. As the duchess had remarked once, a widow might indulge if she was careful and Oliver's blunt suggestion had reassured her that her distraction with his nearness wasn't entirely one-sided.

At the stream, when he'd made his offer to become her lover, she had been so shocked and startlingly aroused by his suggestion that she hadn't been able to form a coherent response. All she'd thought of at the time was that Oliver was remarkably good at seduction for a man who had been locked up for ten years of his life. Or was it because of that seclusion that he'd turned his attention to an easy mark? With her, Oliver had not needed to flatter or tease to get what he'd wanted. He'd merely stated his desire to become her lover and let her choose for herself.

She leaned against the wall as doubt filled her. She had only ever lain with her husband and had thought she could live the rest of her life without such intimacies again. But Oliver's touch and kisses had ignited her dormant desires and her curiosity was stirred to finally know him in every way she could. To do that required courage. He was leaving and so was she. She'd risk her heart simply because she longed for his gentle touch to stir her senses again.

Resolve restored, she looked ahead. Light and the rustle of pages turning came from the chamber ahead. Beth quietly paced down the thick-carpeted hall, her pulse racing at her daring.

When she reached the open doorway, she paused to survey the scene. Oliver sat before the fire, book in hand, glass of whiskey at his elbow, silk banyan parted to reveal his shirt was undone and his cravat missing. Aside from a brief glimpse on the day after his return and then today at the stream, Beth had never seen Oliver informally dressed. He appeared so content on his own that doubts filled her mind again. She could always leave before he saw her.

At that moment, he met her gaze. Beth froze. Her feet would not move and her throat would not form a sound. She couldn't bring herself to smile or say she'd changed her mind. There was no point in running from her desires because they would never go away. She would sleep with him and then she would know for sure what her life might have been like if circumstances had been in her favor. She would barricade her heart against loving him, but she would give her body into his keeping for just one night.

Oliver stood suddenly and crossed the room with long, sure strides. He gently lifted her chin until their eyes met. His eyes were dark, brooding pools threatening to pull her under. Her pulse pounded through her body and moisture pooled between her legs in a most disconcerting fashion. She'd never been so aroused by a touch so gentle and she feared what that meant for her plans to keep her heart uninvolved. She swallowed, suddenly unsure if she could survive this. "One night," she whispered.

"One night," he agreed instantly.

Oliver's thick lashes lowered and then he stepped around her. The snick of the door lock made her jump, but she didn't dare turn. Oliver brushed against her back; the sudden warmth penetrating her gown took her breath away. His fingers rose to her hair and he removed the few pins that held it in place. He ran his fingers through the long strands and then caught her unbound hair and drew it slowly over her shoulder. His breath whispered over her cheek a moment before his lips settled against her throat.

Oliver made love to her neck with soft, tender kisses that belied his lack of communication. He was undoubtedly willing to be a generous lover and take his time. She was grateful speech between them was unnecessary. She curled her arm behind her head to run her fingers through his hair. Her nails scraped his skull and a soft moan sprang from him.

The next moment, her feet left the floor and Oliver hugged her against his chest. He strode to his bedchamber and deposited her on the soft mattress. Beth trembled as he rushed to remove his banyan and shirt. It would be over quickly then. Disappointment threatened to banish her excitement. She had a brief moment to admire his nudity as his breeches and smalls followed after and he joined her on the bed, pressing demanding kisses to her lips.

Beth clung to him, astonished by his urgency. To her mind, he'd been largely indifferent to her kisses, but she supposed something in her expression had alerted him to her need and willingness for anything he'd give. There was no turning back and he knew it. He must be pleased to have convinced her without having to say much at all or be in any way charming. He'd likely known her decision as soon as their first kiss.

She ran her hands over his shoulders, surprised by the lean bulk under her fingers. She'd thought him not so muscular, but the last weeks of frantic activity had changed him. His face, when he raised it between kisses, had a healthy glow about it that proved him better. His arms were corded muscle encasing her in his strength.

A wave of heat swept over her cheeks as Oliver rubbed against her, torturing her nipples with the promise of attention. His hand rose to cup one breast through her gown, his eyes flickering from one to the other as if comparing them to judge their worth. When his thumbs brushed over her nipples, her back arched from the pleasure of it. She wanted his hands on her bare skin but she wore far too many clothes still.

Beth set her hand against his chest and pushed him back.

Oliver gave her space grudgingly, pressing one last kiss to her lips first before he sat back on his haunches, his eagerness to make love apparent when her eyes dipped to his groin.

Blushing furiously, Beth struggled to a sitting position and grabbed the hem of her gown, thankful it required little effort to remove. Oliver's hands joined with hers and together they removed her clothes, tossing them to lie discarded on the floor.

His gaze roamed over her body and she sucked in her stomach as anxiety filled her. She was not a young woman anymore. She'd borne three children and her hips were no longer as slim as they'd once been. Would he find the fine white scars on her belly repulsive? Would he end this now that he'd seen her properly?

A slow smile lifted the corners of his mouth and he pressed her back to the bed. When he lay beside her on one elbow, Beth braced herself for another direct examination. His fingers traced everywhere: between her breasts, over the hard buds of her nipples, lower to dip into her belly button and around and around the softness of her stomach where the worst of her pregnancy scars were. His expression did not change. The same smile graced his lips and when he eventually covered her mound with his hand, she'd had enough of his silence. "Well?"

His smile grew. "As beautiful as I calculated. Perhaps even more so."

He kissed the tip of her nipple softly and then drew the peak into his mouth. The pull of his lips caused her core to throb impatiently. He caressed her stomach before he covered her mound again. As he shifted, the head of his cock brushed her hand and she reached for him, testing the size and feel of his length. He stiffened as she wrapped her hand more firmly about him and when she stroked, he rocked against her hand with a deep groan.

While she fondled him, Oliver made love to her breasts. He shifted to kiss the other and loomed over her. With his body easily accessible, Beth explored him with her hands, too. There was not a spare inch of flesh anywhere about him. His body was firm and taut. She plucked at one nipple until he groaned and eventually he knocked her hands away from his erection. When he covered her, she wrapped her arms about his shoulders and ran her hands over his back. Heat and slick perspiration coated his skin.

Beth bent her legs and pressed her feet to the mattress, holding Oliver's hips firmly between her knees. His mouth claimed hers urgently. Their tongues tangled as her desire for more rose. He shifted suddenly and hooked her legs about his body, falling against her as if he'd done so all their lives. The rub of his hot flesh against the inside of her thighs did terrible things to her patience. She clawed at Oliver's back, digging her fingers into his skin as he rubbed against her. But it wasn't close enough. She wanted him inside her and she whispered her demand into his ear.

The next moment, the head of Oliver's erection pressed against her opening. Her back arched as he possessed her in one slow thrust. His mouth descended on her throat and he kissed and nipped hungrily until they were joined completely. Beth burned as he held still inside her. She waited for him to withdraw and plunge again. Despite his earlier urgency, he waited as if he too was savoring the moment she'd wanted all her life.

Yet if he didn't move soon, she'd have to. There was a greater urgency to their coming together than she'd ever experienced. It was as if her whole life had been empty until this brief moment in his arms. Perhaps it stemmed from her reckless love for him. Beth wrapped her arms around his shoulders and held on. What a fool she was to believe her emotions should be shut away at a time like this. She'd never stopped loving Oliver for one single moment since she'd fallen for him all those years ago.

Beth forced herself to find some control over her feelings and loosened her grip, half afraid she'd blurt out the state of her heart or beg him never to leave her. As with everything, Oliver could not be rushed unless he wanted to be, but eventually his hips retreated and thrust against her in a slow dance that took her breath away.

He leaned up on his hands and stared down at her.

On a usual day, Oliver's silent scrutiny disturbed her. But tonight, knowing he was making love to her at the same time, provided a much more satisfactory reaction. A tight ache formed where they joined. A need demanding to be fulfilled. Oliver caught her right breast in his hand and gently cupped it. "As I suspected. Perfect," he murmured, his voice so deep and warm that her heart skipped a beat.

Beth tightened her legs about his waist, caught his head between her hands, and smiled. He might not make conversation well but he made love so much better and said exactly what she needed to hear most. She tugged until he lowered and pressed his lips to hers. Beth wrapped herself tightly around him, little caring if her behavior was too needy. She wanted him to touch her everywhere.

Oliver moaned and the pace of his thrusts increased. His grip tightened until they were wrapped as tightly together as was possible and still be able to move. Beth ran her hand up and down his damp back, threaded her fingers in his hair, and kissed any part of him she could reach. Just a little harder, deeper, a little faster to ease the unbearable ache. Oliver bucked against her, pressing deeper with each thrust until she cried out and shuddered too quickly. Before she was ready to let him go, Oliver fought to be free of her embrace and he turned aside, spilling his seed on the mattress with a deep, shattering groan.

Disturbed by being presented with his back, Beth laid her hands on him and traced his spine to his waist. Oliver rolled back a touch and trapped her hands beneath him, his breath coming in a harsh, desperate rush. His chest rose and fell rapidly. Beth tugged her hands free and slid one over his chest, brushing his nipples in her need to remain connected, to retain their intimacy. When Oliver remained where he'd fallen, Beth shifted closer and cautiously placed her arm around him. He picked up her hand and kissed her palm before pressing it back to his chest.

A small sigh left Beth as she snuggled against him. He'd surprised her. He *was* a passionate man, but only in private. It was a pity she couldn't have more than this. The thought saddened her momentarily but she was resolved. Just once. Just one brief moment in his arms to last her a lifetime.

She relaxed, lulled by the steady beat of his heart beneath her palm and her own lassitude from his intense lovemaking.

"Marry me," he said suddenly.

Although her heart raced at his surprising proposal, she knew better than to accept at a time like this. He'd given her great pleasure and proved what she'd hoped for all along. She wouldn't marry someone who couldn't love her. She hadn't loved her husband and regret still tormented her. She kissed Oliver's shoulder as sadness filled her. "Absolutely not; there's no need."

A deep rumbling sigh left him and for a moment she wondered if he'd argue his case. When he didn't, she settled again, content with this one brief moment of intimacy with the man she'd always loved. His heart returned to a steady rhythm, his breathing settled quickly. The moment she'd longed for all her life was perfect. She closed her eyes, at peace with her life at long last.

"Don't fall sleep, Elizabeth," he warned a moment later.

Beth pressed one last lingering kiss to his skin, knowing that their time was over too soon. "I won't. I must leave."

"Not yet though." He wriggled free of her embrace and rolled her onto her back. The smile he bestowed took her breath away. "We've only just begun."

Given the urgency of the kiss that followed, Beth concluded Oliver might not be finished with her for some time yet.

Chapter Seventeen

———◆———

Oliver had tried not to think about last night seventeen times before he gave up and returned to his memories of Elizabeth's glorious body held firmly against his. His wicked thoughts and plans for further encounters were so much more interesting than the cold hard facts in his book about Italy or his plans to leave Romsey. Not that he'd let on exactly when he would go. The less his family knew, the better. They couldn't punish his ears with their pleas or wound his eyes with their stricken expressions. Without their disapproval dogging his every moment, he could consider how to lure Elizabeth in his arms once more and hear her sob his name as passion claimed her.

And if he didn't think about leaving, he wouldn't be considering what life might be like if he stayed.

He closed the book and tossed it with the other discarded tomes, sure he was on the verge of making an ass of himself. Elizabeth had been very clear that she'd come to him for one night and that was all he could reasonably expect. Reason, however, had disappeared with the first sight of her beautiful body. He longed to locate her and do something incredibly rash and irrevocable right now.

"What has you so out of sorts?" Leopold grumbled, paper rustling between his hands as he turned the pages. "You've not stopped huffing since I found you here."

He focused on his brother. He couldn't possibly tell him the truth—Elizabeth would not like that, so he scratched around in his mind for a likely excuse he could utter that would prevent further discussion. "A calculation about the length of my trip."

As hoped, Leopold rolled his eyes and returned his attention to his paper.

But Oliver wasn't so easily appeased. Several nights, if he could persuade Elizabeth of the necessity, might not be long enough to satisfy his hunger for her kisses and her perfect body. He'd come undone, all his carefully considered opinions that passion was something he could live without were under threat.

He stood and left the room without a word to Leopold, wandering aimlessly into the drawing room to cool his ardor. He had never believed he needed intimate relations to be content with his life. The path of an adventurer was one of determination and purpose. Surely one night with Elizabeth had been enough to last a lifetime.

But then he heard Elizabeth's voice ahead somewhere and his body hardened all over again as lust gripped him. He followed the sound of her voice until he reached the long hall. She stood outside a chamber, arm moving as she described what she wanted done. Wedding plans for the duchess by the sounds of it. Given her enthusiasm for the subject, she'd likely be busy for hours.

He approached slowly, admiring the body snugly hidden beneath a demure dark wool gown. She faced him and her eyes widened, her breath catching in surprise. Desire sparked in her eyes and then quickly vanished, hidden by wariness and modesty. She dipped into a curtsy. "Good morning, sir."

He eased closer, eyes dropping to the neckline of her disappointingly modest gown and then lifting to her soft lips. His pulse raced anew. One night had not been sufficient to banish his need.

Eamon Murphy's head poked through the doorway and into the hall, immediately halting Oliver's plans to touch and kiss Elizabeth. He schooled his features to show only curiosity and expressed his question to his oldest friend. "What do you do here?"

Eamon lips quirked. "Candelabras. We're on the hunt for several large ones, gold, that her grace remembers from years ago."

"The east wing attic has two, the closet attached to the ballroom has three, and there are more elsewhere should they be required," Oliver supplied quickly, keen to send Eamon off on an errand that would take some time.

Beth and Murphy's brows creased in unison. "There's a closet off the ballroom?" They said it at once and then suddenly looked at each other and burst out laughing.

Confused by their sudden camaraderie, a closeness he had not detected earlier, Oliver nodded slowly. He held his hand out to Elizabeth. "I can show you the ballroom closet if you like."

Instead of taking his outstretched hand, Beth faced Eamon. "Get the ones in the east wing attic and have them polished properly. I'll see what else this closet Oliver mentioned contains and if it could be of any use. We haven't much time."

When Eamon hurried off, Beth looked at him expectantly, one brow rising. "This place needs a map drawn and a proper accounting taken of its possessions. The things we have stumbled across today in the strangest places boggles the mind. Thank you for your offer of assistance." She smiled suddenly and his whole body tightened in anticipation of any small moment he could share with her.

"My pleasure," he said, thinking of her body flush and warm against his last night and her hands tugging at his hair, urging him on. "This way."

He briefly touched her back and then let his hand drop away. "Why are you scouring the abbey in search of candelabras? I thought you were no longer housekeeper."

"The duchess has graciously allowed me to render what help I can." She smiled up at him. "I don't mind. Every woman enjoys weddings."

"Ah," he murmured as he opened a door and allowed her to pass before him. But her comment brought a question to his mind. Had she enjoyed her own wedding to Turner? Had Turner been a good husband and lover? When he glanced at her again, he decided he'd rather not know. If she missed Turner then he would be viewed as a paltry replacement and Oliver rarely liked to be second in anything.

He led her deeper into the house. Listening to the soft tap of her slippers beside him brought a smile to his lips. He almost had her alone, but rather than act intimately in the hall where anyone might see, he elected to wait until they reached the ballroom before he touched her again. The closet off the ballroom was private, secluded from casual observation. He could kiss her there and no one would ever know.

Their footsteps echoed in the empty ballroom, their shadows danced across the floor to the beat their feet tapped out. He looked ahead and caught their reflection in the mirrored wall ahead. His steps slowed. Beside Elizabeth, he appeared ancient and his chest tightened. He'd lost his youth because of the duke's treachery, but he'd lost the path to Elizabeth as his wife all by himself. For the first time ever, he doubted the life he'd chosen for himself. He'd spent all morning wishing to be alone with Elizabeth and it was unlike him to be so obsessed by lust.

His enthusiasm for seduction waned. What had he been thinking yesterday? Making love to Elizabeth, becoming involved in her concerns, was not the way to live an independent life. She continued ahead and the gap that grew between them in the reflection gave him pain. What had changed in him since yesterday?

Elizabeth swung around to see what kept him. "Oliver?"

"Forgive me," he murmured as he hurried to open a discreet panel set in the wall and revealed the closet, shaking off the disconcerting confusion gripping him.

Beth hurried inside the six-foot-square room, smiling happily at the contents surrounding her. Candelabras, silver platters, and crystal wineglasses filled every conceivable space. She clutched his arm and bounced on her toes to kiss his cheek. "I never would have found this. I doubt anyone here now even knows this room exists. The contents of this room fill several other needs on my list, as well. Thank you."

He smiled down at her, wondering why her joy in such a discovery moved him. "There are many such places concealed about the abbey."

"Like the Duke's Sanctuary?"

Her question ended his pleasure in the day. He crossed his arms over his chest. "The sanctuary is gone."

Her brow rose as she stepped closer, hands sliding over his folded arms in a soft, beguiling caress. "It's not like you to give up so easily."

Oliver's heart raced. Had George said something about the model, after all? If so, he was deeply disappointed in the boy. He'd have to answer Elizabeth carefully lest she become even more interested in the subject. It was better that she knew nothing and if she persisted with the topic, he'd distract her until she forgot all about the treasure hidden beneath their feet. "There's nothing to be found."

Her smile fell away. "I suppose there is a good reason you've not disclosed the location for the second entrance."

Her observation surprised him even as he captured her hips and dragged her flush against him, marveling in the pleasure of being able to do so. Yet his unease remained. "What makes you think there is another way down?"

"In this place?" Elizabeth laughed, lifting her hand to gesture at the room around them. "If there *wasn't* one I'd be highly surprised. I can probably guess why you chose to say nothing. There's been enough trouble in the past without confiding in someone who isn't a Randall. Keep your secrets, Oliver. I'm not the one you should share them with, anyway."

She left his arms and faced the shelves behind her, rummaging through a heap of tarnished silverware. Damn but she was a clever woman. She knew him, saw through his lies, faster than he'd anticipated. He moved behind her and slid his arms about her waist, pulling her against him tightly.

A soft sigh left her mouth as she leaned her head against his shoulder. Oliver inhaled deeply of her scent and slid his hands over her gown to cup her breasts, wishing he could feel her nipples hardening. But she was properly dressed; corset and layers of warm wool covered her body. He moved his hand down to her hips and then lower still, splaying them over her upper thighs, delighting when her breath hitched at his caress. He slowly inched her gown higher. What he wanted was her bare skin and warmth against his fingers.

"Ollie, the door," she whispered suddenly.

Oliver quickly took care of their privacy and spun Elizabeth so she could lean against the wall. He fell to his knees, raised her skirts again, skimmed the stockings encasing her slim legs with his hands, and pressed a kiss to every patch of bare skin he could reach. With her fingers tangling in his hair, offering encouragement, he dared kiss higher. Her thighs trembled as he urged them to part and pressed a fervent kiss to her curls. Frustrated by the awkwardness of her position, he eased one of her legs over his shoulder, opening her stance and revealing everything he needed right now. Oliver dipped his head, hungry for the taste of her.

He teased her mercilessly, licking her lower lips with long strokes of his tongue, delighted by her soft moans and how her nails dug into his scalp, keeping him exactly where he wanted to be. She came quickly. A choked cry muffled by her hand. When her tremors had ceased, he rose, freed himself, and slid inside her welcoming warmth with a sigh of relief. He'd needed her all day.

He shifted Elizabeth until she was completely off the ground, legs wrapped around his waist, arms twining about his neck. He moved within her, recklessly pumping his hips with no thought for the next moments or the future. God, she felt good about him. Her passion inspired him to increase his own.

Her lips caressed his jaw, his cheek, the corner of his mouth. He turned his head and claimed those wandering lips, stifling his own satisfied sigh as her tongue skimmed his.

He propped her back against the wall and placed his hands to either side of her head. He wanted to see her expression as he filled her with each slow thrust. There was nothing like her passion in his experience and he couldn't get enough.

She bit her lip as his thrusts slowed. Their eyes met. "Good?" he asked.

"Yes," she whispered and then closed her eyes. Oliver shifted until he held her hips in his hands and slowed his pace even further, prolonging the pleasure and holding off his own release. He wanted Elizabeth to come once more before he did. He wanted to see the expression he'd missed when he'd been kneeling at her feet.

He released her hip and tangled his fingers in her curls. She moaned, a soft complaint that had no real substance, and opened her eyes. Her slit was damp and her clitoris swollen. He rubbed his fingers against the needy flesh. Elizabeth's back arched as she pushed onto his cock, burying him inside her unexpectedly.

The added friction sent a surge of lust straight to his groin.

He surged into her and retreated, each time a little faster and harder than the last. His hand became wedged between them, fingers pressed to her clitoris and unable to move. Elizabeth didn't seem to mind. Her hands clutched at his waistcoat, pulling him deeper with each thrust. When she tightened around his cock, coming with a quiet sob, Oliver lost all control. He slammed into her, roughly holding her against the wall as he took her body fast and hard. Elizabeth met his gaze with sated languor, a soft smile spreading over her lips at his aggression.

That smile brought pleasure within reach. His balls tightened, his loins throbbed and, at the very last moment, he wrenched himself free of Elizabeth's clinging arms and legs as he came. He struggled to catch his breath, fighting the need to plunge back inside her once more. Instead, he dropped his head to her shoulder and kept her body at a distance. "Did I hurt you?"

"No." Her immediate answer brought relief. He couldn't bear to have been too rough, but there were moments with Elizabeth when he couldn't get close enough. When it had happened last night, he'd had the option of rolling away for a moment. But in a closet, standing, there was nowhere else to go but remain in Elizabeth's arms.

It wasn't a bad place to be, but it was dangerous to both of their futures.

He drew in a deep breath and collected his absent wits. "We had better go soon."

Elizabeth grumbled against his shoulder but then moved out of his arms quickly, leaving him cold and abandoned. She quickly straightened her gown, running her hands over her body to see what had been disturbed by his lovemaking. She wasn't too badly mussed and Oliver considered whether he could be a touch more demanding the next time. He had a feeling Elizabeth wouldn't object and that made him long for the evening to come quickly. He would make love to her again. He had to.

Elizabeth faced him, her expression amused. "Get dressed."

Oliver glanced down and, embarrassed that he had been standing there with his trousers at half-mast all this time, daydreaming of their next encounter, he quickly tugged them up, shoving his shirttails in quickly. Elizabeth approached as he fastened the last button on his trousers and smoothed his waistcoat.

"Lean down for me," she whispered.

He pushed his face toward her and her fingers rose to tangle in his gray hair. His eyes closed of their own volition at the tender touch and he held the position until her fingers fell away. The way she touched him held no pity for the aged state of his appearance and when he opened his eyes to view her face, her eyes had grown dreamy. "Perfectly respectable once more," she murmured with a pleased smirk twisting her lips.

She swiped at a dust mark on her gown and then laughed. "Whereas I look like I lost a battle with propriety. At least I have this room's dusty state to blame for the condition of my gown. I'll suggest a maid be sent here before the wedding and that should disperse suspicion of my activities."

Oliver blinked at Elizabeth's fast return to practicality. Were women not supposed to act more affectionate after making love? Last night she'd dozed between bouts of lovemaking and he'd had no time to observe her mood. Had he misunderstood everything about women? He wanted to hold her, but instead he brushed at the dust marks on the dark wool of her gown until they were less noticeable.

Elizabeth wrapped her fingers around the stem of a candelabra and moved to the door. At the last second, she turned her head and winked at him. "Come along, Mr. Randall. I'm sure I can find plenty of ways you can help us prepare for this wedding. Are there any more closets like this, long forgotten and suitably private?"

"I'm not sure."

Her smile widened. "Then you'd better stay close to me while we discover the truth." With her free hand, she beckoned him to follow. Reckless passion stirred in him again as he collected the remaining two candelabras and hurried after her. He was certain there were more forgotten chambers inside Romsey in which he could be close to Elizabeth.

Chapter Eighteen

A secret affair was exactly what Beth had needed to regain her confidence. Since she'd shared Oliver's bed, she rose to face each day with renewed optimism that all would be well, her heart eager to see what would happen next. She wasn't even concerned too much over her son's preference for Oliver's company. Oliver could give George the dispassionate guidance he needed without attempting to take his father's place.

She looked ahead to the tree line and spied three tall shapes striding along the path that led directly toward the abbey. Oliver was out on his daily walk, likely suffering through his brother's demands he remain at Romsey. They would have no luck. Oliver had made his decision to go.

There was nothing anyone could say to sway him from his purpose, which made Beth even more determined to make her time with him as memorable as possible. The wait for George to fall asleep each night, or for Oliver to find her and lead her to a deserted chamber nearby for a brief taste of passion, consumed her every thought. She did not know how the outwardly reserved man did it, but one glimpse of his lean profile turned her thoughts to wickedness and the best way to get him alone.

"I've booked passage for us on December third," Henry said suddenly as they entered a barren archway, waiting for spring to fill it with the color and the scent of wisteria in bloom.

Beth, who'd been lost in her memories of Oliver's lovemaking, stared at her brother-in-law in shock—that was the end of the week. He'd been at Romsey for over an hour and hadn't given a hint that their departure was imminent at any time before that. In fact, he hadn't mentioned returning to America at all. He'd just walked and huffed occasionally at each pretty spot they came across. She swallowed the lump in her throat. "That's very sudden."

Sensing the panic in her voice, George returned to her side and his hand slid into hers, squeezing tightly.

Henry, never one to hide his scorn for her reluctance to embrace his plan to relocate, rolled his eyes disdainfully. "I've a business to return to and no more time to spend on nonsense such as this."

He waved at the gardens around them. The sun had come out today and since the weather was so pleasant, they'd been strolling, giving George a chance to stretch his legs and get to know his uncle. At least Beth had thought it was pleasant. "I've barely considered what to pack for us. We cannot be ready to sail on Friday."

Henry stopped and set his hands to his hips. "What could you have to pack? From what I've heard, you sold off practically everything my brother valued as fast as you could."

Beth's temper rose at the accusation underlying his words. "I sold the things from my dowry in order to survive."

Henry made an indelicate sound that had George clutching her whole arm and crowding her back. Her son wasn't warming to his uncle the way she had imagined and she didn't blame him. Henry wasn't particularly likeable. Once, they'd talked about Henry's return with hope and optimism for his presence. How badly had they got it wrong? Henry wasn't the family or savior they'd longed for. He meant to break them to his will.

He wagged a finger in her direction. "Well, there had better not be too much useless rubbish coming with you. I've no time or patience for extravagances."

Beth drew herself up straight, determined not to cower to such a bully. "We'll take what we own."

Henry snorted again and looked about him, his expression one of extreme distaste. "I'll come for you early, as the sun rises on Thursday. We've a goodly distance to travel and no time to shilly-shally about. Do not keep me waiting."

A movement caught her eye across the garden and three tall forms came into view, moving toward them: Oliver in the company of his two brothers. Her heartbeat sped up a touch. Oliver's steely gray hair was mussed from the wind and a healthy glow lit his cheeks. He appeared the picture of health at last.

Warmth pooled between her legs and she scrunched her toes in her slippers to fight the reaction. Since he'd kissed her, made love to her, she'd had a great deal of trouble getting her traitorous body to forget during the daylight hours what his touch did to her senses. A riot was the best description and she couldn't afford to show any hint of it before others. Especially not now.

Oliver could never know that she was in love with him, had been in love with him her whole life. He wanted none of that and, with Henry standing at her side watching her behavior for signs of wickedness, she couldn't even risk hinting that she was pleased to see him looking so well.

Thankfully, it was Leopold Randall who hailed them and approached first, Oliver and Tobias were engaged in deep conversation and trailed behind.

"I wondered when you'd call again, Turner," Leopold began as he thrust out his hand. "I was about to send word to you. Care to come shooting tomorrow? I can lend you a prime piece if you require one."

"That sounds a fine idea," Henry agreed and the two soon fell into a conversation of guns and hunting that excluded everyone else. Tobias and Oliver joined her.

"Never much cared for shooting," Tobias muttered as he caught Beth's eye and winked. "Especially not once I'd had the whole estate pointing guns at me."

She held in a laugh at his outraged expression. "Then you should have knocked on the front door rather than climbing the trees, you ape," Beth said quietly, keeping an eye on her brother-in-law to check that he wasn't listening.

She didn't think it right to tell tales, even to her own family, about the Randall's past problems. Once Tobias had been unmasked as the troublemaker, the family had grown closer than ever before. And when Oliver was returned, weak but unharmed, everything had almost appeared normal between them.

Tobias clutched his chest dramatically. "Wounded, and by such a tender blow."

George relaxed his grip on her hand and stood straighter. "Do you still climb the abbey, sir? I've not seen you do it and they say you're a wonder to behold."

Tobias ruffled his hair. "Sorry, lad, you won't. My feet are firmly planted on the ground now. There's no one left to rescue." Tobias cast a sly glance at Oliver, who'd remained silent on the subject of his adventurous younger brother's antics.

"There is Rose still to locate," Oliver said abruptly, a frown forming over his face.

Tobias sighed morosely. "I wish Rose was here. Leopold is going to have no hair left soon. There'll be just one tuft left at the top that he musses every time another letter arrives with no news of her."

Beth rubbed her hands up and down her arms as a sudden chill swept her skin. "I miss her, too. But she's still alive. I am sure of that."

"But why doesn't she come?" Tobias grumbled. "Leopold has had an advertisement running in every paper with no success. She's vanished without a trace."

"Give her time, Tobias," Beth murmured gently, concerned by the rising of his voice. "Who knows how far she ran ten years ago? The one thing you should remember is she could look after herself better than any girl I knew. Trust that she's safe."

Oliver met her gaze directly. "She might not believe the messages are true."

Tobias groaned loudly. "You mean she may not even believe we posted them?"

"It's a possibility I've been considering this past week to account for her silence." Oliver shook his head suddenly. "If I come up with an alternative wording next week I'll write immediately."

Tobias fell silent and Beth risked a glance at Oliver. His expression hinted he was far away in his thoughts and she quickly looked elsewhere before she was caught staring.

"Wait," Tobias said suddenly, waving his arms to draw Oliver's attention. "What do you mean you will write next week? Next week you'll still be here."

Beth steeled herself for pain as Oliver let out a long sigh that could only bode ill news for his brothers. "I received a response today to my enquiry about a passage to cross the channel," he said. "My ship sails on December second."

Beth sighed. "A bare day before we sail."

Tobias glared. "You're leaving so soon, too?"

Oliver's attention shifted to her and his stare grew uncomfortable. There was something unusual in his expression that she hadn't seen before. Disappointment? Sorrow, perhaps. She nodded quickly to dispel the illusion. "I was informed of the date of our departure just before you joined us."

George clutched her hand again and laid his cheek against her arm. She hugged him quickly. "Looks like we are all bound for adventure within the week. I am so sorry that I will miss your wedding, though, Tobias. I'll wait and hope for a letter to follow me so I may hear all about it."

Tobias looked between them. "You're both mad to think you'll be happier elsewhere. You've spent too much time in the sun." He threw up his hands and stalked away, heading for the abbey and, Beth guessed, for the likely comfort of his future wife.

She followed Tobias's progress until he slammed through the terrace doors. When she faced Oliver again, he was watching her intently. He drew closer. "You do not sound excited about America."

She smiled quickly. "We haven't had a lot of time to prepare."

Oliver slued around to study her brother-in-law, his lips pursed. Eventually he huffed, a sound she'd heard from him quite often of late. "And he's hardly been forthcoming. If you have doubts, you should remain here. There's plenty of time for George to join his uncle and learn his business, whatever that may be, when he's grown older."

She didn't like that Oliver's thoughts ran with her own. But what she did with her life wasn't something he should concern himself over. He hadn't wanted a say in her life years ago. He'd allowed her to marry someone else. She wouldn't give up her independence now; no matter how well he made love or how many times he could entice her to share his bed. "There's no reason *not* to go now. Do not give our happiness another thought, sir. You must be quite anxious to be on your way, too. After all, it's everything you've dreamed and spoken of your entire life."

His eyes lowered. "I suppose it was. If you'll excuse me, I have my own packing to do and a brother to reconcile with the news. Until later."

He strode toward the house and Beth wrenched her eyes away before they filled with tears. Their time together was almost over and she must prepare for that, too. She would not blubber like a lovesick ninny as his carriage carried him down the drive. She would be strong and wish him well on his adventure. She would wish him every happiness.

She hugged George to her side and then smoothed his hair from his eyes. "We have much to do and a haircut appears to be the first order of business."

"I don't want a haircut," George said petulantly, scrubbing at his head as if her affection was annoying now. "I want to stay with Mr. Randall."

"He's leaving, too," she reminded him gently.

"Then I want to go with him."

Pain sliced through her. What she'd feared most had come to pass. George was far too fond of Oliver. His heart was going to be as broken as hers when Oliver left them behind. She bent down to her son's level and met his gaze squarely. "As I told you before, that is not possible."

He shook off her touch and lifted his chin defiantly. "It would be if you didn't speak so meanly to him all the time."

Beth's brows rose. "I do no such thing."

George scowled at her. "It wouldn't hurt you to be nicer to Mr. Randall. I want to go with him and see the coliseum, to see the things he talks about in Italy and Turkey. You spoil everything. I didn't want to believe him, but Uncle Henry was right. Women say one thing and mean another." His words came out in a disgusted tone and he stomped away, headed for the house too.

Beth glanced swiftly at her brother-in-law to see if he had noticed the mode of George's departure and saw a smile flit across his face. Was that his game? To turn her son against her by undermining their relationship? Rage filled her. She had gone without for many a night, stomach rumbling in hunger to ensure that her son's belly was full so he wouldn't cry himself to sleep.

She'd buried a husband and two children, barely old enough to be out of her arms, and would not give up her son without a fight just because a man had waltzed in with money and power and thought he had the right to take what he wanted.

Beth remained at a distance from her brother-in-law and Leopold Randall until they eventually paused in their discussion, forcing her anger away and plotting her resistance. When he noticed her standing alone, at least Leopold appeared chagrined. "Forgive me, Beth. I thought my brothers were still with you. Henry, I don't mind telling you that Beth will be sorely missed when she leaves us. The duchess was remarking just last night at dinner that Beth has become indispensable."

Henry's brow rose. "Well, we cannot have the duchess inconvenienced. Beth may remain. It makes no difference to me. I'll suggest George write to her every once in a while."

Beth glared at her brother-in-law, the flippant comment adding to her outrage. How dare he? "George goes nowhere without me."

The seriousness of her tone had little impact. Henry merely laughed and looked around. "Clearly not all the time. Where exactly is George now in that monstrosity, eh? The boy will do well enough without you, should you prefer to retain and cultivate your relationship with the duchess. I'll look out for him now."

She met Leopold's gaze and swallowed. Had Henry been aiming for this all along? He would take George away and remake him into his own son without her interference. She couldn't let that happen. She would not. "The duchess is too kind, but I will not be left behind to wonder if your estate is as grand as you claim."

Henry's jaw clenched at her accusation. She had no proof of his wealth or situation but his own few words. She was tired of giving him the benefit of the doubt. If he lied to them and they moved, they might never escape his control again.

He took a pace forward and Beth glanced down. His hand had curled into a fist at his side. She raised a brow and dared him to follow through with his desire to shut her up. He'd learn she wasn't any man's victim. Rose, of all people, had taught her how to fight back once and she still remembered enough now to feel confident.

"She will get over the loss of you if you promise to write as often as you can," Leopold added quickly, stepping between them smoothly. He slapped his hand to Henry's shoulder and turned him in the direction of the stables. "Excuse us, Beth."

Beth took the opportunity to flee, walking away with her back straight as if the encounter had been commonplace. Once she reached the safety of her bedchamber, however, she closed and locked the door behind her and sank to the floor.

She did not want to go anywhere with Henry but she could not be left behind to wonder what kind of man her son would turn out to be. She covered her face and burst into tears. It was bad enough that she'd never see Oliver again, but she wouldn't survive the loss of her son, too.

Fate couldn't possibly be so cruel as to take the two greatest loves from her life at the same time.

Chapter Nineteen

———◆———

Oliver let himself into his apartment and locked the door behind him so he might secure his peace. The day had not ended particularly well. The worst of it was that he only had himself to blame. He had not expected news of Elizabeth's imminent departure to trouble him as much as it did. After all, he was leaving England before her and he'd had days to accept her path would greatly diverge from his.

The forced cheer he'd witnessed in the garden had been for her son's sake and he'd wanted to tell her she was wrong about his dreams. The endless arguments with his brothers about his departure had stolen any chance for private speech with her after dinner. Her happiness *was* important to him. He would think of her often, as he had always done, when they parted company in a few days.

The door behind his back rattled with the force of a blow. "We've not finished this discussion, sir. Slinking away while my back was turned will not save you. Get your ass back out here and talk to us," Leopold yelled.

Oliver moved away from the door and raked a hand through his hair as irritation seized him. His elder brother had taken the news of his imminent departure less than well. It was quite a shock to Oliver to be set upon by his own family. He hadn't felt this anxious since his days at Skepington. He swallowed the bile that rose in his throat at the memory of that evil place.

Bargaining for the key to his chamber there had been an absolute necessity. He'd not enjoyed waking to find a fellow inmate leaning over his bed or rifling through his possessions.

He pulled the ribbon he always carried from his pocket and stroked the once-lustrous material. It had darkened since he'd first acquired it, but it still retained the same ability to soothe him. The door rattled one last time and then Leopold's footsteps hurried away.

"Will he be back," a small voice asked suddenly.

When Oliver looked about, he spotted George huddled by the fire. Puzzled by his presence at this time of night, Oliver moved toward him, tucking the ribbon back into its usual resting place. "It's likely, unfortunately. He will be even more cross with me by then. You may want to take the opportunity to leave before he returns or else be faced with a terrible scene."

Oliver was the only one with keys to this room. As soon as he'd decided to move in, he'd taken the housekeeper's copy from Elizabeth when she hadn't been looking in order to ensure his privacy. Leopold was about to discover that fact for himself and he hoped he wouldn't rant at the new young housekeeper too ferociously.

"He's mad at you for going away?" George asked, still curled up where Oliver had discovered him. The wistfulness in his voice caught him by surprise. Shouldn't he be happier that he was bound for adventure too?

"My brother is bossy. A side effect of being the eldest." Leopold was turning into a damned nuisance.

"I was the eldest once," George said as he laid his head against his knee and stared into the dancing flames. "A long time ago I had a little brother and sister to take care of. Papa said I had to look out for them."

There was nothing Oliver wanted to say to that. He'd decided that to ask after Elizabeth's other offspring, George's siblings, would stir up emotions best left at rest, so he made himself comfortable in a chair not far from where the boy perched. But the boy's presence and sober mood could not be ignored. "It's late. What brings you to me at this hour?"

The boy shrugged and didn't answer. That was unlike him. Usually George was quite forthcoming with information and conversation. "Your mother will worry where you are soon and come looking to fetch you to bed."

An expression of distaste crossed his face and Oliver's contentment vanished. The boy had never before reacted to the mention of his mother in such a way. The lack of respect bothered him a great deal. Why would George be disgusted by Elizabeth? It couldn't be that he knew they were lovers or the boy would never have come to him tonight. It must concern something else, and the only other event in his life presently was his uncle's plan to take him away. "Are you anxious about leaving England?"

"No." George shrugged. "Sort of."

Oliver moved until he was sitting on the floor beside George. He stretched out his legs until he was comfortable. George copied him and a strange sensation crept through Oliver's being. Happiness. He was happy to be sitting on the floor beside his lover's son, whose character was a great deal similar to his own. An impossibility, but Oliver continued to see similarities between their natures. Or perhaps, he merely wished they were there. If he had married Elizabeth when his parents had hinted at the match, would his own flesh and blood be like George? He'd never know and considering such a theory would lead exactly nowhere.

"Explain," he demanded of George.

"I don't want to go to America."

"Ah," Oliver said slowly, still puzzled. "Change can be difficult to accept, but you will grow from the experience and find your place again."

George pulled his legs up and hugged his knees. "If Mama had been nicer we wouldn't have to go."

"Your mother has an exceptionally agreeable temperament," Oliver corrected. "What could she have done differently? Your uncle is here and you are his heir. It is logical that you go with him to learn of what you will inherit."

"I don't want to be his heir. I want to stay with you," George blurted out.

Understanding slammed through Oliver. He swallowed the lump that formed in his throat and glanced at the boy huddled miserably at his side. What could he possibly say? He would gladly have the boy as a companion on his trip, but Elizabeth would not allow it. She had already protested that the time they spent together in study would strengthen any bonds beyond those expected between a student and tutor.

Perhaps she'd been right to protest.

She did know her son better than he did.

In all of Oliver's life there had never been a time when he hadn't known exactly what to say. He preferred honesty, but telling young George that his mother would never let him travel with him would only cause more problems between them. If George had already told Elizabeth of his wish, then it was no wonder she had dismissed his earlier concern as if he wasn't important. She was trying to protect the child and help him accept the direction the future was taking him. Oliver would do anything he could to help Beth in that regard. "Everyone outgrows their teachers at some stage. I had several and still think of them fondly."

George's shoulders hunched further.

"I remember one fellow, Mr. Pierce, insisted every response be followed with his name. It grew quite tiresome. He thought very well of himself, but he did know his mathematics."

Oliver bent one leg and set an arm to his knee, warming to the topic. "Another, Mr. Reeves, could discuss theology at any hour of the day or night. It was his belief that animals had souls and carried them to another body when they died. My father dismissed him when he overheard our discussion just when it was becoming interesting."

"They sound very silly." George peered up at him. "But you're not like that."

Oliver chuckled. "Everyone is silly at one point or other in their lives. But still, silly or not, right or wrong, they still deserve our respect for the kindness they show us in sharing their opinions. But there is also a time for all things to end. We grow from new experiences. Why are you upset with your mother, lad?"

"She could change things, but she won't."

Oliver frowned. "From what I've observed, she has chosen the path she wants to take. It is not for us to question her. She has your best interests at heart, always."

"If she married, she wouldn't have to go," George insisted. "My new father could protest and insist we stay here and not go to America."

"Who do you imagine your mother might marry, lad?"

George's face pinked and he looked down. Realization dawned slowly for Oliver. If he were inclined to ask Elizabeth to marry him again, George would not protest were she to accept. George would have what he wanted, avoidance of America and to travel with him to the continent. His logic had merit except Oliver perceived the preparations for Elizabeth and George's departure had progressed too far to be halted by a mere offer of marriage. "A marriage would not stop you being Mr. Turner's heir. He would still want you to go with him."

The air left George's lungs in a rush and he turned away, disappointment clear in his crumpled posture.

Oliver nudged him. "But if I ever had a son, I should hope he was like you. Let's not spend our last days together in a sulk."

When George wiped at his eyes, Oliver was surprised. Was he that set on a tour of the continent that he would succumb to tears when denied?

"What shall we do tomorrow?" he asked gently, determined to soothe him with the lure of a local adventure. "Shall we fish or take a walk, or perhaps go riding? It's been many weeks since you've visited the stables or the Allen boys. We could all go riding together if you like?"

The boy shook his head quickly, giving Oliver the idea that the lesson's abrupt end had been his choice all those weeks ago. Was that why the boy hugged his shadow so closely? Had he had a disagreement with Charles Allen or his sons? When morning came, should he speak to Allen about the matter and ensure the issue was resolved? A father would undoubtedly do that for his son. The question was did Oliver have the right to interfere?

If it wasn't a simple disagreement, easily set aside, he'd find some other way to entertain the boy. Perhaps he could fulfill his promise to show George the secrets of Romsey. Although he acknowledged now that offering to take George to the Duke's Sanctuary was extremely dangerous and oddly sentimental, he had made a promise. He would keep it. "If your mother agrees and there are no visitors to be met with, you and I shall take a short trip tomorrow."

George frowned. "Mama never lets me go very far without

telling her where I'll be. Uncle said women are meddlesome creatures."

Oliver tossed the statement over in his mind, vastly troubled by it. Henry Turner's opinion would poison the boy's mind against women. Was his first step to be making Elizabeth an outsider in George's life? Oliver would not allow it. "Men of sense do not disregard women, George. Your mother gave you life. It is small-minded of you to believe her concern for your welfare is meddlesome."

George had the sense to look chagrined. He nodded slowly and mumbled a contrite "yes, sir." When he lifted his head, his expression was once again hopeful. "Where will we go tomorrow?"

But before Oliver could answer, footsteps rushed toward them and the doors burst inward. "Don't you ever do that again," Leopold growled. "You ba…"

His angry words died as his eyes slipped to where George sat. The boy's presence actually seemed to deflate his brother completely of anger, a fascinating process to watch. Yet Oliver knew better than to believe he would be spared completely and waited for the tirade to resume.

"Forgive me, I had no idea you had young George here with you," Leopold said quickly. "I thought you to be alone."

Oliver peered at the splintered wood of the doorframe. "Breaking down the door was a touch excessive. You could have resumed your sermon tomorrow over breakfast on the merits of delay and at least given me a respite to speak with George in peace."

Leopold turned red and held up one hand. "Now, look here."

Oliver stood. "It's late. The boy is tired and should be returned to his room. We'll speak again tomorrow. Go to bed, Leopold, and search for control of your temper."

He gestured for George to come to him and then swiftly led the boy away. He placed his hand on George's shoulder as they traveled the distance to his bedchamber. "Never mind about Leopold. He'll calm himself soon enough."

"They really don't want you to leave, do they?"

Oliver smiled ruefully. "Not one bit, but it is my life and I'll choose the direction it takes without their interference."

"I wish…" George drew in a deep shuddering breath. "I wish I had a father to speak up for me."

Sympathy filled him. At this age, a boy still needed reassurance on occasion.

George let himself into his bedchamber and beckoned Oliver to follow. When Oliver crossed the threshold, his eyes were immediately drawn to the connecting doorway. Through the gap, he could see Elizabeth moving about her chamber. She must be packing in readiness to leave. He tamped down the flame of desire that always ignited when she was near now and cleared his throat, drawing attention to his presence.

Her head snapped up and she faced him. Her eyes were red, her skin blotchy. She'd been crying again and this time he thought he might know why. With George nearby, he could do or say nothing to comfort her. He tipped his head toward her son and remained where he was.

Elizabeth hurried toward him and stopped short when she saw George. She seemed to stiffen and instead of rushing to George's side as she always did, she hung back. Oliver swung his head to see George's reaction to his mother's arrival. The boy bit his lip and, after a moment, he rushed into his mother's opening arms. Oliver's heart swelled. Whatever disagreement existed between them was on the mend. At least he'd done one thing right today.

Elizabeth met his gaze over her son's head, her eyes watery bright. Her lips moved to say thank you. That one small acknowledgement was everything he needed. He smiled broadly and departed, retracing his steps to his bedchamber. He checked the damage to the door as he passed. A carpenter would be needed for it to ever lock properly again. More unnecessary interruptions. He hadn't really wanted his last days to be filled with the sound of hammering.

He moved from the door, only to be brought up short by Leopold pacing before the fire. They stared at each other across the space and Oliver tensed, waiting for the next volley of demands that he must refuse.

Chapter Twenty

———◆———

Warmth from the sun streaming through Beth's bedroom window warmed her back as she surveyed her possessions strewn over her bed. She frowned at their number. When had she acquired so many fine gowns? Of course, she knew the answer to that immediately. Her employer and the duchess had recently reviewed the contents of their wardrobes, most gowns seemingly never worn, and she'd been the happy recipient. But that generosity did give her problems now. She likely couldn't take them all with her. She'd have to choose her favorites from among them and leave the rest behind, and that did not seem right.

She rubbed her brow and fought off the weariness that came from a night spent tossing and turning. Not the kind that came with a night spent in Oliver's bed, but one where her mind refused to settle. She'd stayed away from Oliver in fear of Henry finding out about them. It pained her, but she had no choice. She had her memories to cling to now. They would have to be enough.

Thanks to Henry's refusal to impart any essential information on their future living conditions, Beth had spent the night fretting over what to take. She fingered her herringbone-stitched spencer, wondering if it was too fine for her new circumstances. The pink silk gown with narrow, smocked panels down each side was a favorite she would leave as a gift for the new housekeeper to wear on special occasions.

Beth lifted another gown and held it before her. Plain and unadorned, a simple dark blue cotton with full-length sleeves was as serviceable as any gown she'd ever owned. Yet she would keep this one in particular because she'd been wearing it when Oliver had kissed her. A reminder of what could never be.

A timid knock sounded on the door and she bid her visitor enter.

"Are we disturbing you?" Mercy asked, leading her sister into the room.

Beth dipped a quick curtsy. "Of course not—is there anything I can help you with?"

Mercy's gaze swung around the room, a small frown line forming between her brows but smoothed away when she'd finished her inspection. "Nothing for me, but I thought I might be of use to you."

Beth threw a quick glance at Lady Venables but the countess gave nothing away. "Oh?"

"I have friends, ones I have not seen in many years, residing in America that I should like you to call upon if you encounter any problems in your new life." She pulled a letter from her pocket and held it out. "Ducky is a dear friend, much involved in society in Boston. This letter of introduction will ensure you're looked after and I've asked him to provide the means to send you home to us should you request it."

Beth swallowed at the duchess's unexpected generosity. At every turn the woman had proven herself a kind and thoughtful friend. She knew that Beth's greatest fear was to be without means to protect herself and her son. In the New World, she wouldn't know anyone but Henry and his as-yet-undisclosed acquaintances. What if they were separated from him?

She shivered as she took the note. "Thank you. I do not know what I've done to deserve your favor, but I treasure your gift most certainly."

Mercy moved forward and embraced her. "I cannot bear the thought of you going away. You've come to mean so much to me, to all of us, that I hate to say goodbye."

She squeezed Beth as if she would never let her go. Beth closed her eyes, moved to tears and unable to prevent them from spilling over. "I will miss you, too."

"If you ever wish return home to England we'll be waiting for you with open arms," the duchess whispered close to her ear.

"Thank you, Mercy." Beth blubbered, unable to remain formal in the face of such obvious affection. "I will."

Mercy released her and caught her face between her hands. Tears slid down the duchess's cheeks unattended. "I'll hold you to that."

With one last hug, Mercy hurried out the door, a sniff and a sob drifting to Beth's ears just before the door closed.

Lady Venables shook her head. "You'll have to forgive her tears. Mercy never likes to part from friends and in her condition she's less likely to refrain from saying what's on her mind."

Beth frowned. "Her condition?"

A sly smile twisted the countess's lips. "I believe she may be with child, though she's not said a word. However, her emotions are running high right now because of you and Oliver leaving, so allowances for her theatrics must be made. For myself, I never noticed my emotions changing one way or another during my confinement."

Beth thought back over her pregnancies, wondering if she could remember how it felt to have a life growing inside her. The memory was vague, but she thought she'd never been happier. "Now I feel worse for leaving at such a time, my lady."

"Blythe," Lady Venables corrected. "There is no point in adhering to the formalities now."

More tears raced down Beth's cheeks and she quickly dabbed them away.

"Mercy is more worried about your happiness, and I must say I agree with her," Blythe said as she picked up a wrapped parcel and began to uncover it. "With some difficulty, I have pried information from Tobias about life both at sea and in America and he has some suggestions for you. The first, keep my sister's letter on your person at all times, including any money you have. It is far too easy to become separated from your baggage and the docks are rife with pickpockets."

Beth glanced at her gown. If her pockets were not safe from thieves, where else could she hide her few valuables?

Seeming to read Beth's mind, Blythe picked up the muff and gloves and set them aside. "Not inside something so easily discarded or lost as these." When Blythe picked up her warmest pelisse and studied the garment, Beth drew closer. "This could be the perfect hiding place. However, you would always need to wear it during your travels."

Fear of pickpockets and thieves filled her mind. Beth agreed quickly. "I can do that."

Blythe examined the stitching. "If we unstitch the hem here in the front, we'll be able to make concealed pockets for some of your valuables. Also here at the sleeve cuff. Show me what you will take with you."

Beth scrambled for her meager collection of coins and her wedding ring. She laid them out on the bed, set Mercy's letter of introduction beside them, and stood back. There really was little value in her possessions. Most items she had were sentimental rather than financially valuable. The lack caused a blush to climb her cheeks.

Blythe removed a narrow length of blue silk from her pocket and unwound it slowly. When she was done, two thin ties could be seen and it issued an odd crinkling sound. "Another of Tobias's suggestions. Wear this belt tied about your waist snugly, beneath your gown, and don't let anyone know of it."

She held out the strip and Beth took it, examining the belt's construction. Two long ties, a thicker section in the middle, and long enough to tie about her waist and wear in reasonable comfort. She saw an opening and peered inside a cleverly designed pocket. The edges of paper notes could be seen. Her heart raced as she checked each pocket in turn. The whole belt was filled with more money than she had ever had in her life. She handed it back. "I gladly accept the belt, but nothing else."

Blythe sighed and refused to take it. "My gift to you is the means of hearing you are well. Some of it is paper to write upon. Do you honestly believe Henry Turner will allow you to correspond with a duchess for whom he barely hides his contempt? I do not. Take the money so you may at least be able to write to us to say you are well and happy. The way George reads, you may need the remainder to feed his intellectual appetite."

Beth could see the sense in her suggestion, but yet again, she was taking charity. It had never sat well with her. Would she ever have the means to repay them? If not for George, she would refuse outright. But she did have a son to consider and he counted on her to make his world right. She curled her fingers over the belt and held it tightly. "Thank you."

Blythe quickly embraced her and then set her hands to her hips, glance sliding to the bed. "We've a lot to do today."

Beth shook her head. "There's no need. I'll be fine on my own, thanks to your suggestion."

"Nonsense. I'll not listen to Mercy's weeping for the entire day." Blythe laughed. "Besides, I'd enjoy spending one more day with you. George is otherwise occupied, isn't he?"

Beth nodded slowly. "He went for a walk with the Randall men and then he'll probably return to the library."

"Or stay in Oliver's company," Blythe replied with a direct look that unnerved Beth considerably. Did she know that Beth had spent several pleasant interludes in Oliver's arms? She must not or she wouldn't be so friendly.

Beth hated lying or withholding the truth from people she cared for. She fingered the belt and then set it aside. She should get started on altering her pelisse. She fetched her scissors and needle and thread and then laid the garment over the bed.

Blythe said not one more word more on the subject of Oliver Randall while they worked through the morning. Luncheon was sent up to an unused room nearby and they paused to eat and talk when Tobias joined them. His mood was somewhat bitter and eventually, Blythe left them in a huff over his surliness.

Tobias stared after Blythe's departure with glum expression. "Now she's angry with me."

"Hardly," Beth murmured. "She just cannot help you convince Oliver to stay and sees no point in a conversation that goes nowhere."

Tobias leaned back in his chair, hands sliding over his skull in a way that showed his frustration. "He's just so damn stubborn."

"And are not all Randalls stubborn, determined to go their own way? If I remember correctly, you never backed down from a dare."

"No one is daring Oliver to leave Romsey."

Beth smiled. He made his own rules and to hell with anyone else. "Oliver is different. He's always set his own challenges."

Tobias snorted. "He should have married you. You understand him better than anyone."

She choked on the tea she'd just sipped and had to cough in order to breathe normally again.

Tobias's expression grew smug at her discomfort. "Well, it's bloody obvious there's been a change between you. I've never seen him smile so much. And he has never liked children, but your child is always in his company. What else could account for such behavior?"

Beth set the cup down carefully, horror trickling through her. She did not care to have this conversation with anyone, least of all Oliver's inquisitive younger brother. "He is merely helping George find material for study."

Tobias sat forward, peering at her intently. "Is he Oliver's son?"

Beth stood, shock thrumming through her. "Do not insult me."

"That wasn't meant as an insult. That was hope." Tobias winced. "He's a fine lad and doesn't look a bit like William Turner."

"Well, he certainly is William's son and you should not repeat that question to me again. I thought you were my friend."

"I am." He grimaced and raked his fingers through his hair again. "I just hoped we might be family and you could prevent Oliver from leaving."

Beth pressed the heel of her hand to her temple. "Oliver alone will choose his future, just as I have chosen mine and George's. We leave for America in a few days and I'd like your promise not to mention your hopes again. It is doubtful we will ever see each other again once we go, but I should not like bad feelings between us."

Tobias stood and took her hands in his. The scars on them reminded her that he'd lived as harsh a life as her brother-in-law. Yet Tobias had retained his good temper and kind nature. Except for his insulting suggestion that she'd cuckolded her husband or married another man after being intimate with Oliver, they'd never seriously disagreed. Beth would hate to part at odds with him.

"Forgive me. I spent my life hoping for miracles and when one is just out of reach, I struggle to bring it to life." Tobias folded her in his arms and crushed her against him. "I'm sorry to have upset you. Be safe, my dear girl. Don't forget to write us of your journeys and let us know where you are. When Rose comes home, she'll want news of you, too."

Beth looked up at Tobias when he released her, sympathy overriding her outrage. "I'm so sorry she's not come. Have your brothers made any decisions on how else to locate her?"

Tobias shook his head. "Leopold will go to London in the spring and hire runners, but without leads I'm not optimistic. Maybe she is dead."

Sharp pain squeezed Beth's chest at the idea. Rose couldn't be dead. The idea was preposterous. Beth pressed Tobias's hand in hers, trying to instill hope in him. "She's alive and will be home before you know it. Just remember when she is, you'll likely wish for peace again."

Tobias laughed at her prediction. "You and Rose were the best of friends. As good as sisters, or would have been if my brother had shut his books long enough to consider it. Where do you think she could be?"

"I've done nothing but worry for her welfare for ten years, too. I've no idea where she'd go. What of your mother's friends? Do you remember any of them?"

"No."

She sighed, unable to think of a single name that would not have already been investigated. "If she doesn't see the advertisements placed in the papers, and her whereabouts is not known by any past acquaintances that Leopold or Oliver can recall, then all we can hope for is that Rosemary chooses to return on her own."

"Getting Rosie to do anything in the past was an uphill battle," he quipped morosely. "She's likely to be even more stubborn now."

Beth laughed to lighten the mood. "Have faith. I'm sure the right incentive will occur to one of us soon."

Tobias gestured to the chairs again. "Will you sit with me until Blythe comes back?"

As much as she'd love to sit and talk of times past, she couldn't bear it. The last few days had been exhausting and emotional and she just wanted to prepare herself to leave. Part of that was a trip to the churchyard to bid farewell to her children buried there. She wanted no company for that journey, not even George. She was sure she would break down and cry if anyone was with her. Leaving them would be painful and she'd been trying not to think about it.

She straightened her shoulders and faced Tobias with a smile. "There's nothing else to be done but to pack for my son now. Blythe had mentioned spending some time with the young duke. If you wanted to find her to mend things between you, she'll likely be there."

"You know, my brother may consider himself remarkably clever, but he really has no sense." Tobias sighed and moved to the doorway. As he opened it, he glanced over his shoulder. "You really would have made the perfect wife for him. No one knows the Randalls better than you. You'd have kept us all in line just as Mama used to do."

He ducked out before she could chastise him for bringing up the subject again. Beth waited until her heartbeat slowed before she made her way out of the abbey and down the drive on her way to visit the little graves for the last time. Clever or not, if Oliver couldn't express love then she didn't want to marry him. He hadn't meant one word of the proposal he'd made. There were no words to describe how sad that made her.

Chapter Twenty-One

The secrets of the Dukes of Romsey were always hidden in plain sight. A man only needed to walk about with his eyes off the finery and look to the bones of the house to discover the truth for himself.

"Quietly now," Oliver warned as he cast an anxious glance along the deserted long gallery behind him. It had taken an hour to shake off his brothers and Eamon too, without alerting them to his intentions. Thankfully, Elizabeth and the ladies were occupied elsewhere and the boy had freedom enough to sneak away from the library with him at short notice.

He hurried George to the far end of the long gallery, past the benign painted smiles of former dukes of Romsey. Let them smirk in their gilt frames. Oliver was about to disclose the greatest family secret to a child unrelated by blood and there wasn't a thing that could be done now to stop him.

He approached the tall windows leading to the west gardens, checking that no servants toiled beyond the glass. Thankfully they were completely isolated from others and could proceed as he hoped. He approached a blank piece of wall and studied the moldings running down the wall. There was a slight difference in hue to one small section. A man only had to be observant to spot the discoloration. Press, turn, slide, and the narrow entrance to the sanctuary was revealed.

"Blimey," George whispered in awe as the door swung open with the slightest groan of protest. His eyes widened impossibly and then his smile grew. "I hit a ball against that panel the other day while playing ninepins and you didn't even blink. You're very good at keeping secrets, sir."

Oliver quickly oiled the hinge to stop further noises sounding and set the oil bottle just inside. When they came back out, it was essential to be quick and quiet. Any shriek would draw unwanted attention.

"A useful trait when you want your way. Remember that." Oliver lifted the lantern he held above the boy's head and lighted the way. "Quickly now. Inside."

George hurried in and Oliver quietly closed the doorway behind him so their adventure couldn't be interrupted. He drew in a deep breath and shuddered. He'd never liked the scent of underground spaces. The cloying damp of earth and stone made him want to turn about and leave immediately. However, he'd made a promise to the boy that he wouldn't break.

They made slow progress down the narrow staircase, headed for the large cavern below. Each shallow step brought darkness closing in on them. The roughhewn walls brought apprehension. Although Oliver knew full well the design and space ahead was large and perfectly safe, tension still caught him in its grip and he longed for the bottom step to be closer.

George's footfalls grew slower and slower until he stopped completely, blocking the path ahead. He barreled around, breath rasping from his lungs in a quick pant. "It doesn't go anywhere. We'll be trapped."

Oliver drew the boy against him to ease his panic and held him close. "I did mention there was a long flight of steps. Very soon we come to a corner in the staircase and then you'll see light ahead. There's no need to be afraid. I'm here with you."

When Oliver released him, George reluctantly let go but slipped his hand into Oliver's free one and clung. The odd sensation brought a smile to his lips. How funny that such a small gesture could make his day so much brighter. He doubted Elizabeth would smile with him if she saw them like this, but Oliver was very glad to have earned the boy's trust.

With a bit of shuffling, they switched positions so Oliver led the way down. As he'd predicted, the corner was close, just beyond the reach of the lantern, and he drew George toward the faint light ahead.

They stepped onto the landing and, after another three shallow stairs, stood in the dim light of the Duke of Romsey's Sanctuary, the room that had caused so much trouble.

Sunlight filtered down from the ceiling through cleverly concealed air vents, casting a dim glow that revealed shapes and lumps untidily stacked ahead of them. But that meager light wasn't sufficient to view the contents of the chamber properly. Oliver handed George the lantern, drew a taper from inside his coat, and held it to the flame until it caught. He then turned to light the lanterns set on each side of the staircase and moved about the chamber until the remaining dozen shone with welcoming light.

He faced George, saw him craning his neck in every direction, and gestured to the room. "Be my guest. There's no danger here. Well, maybe a rat or mouse at most," he added a touch ruefully. There was no getting away from them in a place like this.

The boy didn't look impressed by his observation and slowly shuffled deeper into the room. Curious as to what the boy would do when faced with another man's spoils, Oliver opened a chest containing gold coins and beautiful gems, most set into jewelry, likely stolen from past friends, and waited to see his reaction. George ran his fingers through the profits of the family's unspoken profession without too much interest in the wealth stored there. People had likely died for these treasures. Blackmail and revenge had been the former Dukes of Romsey's preferred mode of business. In Oliver's opinion, that was adventure of the worst kind.

George stared at the chest a long time. "And this is all *his*."

"The young duke's? Yes. Every bit of smuggled or stolen goods in this room are part of his inheritance." Oliver sighed at the likely impact of that confession to come. The young duke would be intrigued, but Oliver hoped the boy would be wise enough, thanks to Leopold's influence on his life, to keep the secret of this chamber from others—only passing it along to his own son one day when the child was old enough.

A sudden chill swept him. He was still a pawn in the old duke's game. With his cousin dead long before he could share the secret of this room with the young duke upstairs, it now fell to Oliver to reveal it when the time was right. He cursed at the idea of being caretaker to this terrible legacy. If he never returned from his travels, if he settled elsewhere, this room and its contents would likely be lost to generations of Randalls.

The boy moved along the row to some paintings propped up against a wall and rifled through the smaller ones he could easily manage without help. George set each back carefully, wiping his hands together when he was done.

Oliver closed the chest, rather proud that his instincts about the boy's honesty were sound. He'd made the right decision to befriend the child. Elizabeth's son might be young, but he had a good heart and could be trusted.

Racks of guns and boxes containing dueling pistols lined another wall. There was enough to furnish a small uprising and Oliver wouldn't be surprised if they had been used for that purpose before. George stopped before them but didn't touch. "My father died from a ball in the leg," he said, breaking the hushed silence with his abrupt confession.

A poacher's shot if Oliver recalled correctly. William Turner's death would have been slow and painful, a terrible experience for the young boy to witness. "I'm sorry. You must miss him."

George shrugged. "I suppose. Everybody dies."

The toneless statement was so at odds with the boy's usual mode of speaking that Oliver suspected the words mimicked the sentiments of another man. He drew nearer and set his hand to the boy's shoulder. "George, there is no shame in missing the people who are no longer with us. From all I've heard, your father loved you very much."

A shudder went through George. "He never did anything with me. Not like you do. He was always too busy to go fishing or to talk to me."

Ah, so that explains why Elizabeth was wary of his influence on the boy. William Turner had not shared the same interests as his son. No wonder being accepted and included by him and his brothers must have worried her. "You and I have much in common, but you must remember I do not have the responsibilities of a family to claim my time and attention. Should I have been married with a wife and children to care for, perhaps we would not have spent so much time together. I like to hope we've become good friends."

George brightened at his words. "I'd like to be your friend."

"Good." Oliver gestured about them. "Then I suggest you continue your examination of the room. We cannot stay long, for fear of you being missed. This place cannot be discovered. Such a thing would be disastrous to my plans."

George, however, remained where he was. "I've never seen men so angry. Your brothers, I mean, not the ladies."

Oliver rolled his eyes and laughed. "Family. I could use a little peace from them at the moment."

George laughed along with him and resumed his exploration. Oliver followed behind, picking up things that caught his eye before he returned them to their former place. Tarnished silver, the flicker of a gem under layers of dust, and a hundred other odd trinkets littered long trestle tables strewn about the room. He peered at a foot-square box under one. The half-hidden carving seemed familiar, so he dragged it toward him and wiped the dust away.

A bunch of rosemary sprigs, tied with a white ribbon, appeared.

Oliver wrenched the lid open, ignoring the hinge's shriek of protest. Inside lay a gentleman's silver pocket watch, an opal ring, and a small jade brooch on a black velvet cushion. He picked the pieces up and laid them on the flat of his hand. Time had dulled their shine, but Oliver recognized them instantly. There was a portrait of his parents wearing all three hanging in his father's study at Harrowdale, a room he'd made his own when he was young. These pieces had belonged to his parents once, but Rosemary had been given the brooch on her last birthday before they were separated. She'd *always* worn it with pride.

He covered his mouth. The obvious conclusion that Rosemary was dead choked him. She would never have willingly parted with her most treasured possession. If she were alive, she would still have it with her.

"Mr. Randall, are you all right?

Oliver looked up and blinked through his blurred vision.

George touched his shoulder. "Why are you crying, sir?"

"Am I?" He touched his face and wiped away the wetness coating his cheek. His fingers curled around the piece in his hand and the pin pricked him. He winced and opened his palm to show George what he'd found. "My father's pocket watch. My mother's ring." He swallowed past the lump in his throat. "My sister's brooch. They are indeed dead."

George remained quiet as Oliver stood, grief and anger coursing through him. There was no one else. Rosemary was no more. All that remained was himself, Leopold, and Tobias. The urge to find his brothers and confess everything he'd withheld stirred. He'd not intended to tell them of this room's location or how to access it, but if he showed them the brooch he might have no choice. He shoved the items into his pocket. "I need to think. Excuse me."

He moved away to the far side of the chamber and picked up a perfectly polished crystal orb. He turned the globe over in his hand as he sifted through possibilities. Assumptions often led to incorrect conclusions. The presence of the brooch with his mother's ring proved only that his sister had been with their parents on the day they died. It could have been left on a fallen shawl that was trapped in the carriage wreckage with them. Or in the flight to get help, Rose could have dropped it and one of the duke's henchmen had found it and brought it back to the duke.

Oliver shook his head. Either way, his discovery today made no real difference. The presence of the jewelry only confirmed what they already knew. His parents were dead and Rosemary was far beyond their reach.

He removed the items from his pocket and held them tightly in his hand one last time. He wouldn't risk upsetting his brothers any further. Not when he was to depart tomorrow. He retraced his steps to the box and placed the items inside, brushing his fingers over them once. As he shut the lid, he sent a prayer of contrition to his parents. He hadn't grieved them enough. They had done as much for him as was within their means and his inquisitiveness had gotten them killed, and possibly Rosemary, too.

He vowed that from this moment on he would not embroil himself in other people's secrets. He would mind his own damn business and get on with his life. To do otherwise would only cause problems. He crossed to where George stood, peering at a map set behind dirty glass. "Come along, lad. It's getting late."

"Yes, sir." George hurried for the stairs, but stopped before he'd ascended. His expression when he turned was full of questions. "When will the young duke be old enough to learn about this place?"

Oliver extinguished the lanterns as he came, considering the future task with a sense of dread. It would be many years before he could be relieved of his burden. His future was still tied to this place by a tenuous thread. "When he reaches his majority will be soon enough."

George frowned. "What happens if something were to befall you before he's old enough to be told of this place? Will you leave a note behind?"

"Notes can be dangerous in the wrong hands." He picked up the lantern they'd brought with them and studied George. Had he made a mistake in confiding in the boy? Had he shared the burden of this knowledge with someone too young to bear it? As he stared, his heart could not believe what his mind suggested. He did not want to tell anyone else. He leaned down to the boy's level so they were eye to eye. "If anything were to happen to me, I suppose I'd have to rely on my young friend to pass the discovery along to the duke at the appropriate time."

George smiled brightly. "I'd like that. But how will I know what befalls you, if anything? Will you write to me in America and tell me about your travels? I should like very much to hear of your discoveries."

"I'd like that as well." Pain returned to his chest as he smiled down at the boy who might have been his son had he chosen another path for his life. Now he understood. The pain was one of regret. "I'd like to hear how you and your mother settle into your new life."

He set his hand to George's shoulder, sorrow suddenly filling him. If he'd decided differently, would he be happy without the prospect of this adventure ahead? When once he'd been so certain of the answer being no, now he wasn't so sure.

"Maybe Mama won't cry when we're in America," George said as they trudged up the steep staircase.

Elizabeth would cry wherever she went. She did not forget the past and a part of him hoped she wouldn't forget him easily when the lure of her new life trounced the sorrows of this one. "I'll pray for that, my boy. With all my heart I wish her happy."

Chapter Twenty-Two

———◆———

Beth placed the last altered garment in her trunk and closed it tight. There. Done. She was as ready as she would ever be to face this great new adventure in her life. She couldn't have completed her preparations in time without Blythe's help today and she wished there was something she could do to repay her kindness.

But even with that help, Beth still felt as ill prepared as a newborn babe. She'd barely scratched the surface of what she'd need to know to rebuild her life so far away from England and the district she'd never left before. She sank onto the edge of her bed, misery rising. No matter how hard she tried to convince herself that she wanted to go, she'd rather stay here with the new friends she'd made. Even working as a drudge in the bowels of this great house scrubbing pots would make her happier than she was now.

Not since Rosemary Randall had included her in her rambles had she ever felt she belonged or that her company was wanted so often. And it was not losing her heart all over again to Oliver Randall that made her want to remain, waiting for the day he eventually returned. The duchess and her sister were remarkably warm people. She truly cared for them and wanted to see their lives unfold. The prospect of new life that Blythe had hinted at had made her long for another child of her own.

Beth wiped tears from her eyes in frustration. Oliver would leave tomorrow, bound for adventure, new vistas, and possibly danger. She tamped down her anxiety for his future. Oliver had Eamon Murphy traveling with him and she couldn't imagine a better companion to keep him out of trouble. But who would look out for her and George in this new world? She couldn't help but be worried.

Henry had called again late in the afternoon, taken a look at her luggage and demanded she economize. Five lovely gowns were to be left behind so her baggage needs were less on the carriage. George was spared censure. He would take everything he owned. Henry had not requested he compromise one item, not even for a childhood toy he'd long outgrown. Henry's indulgence for sentiment began and ended with his nephew.

Beth rubbed her temple, weary and afraid, so tired of being alone and making every decision herself. She was grateful she didn't have to pretend an excitement that she just couldn't feel. During dinner it had been difficult to maintain the farce that she was unaffected by Oliver's leaving. She slowly worked the pins from her hair and teased the long strands straight. In two days she'd be trapped aboard a ship with little luxury or comforts beyond a bed, with strangers lurking everywhere. She might never be as alone as she was now. She might never feel free to be herself again.

She crept to the doorway connecting her room to her son's and leaned against the doorframe. George had fallen fast asleep tonight the minute his head had touched the pillow. Whatever he'd done today must have been exhausting. But for a change, he had not boasted of where Oliver had taken him or the sights they had seen together. Today her son had kept their activities secret, even from her. For the first time, that didn't make her unhappy. Oliver would never place him intentionally in danger. She'd seen enough of his behavior to note he wasn't entirely absent-minded when her son was around.

She pulled the door closed, wondering what to do next. Should she go to Oliver Randall again one last time to say a private goodbye or should she end their affair now and spare herself a painful parting? Even the idea of standing on the front steps of Romsey Abbey and saying goodbye before everyone made her sad. She feared she would fall apart and weep openly at the thought that she'd never see him again.

Beth wiped at the moisture blurring her vision. She'd not go to him. She'd stay here and sleep alone in her own comfortable bed and cling to her memories.

She slipped her gown from her body and laid it across the chair, next she removed her corset and shift until she stood naked, the chill in the air making her nipples harden. She walked to the mirror and viewed her body. Still slender, breasts only slightly less firm than before her children had been born. A body that had discovered passion again in the last place she'd ever imagined.

Oliver had liked her body well enough. Perhaps in the New World she would fall in love and marry again. Her stomach dropped like a lead ball into a river. She turned away from the mirror, unable to accept she could love anyone else. Oliver might be annoying and rude occasionally, but she knew exactly what he would do and say most of the time. There were no surprises with Oliver Randall except for the passion they shared. What he wanted, he took, and gave in equal measure, but he was never cruel about it.

She slipped her nightgown over her head, and as she freed her hair the door to her bedchamber creaked. She turned as Oliver closed the door behind him. He was barefoot and half-dressed, his eyes dark and thoughtful.

He crept toward the adjoining bedchamber door, stared at her son a long moment, and then closed it and turned the key in the lock. When he drew close, he reached out to cup her cheek gently, the pads of his thumbs wiping gently across her cheeks.

She forced a smile to her lips, determined not to shatter before him now. "How long were you at the door?"

A smile lifted the corners of his mouth. "You are beautiful with or without clothes. Are you all right? You seemed in a daze when I came in."

Beth leaned into his touch. "I'm afraid and I don't know what to do about it."

"Then stay at Romsey," he suggested seriously. "Don't give in to Turner's demands. George would never willingly leave without you. He tells me he'd rather not go to America."

Beth sighed. "That's not strictly true. I'm afraid he'd much rather travel with you and see the sights you keep telling him about."

Oliver drew her into his arms. He held her tightly and they stayed like that for a long time. "I'd gladly take him if you gave your permission, but there is no time to arrange it," he whispered against her hair.

Beth closed her eyes. The prospect of losing George to Oliver was far less painful than losing him to her brother-in-law. But both were still out of the question. She wouldn't lose her son so completely to either of them. She would not be cut off from his life, never knowing how he fared.

Oliver's hand shifted over her back, soothing her with the warmth and gentleness she'd grown used to and needed now. His head dipped and he pressed a soft kiss to her brow, her cheek, and then bent to kiss her lips. His eyes met hers, darkness pulling her into his passion. She splayed her hands over his chest and then slid them upward until she could wrap them about his neck.

When he kissed her with greater passion, she clung. She'd been fooling herself to think she hadn't needed this one last night in his arms. While there was time to love again she would. He lifted her suddenly and carried her to her bed. He set her down gently, snuffed the candle, and slid in beside her without a word.

They lay together, side by side, barely touching, until Beth couldn't stand it. She thrust out her hand and found his laying close to hers on the mattress. Their fingers threaded together and his grip tightened. "I'll only stay a little while," he whispered. "I know I shouldn't have come at all, but I had to see you again."

Beth rose up on her elbow. "I'm glad you came."

She touched his chest and discovered he was still as dressed as when he'd stepped through the door. She smiled at his behavior. It was kind of Oliver to have come with no expectations of further intimacies. But on their last night together, she wanted to touch every part of him and for him to do the same to her. To be as close as they could ever be to each other.

She pressed a kiss to the center of his chest. "You're wearing too many clothes."

He sat up, shirt rustling as he pulled it over his head. "So are you," he whispered in return.

Beth scrambled from her nightgown and sat on the bed, waiting for Oliver to come back to her. When he did, they kissed each other as if they had all the time in the world. Slow, languorous kisses that sent chills racing everywhere. Beth ran her fingers over Oliver's chest and arms, down his legs as far as she could reach, and back up. In the quiet of night, Oliver's groan sounded very loud and needy.

His fingers threaded through her hair as they kissed, holding her to him. When she touched his length and stroked, he hissed against her lips. Beth kept her pressure light, teasing Oliver to greater heights of passion as she'd discovered he liked. His lips moved to her throat, his hand to her breast, kneading her flesh and arousing a fever in her that would burn forever. She rose to her knees as she kissed his neck, his jaw, and finally his lips again. Their tongues tangled in an intimate dance, but she was determined to take charge tonight.

He shifted until he sat propped against the bedhead while Beth arranged herself above him, knees positioned on either side of his hips. Before she could grasp his length again, he pulled her against him and held her tightly. His skin burned.

"Elizabeth," he growled quietly against her neck, hot breath scorching her skin. His teeth nipped and teased, heightening her desire. "My angel. My..." His words cut off abruptly as she brushed against him. "I need you."

Beth held his mouth to her neck, fingers threaded through his hair, enjoying his passion and accepting that her love for him would never fade. "I'm here, Ollie. I've always been here."

He lifted her suddenly and then lowered her onto his hard length. Instead of moving, Beth remained still. A sudden chill raced down her spine as she imagined a lifetime ahead without him inside her. She might go mad from wishing and imagining.

At Oliver's prompting, Beth rose, sliding him from her body, and then fell again, bringing him deeper and dragging a groan from his lips. She quickly covered his mouth with her hand, eyes darting toward the door to her son's bedchamber and then back. She lowered her hand as he pressed a kiss to her fingers.

In the faint light from the fire, she saw that he was smiling up at her. The expression was one Beth had longed to see all the days of her life. She set one hand to his chest, one to his shoulder, and rode him, letting her body have him the way she craved. She'd never been this demanding before, but Oliver appeared aroused by her boldness. His hands fluttered over her body, fingers brushing her peaked nipples before he squeezed them. He shifted to take one into his mouth, suckling firmly as she shuddered and moved on him.

Tension coiled up her spine as she brought Oliver deep into herself. The way he made her feel was incredible and when his fingers slipped between them she bit off a choked cry. Oliver's hand pressed to her mouth gently, cutting off her moans for mercy. He teased her while she rode him, heightening her desires tenfold. His mouth returned to her breast and Beth held him there, threading her fingers into his gray locks so he could not leave her.

Beth bit her lip on the demand that almost followed that thought. She wanted to have this with him forever, even if it had to remain their secret. Sweat broke out over her body. Her release remained maddeningly out of reach. Oliver's lips left her breast and he faced her. Beth continued to move but she couldn't come. She just couldn't let go of the moment and begin to lose him.

His head pressed to hers, his fingers stroked her clit with more gentleness, concentrating on drawing small circuits with his fingertips. His mouth hovered beside hers as she panted. "Let go, my angel. Let me hear and feel you be happy in my arms."

His mouth sealed to hers as gooseflesh rose over her skin. Her body tensed, clamping around Oliver, and she sobbed against his mouth helplessly. He kept her close, smoothing her skin and playing with her long hair. When she relaxed, he rolled her onto the bed and withdrew from her body.

When he fell onto the other side, panting hard and making no attempt to find his own pleasure, she leaned into him.

He caught her hand again and raised it to his lips. His breath was a fast pant against her skin. "You are," he mumbled as he kissed her knuckles, "the most breathtaking woman I have ever known or should ever want to make love to."

Beth smiled at his compliment. They were so rare that she believed he meant every word. It didn't prove that he might finally love her, but it was as close a confession that she was special to him as she might ever get.

When Beth ran her eyes over the lean flesh revealed by the flickering firelight, her daring grew. She reached out to touch him. He was still hard. Still unfulfilled. She tightened her grip about him and stroked. It didn't take long before his muffled groans filled the room and his release splattered over his chest.

He rose to use the washbasin and returned quickly, pulling Beth back firmly against his chest and wrapping her tightly in his arms. She smiled as contentment washed over her. One last night. One last embrace. One last confession. She closed her eyes to memorize the moment. Oliver sighed and his arms grew heavy.

"I love you, Oliver," she whispered softly, daring to believe he might want to know how much she cared.

Beth waited for a response. He didn't move. His breathing was even and deep as if he was already asleep in her bed. She eased out from under his arm to look at him. Oliver stirred, legs moving restlessly, and then grew still.

Beth lay back against the pillows as disappointment filled her. She'd finally dredged up the courage to reveal her deepest affections and Oliver wasn't even awake to hear. She angrily wiped at the tears pooling in her eyes and thumped the mattress with her fist.

Oliver sat up. "What is it, my love?"

Beth's throat tightened at the endearment he used. "It's nothing."

"Good." He pulled her back into his arms and instead of being angry anymore, Beth smiled. He might have missed her declaration of love but, sleepily said or not, she hadn't missed his. Oliver always spoke true of his heart.

Chapter Twenty-Three

———◆———

The day of Oliver's departure dawned clear and bright and he was glad to be going. Restlessness had seized him from the moment he'd woken in Elizabeth's rumpled bed some hours ago as the first of dawn had lighted the horizon. At first he'd watched her sleep, counting her breaths and the little sounds she made as she moved. Most often though she had been so still and content that he feared waking her at any moment.

Impulsively, he'd pressed a kiss to her hair, her shoulder, and the upper swell of her perfect breast as he considered whether he could make love to her one more time before leaving. But he came to his senses quickly—the boy and a great many others in the house were early risers. He didn't want to be caught and embarrass Elizabeth. So he had crept out of her bed before she'd awakened, closing the door on a chapter of his life that would always remain a mystery but very dear to him.

It was time to go. Oliver threw one last book into his satchel and fastened the buckles. "This is the last."

His fingers dipped into his pocket and touched the ribbon nestled there. Leaving Elizabeth behind was going to be harder than he expected and the knowledge that she'd soon be traveling in the opposite direction sat ill with him. He feared he would await the first news of her successful journey and new life very anxiously. A circumstance that he'd never considered possible when they'd begun their affair.

Leopold snapped his fingers before Oliver's face, breaking him from his thoughts. "I said why are you packing a book on America?"

"I hadn't finished reading it," Oliver answered as he swung the satchel over his shoulder and looked about him to check that he hadn't forgotten anything he needed. After weeks of planning, he couldn't imagine what might be mislaid but it paid to be vigilant.

"But you are not going to America, are you?" Leopold argued. "Surely your journey will not take you away for even longer."

Leopold was still against his leaving and had not stopped arguing his case since he'd arrived. Oliver set his hand to Leopold's shoulder and met his brother's troubled gaze. "I will be back the moment I want to be."

Leopold's shoulder rose beneath his hand as he took a deep breath. "And where the devil were you last evening? I searched the abbey and couldn't find you. No one could."

A sliver of disappointment filled him at the idea that he was being hounded as if he were a small boy with no sense or freedom. He didn't want his brothers keeping a close watch on his activities. They might discover he'd spent one last glorious night in Elizabeth's bed and spoil everything that existed between them. "Can a man not have a moment of privacy without your whining? Stop being so difficult. It's tiresome. Are we to argue, shouting through the carriage windows, as I'm leaving the estate, too?"

Leopold frowned. "You don't know what it's like beyond England's borders. You could die and I'd never know where your body fell."

Dear God in heaven. Not this again. Leopold was growing repetitive in his arguments. "I'm sure you already thought me dead before Tobias found me," Oliver observed, struggling not to snap at Leopold's ridiculous sentimentality. "People die every day, near or far away from loved ones. I will not live out my life in swaddling clothes according to your will. There is too much to see and do yet. I'd rather be dead than idle."

Leopold's face drained of color. "I never believed you dead. I always had hope." He thrust his hand in his pocket and removed some papers. When he held them out to Oliver, his hand shook. "I took every avenue possible to find you. I even drew these in the hope that someone might recognize you as you are today."

Oliver studied them in silence. His brother possessed a good hand at sketching and his attempts to draw them as they might be as older individuals were not without some success. His drawing wasn't completely inaccurate, but he didn't have a receding hairline and rather unflattering bags beneath his eyes like this. He returned them to his brother. "Then find your hope again and cling to it. I will be fine and return or write whenever I can." Oliver gestured to George, who'd huddled by the window watching his preparations glumly, to come to him. "Now if you'll excuse me, I have farewells to make and a ship to meet in Portsmouth."

He pushed George toward the doorway, ushered his brother out, and closed the doors behind him. "Keep out of my possessions. I will be back for them and will know if anything has been removed."

"Oh, fine. Go. Just don't think I'm going to stand on the front steps and wave a tearful goodbye," Leopold said, weariness etched into every word. He slumped into the first chair they came to and didn't appear willing to take a step farther.

Oliver handed his satchel to George and returned to Leopold. He leaned down and awkwardly hugged his brother around his shoulders. "I'll be home before you know it, and I promise I will write often."

Oliver turned away as his eyes watered. Foolish emotions like tears were an inevitable encumbrance at the beginning of any adventure and the sadness would pass in due time. He and George hurried for the stairs and the waiting small crowd below. Her Grace came forward first and embraced him without a word.

Blythe was next. "Be very careful, sir. Tobias didn't risk his own neck just to hear of you in peril abroad."

Oliver gave her a quick squeeze. "I will. Keep yourself well and him out of trouble if you can."

When he came to Elizabeth, Oliver's heart thudded and he didn't know what to do. Nodding seemed an inappropriate farewell for a lover, especially one so tempting.

Elizabeth stuck out her hand. "Goodbye, Mr. Randall. I wish you smooth sailing and many wonders for your starved eyes."

Oliver took her hand in his, noting the cold clamminess of her skin and the slight tremble that flowed through her. He stepped closer, tightening his grip to instill his warmth. "Farewell,

Elizabeth. Take care of yourself and that clever boy of yours."

He released her hand slowly, imprinting the moment on his memory. Her eyes grew glassy and he turned away rather than have his last sight of her be one of tears. She cried too much.

He turned for the front door and stepped into the light, eagerly striding down the stairs on his way to the carriage. Tobias waited beside the open door, his eyes downcast. Oliver tossed his satchel into the carriage and embraced his younger brother. "Thank you for saving me so I might have this adventure."

Tobias tightened his grip. "Just don't get into trouble this time. Save yourself rather than waiting for me to do the hard work."

"You can be sure I will. I'm not as completely helpless as you all like to make out. I did spend ten years holding my own against a largely unstable element among the inmates. I've a trick or two up my sleeve for when I want to have my way. You merely caught me at a bad time. Besides, how do you think Rosemary learned to fight if not from one of us? I assure you, it wasn't Leopold who taught her."

Understanding dawned in Tobias eyes and he actually began to chuckle. "You sly old devil. I always thought Rosemary had been born with those skills. Leopold's convinced you're bound for trouble."

He thumped Tobias's shoulder. "Leave off the old bit. I'll see you in a while."

He glanced down at George and rolled his eyes. "Family. They always fret no matter how much you tell them not to."

George wrapped himself around Oliver tightly. "Goodbye, sir. Don't forget us."

A lump formed in his throat as he returned the embrace. "Never, lad. Mind your mother and make her proud."

He removed the grasping boy from around him and climbed into the carriage where Eamon Murphy waited. When he was settled and a footman had secured the door and folded the step away, Eamon thumped on the carriage roof. As the carriage lurched into motion, he turned to those gathered on the stairs and lifted his hand in farewell.

Elizabeth and George huddled together. Tobias had his arm about Blythe's slender shoulders and his brother had, in fact, joined them on the stairs after all, the duchess tucked snugly in his arms. It was a pretty memory he'd treasure during the long journey ahead.

He faced Eamon when he was nudged. "Yes."

Murphy held out a square of linen. "You've tears on your face, my friend. Very unaccountably emotional of you."

Oliver patted his face and gave Murphy his own handkerchief to replace the one he'd used. He adjusted himself on the seat and watched in silence as the Romsey estate slipped past his window. All his life he'd dreamed of this moment. Seeing new fields, towns, people.

He glanced across at Murphy and was disappointed to find him dozing already. Did he intend to sleep the entire way?

An hour later when Eamon still hadn't woken on his own, Oliver kicked his shin to point out a charming dovecote on a faraway hill. Eamon spluttered to wakefulness, glanced at it briefly, and then harrumphed. "Nothing new yet."

"There have been many new things that you cannot see by falling asleep."

Eamon scratched his jaw as he looked outside. "If you find the scene outside fascinating, why are you risking our necks beyond England's shores in search of adventure? You could easily spend half a year each year traveling to the far counties and Ireland. The duchess has good connections everywhere so you'd have many welcoming places to stay."

Oliver hadn't honestly thought that enough of an adventure to suit his needs, but the idea was intriguing. He could always undertake such short jaunts when he returned from the continent. As the carriage jostled and swayed along the road to Portsmouth, he stared at a distant manor house and wondered at its occupants. At a creek crossing, two boys sat beside the stream, long poles and strings dangling in the water in search of fish. He'd done that recently with George and he wondered what the boy was doing at this very moment. He turned to Eamon to pose the question, but his friend was sound asleep again, which made him wonder anew where he'd spent his last evening at Romsey.

In truth, Oliver hadn't paid much attention to Eamon's romantic pursuits for the past few weeks, especially once he'd begun his affair with Elizabeth, but he suddenly wondered if Eamon was sorry he'd agreed to join him on this journey. Was he leaving a sweetheart behind? If he was, he'd given no indication, but Oliver was coming to understand that complete honesty was a trait few shared. Was he being selfish to take Eamon with him? Oliver had not suggested it, but he rather thought his brother's protests had been the catalyst for Eamon's decision to come.

Troubled, he tried to settle and enjoy the new discoveries as they passed him by. When they stopped for luncheon and to change the horses, he ate and drank in the public taproom, watching those around him with interest. When they stopped to change horses again later in the day, he walked to the edge of the village to stretch his legs. He looked across the valley, squinting to see if the ocean was within sight yet, but didn't believe so.

Disappointed, he returned to the carriage moderately happy and ignored Eamon's grumble that his backside had gone numb. As Eamon's complaints grew more and more elaborate, he decided to send his friend home once they reached Portsmouth. He valued Eamon's companionship, but it was very easy to see that his heart and soul weren't in the adventure of the trip. He would have found greater pleasure and companionship should he have taken George with him. The boy had never been beyond Romsey. They would have had much to comment on.

Thoughts of George turned to thoughts of his mother. Would Elizabeth be weeping over his departure? Would she come to enjoy the thrill of travel? He dug in his pocket and removed the ribbon he'd kept with him these dozen years. He ran the slick strip through his fingers, his mind turning to their lovemaking and her passion.

He'd spent ten years trapped with madmen and women and never once had he let this slip of ribbon be taken from him. When his thoughts had turned maudlin, the ribbon had given him comfort. He had imagined Elizabeth at Romsey, laughing and happy in her life.

Yet he'd been wrong. Elizabeth had not always been smiling. When she cried, Oliver had been glad to hold her and turn her mind from her troubles. He hoped she had no need of comfort again. He wouldn't be there to hold her anymore.

After a time, traffic around them grew denser. His coachman grew surly at other drivers getting in his way. They drew to a stop before an inn on the outskirts of Portsmouth that his brother had mentioned was acceptable and waited their turn to enter the yard.

As his luggage was handed down, he glanced about him curiously.

"Watch out," someone shouted.

Eamon grabbed his arm, wrenching him against the stone inn wall.

A horse hurried past, tail flicking and striking Oliver across his chest.

Eamon laughed suddenly. "Keep your eyes open my friend lest you get run down before your adventure begins."

Oliver frowned at Eamon, but concluded he was correct. He would make sure next time to stay out of harm's way before he studied his surroundings. He followed Eamon into the coaching inn and waited while his friend bargained for a cheap set of rooms, dinner, and water for washing. Their chambers were neat and bare, the taproom crowded and noisy.

Eamon slid an ale across the table and drank heartily from his own. As Oliver sipped his slowly, he studied the room. Merchants, a few sailors, and important-looking men propped up their tables with either laughter or solemn expressions. Dinner was adequate, a trencher of fowl and green beans and day-old bread that stuck to the roof of his mouth and made swallowing uncomfortable.

When night fell and Eamon gained the company of a willing tavern wench across his lap, Oliver returned to his bedchamber alone, ears ringing from the noise of the taproom below, and considered how Elizabeth would spend her last night at the abbey. Dinner with the duchess, tucking her son into his bed with a kiss to his brow, sliding into the cold sheets of her bed and maybe sparing a thought for their time together.

As he lay down, he distinctly heard singing and laughter coming from the room next door. He held a pillow over his head as the laughter turned to moans of pleasure.

Yet sleep was denied him. He tossed and turned but couldn't get comfortable in the strange empty bed. As he lay there, he wished for Elizabeth's soft body to be nestled against his own, warmer and more welcoming than the ribbon he carried could ever be.

Chapter Twenty-Four

———•———

There was nothing gloomier than to sit in a room full of people you loved and exchange soft smiles with those who were to be left behind the very next day. Beth shivered and drew her shawl tighter about her shoulders to banish her fears. She would leave Romsey and the people she'd come to admire tomorrow and would never see them again.

Although she wished to thank Leopold Randall for all he had done for her and her son, she decided to wait till morning to speak with him. He had been surly with everyone since Oliver's departure. Beth had heard the servants' whispers of their discussion and had been shocked to her core. The strength of Leopold's arguments had not swayed Oliver one bit. He'd told his brother in no uncertain terms that he was glad to be gone from this place.

She glanced across the room at Mercy and forced yet another smile to her face. The poor woman didn't seem her usual glad self tonight either. No one did. Oliver's departure had affected everyone's spirits for the worse. If not for Henry being invited to dine, Beth would have begged pardon and retreated to her room to nurse her disappointment and worries in private.

A sudden happy giggle turned her gaze across the room. The young duke played with George, blissfully unaware of the miserable faces around him. George caught her eye, smiling a little sadly as the young duke rushed across the room to his family to show them his toys. She'd never fully realized the deaths of his siblings and father affected George so badly still. Her heart went out to him. At least they would have each other to cling to in the years to come. They would be all the family they needed.

"Edwin will be so lonely when George goes," Blythe murmured. "They've become the best of friends."

"He won't be lonely for too long. Aren't Lord Grayling and his daughters expected soon?" Beth hoped her question would hold off any discussion about their imminent departure. She was doing her best not to dwell on it or burst into tears.

The sisters exchanged a look. "Still no word and we've decided not to wait for him any longer," Blythe confessed, a pleased smile lifting her lips as she glanced at Tobias where he sat beside her. "If Gray misses our weddings it will be his own fault."

"Happy to wait as long as you need, sweetheart," Tobias assured Blythe with a cheeky wink. "I am yours to command."

Beth couldn't help but laugh at the changes wrought by a few short weeks. Instead of surliness and reluctance, Tobias appeared ready to do anything Blythe demanded of him. So far, all she'd asked was that he dress as a gentleman, so gloves and hat had become essential for him at all times. Occasionally he had to be reminded, but Beth had a suspicion he enjoyed his future wife's fussing so much that he forgot on purpose.

The drawing-room doors opened after a brief knock and the newly promoted butler announced their guest had arrived. Henry strode in, a pleased grin fixed to his face, and bowed to the duchess extravagantly. "Your Grace, you look as lovely as ever."

Even that small compliment didn't lift Mercy's spirits enough to do more than cause her lips to turn up slightly. "You're too kind."

He greeted everyone else in turn, made a fuss, and had George come to shake his hand so he could speak a few private words to him before he faced Elizabeth.

His brief nod was curt and then he immediately faced Leopold to discuss the success of the day's hunt as if there was no one else in the room. Beth's cheeks flamed with heat at his rudeness and she bit her lip, appalled that her brother-in-law could behave so badly so very easily.

Mercy smoothly interrupted the gentlemen when their conversation appeared never-ending. She coiled her arm about Leopold's and offered a hesitant smile when they fell silent.

"You'll have to forgive our odd moods tonight, sir. Oliver's departure for the continent has made us all a trifle sad this evening," the duchess confessed.

"In my book that would be cause for celebration." Henry laughed. "Always such an odd fish. Never one for carousing or charming the ladies as all men do. Always had his head in a book and couldn't be bothered with manly pursuits."

Leopold's lips lifted in a wry smile as if he agreed. Clearly Leopold did not know that Oliver could turn a lady's head quite effectively once he put his mind to it. "Everyone has their own interests, Turner. Tell me, what is there to do in America that occupies your free time? Do you go to the races or hunt?"

"There's races aplenty, and hunts if you're well connected and know where to find your quarry. A man can always find sport of some description, just as you can on any great estate." As he spoke, Henry's demeanor shifted ever so slightly as if remembering the thrill of the chase pleased him immensely. His gaze slid from Mercy to Blythe with a barely veiled hunger glittering in his eyes that sent alarm bells racing through her veins.

"Shooting parties are rare at Romsey," Mercy said with a merry laugh as she missed the sly look completely. "In fact, I believe your outing with Leopold may have been the first in many years."

Henry peered at Tobias. "Really? That's not what I've heard. I was led to believe you had trouble some time back with a ruffian and had the whole village on the hunt."

"A misunderstanding," Leopold said quietly. "And not something on which we will dwell."

"Not surprising." Henry nodded sagely, hand sliding into his pocket. The sound of coins clinking together was very clear. "After everything I've heard, you must be keen to ensure the whole of it is forgotten and behind you."

The coins clinked again as Henry's gaze flittered about.

Both Randall men drew closer to her brother-in-law, their eyes alight with anger. "If you've something to say, Turner, then say it."

Beth stood, suddenly afraid that the gentlemen would come to blows on her last night here. She didn't want any unpleasantness left behind when she departed, and certainly none instigated by her unpleasant brother-in-law. "Please," she said quickly. "Shouldn't we all go in to dinner now?"

Henry laughed, a cruel sound that made the hair on the back of her neck stand on end. "Keep your wig on, woman. I was just fishing to see if the gossip is true. Lord knows a man must protect his family from idle tongues or the influence of an improper person on their family."

Mercy and Blythe quickly crossed the room to her side and together they ushered the children toward the dining room. On their last night here, George was to eat with the adults. And since George was here, so too was young Edwin.

When Beth attempted to sit at Henry's right, he insisted George take her place. She moved to accommodate his wishes without a fuss and tried to slow her frightened heart.

Throughout the meal, she couldn't miss the way he kept his conversation fixed on George, occasionally casting scowls on those around him as they talked of local matters. His glass was refilled more often than anyone else's. His manners at the table slipped.

Not even the young duke was overlooked for Henry's amusement. When Edwin accidentally knocked his mother's glass over, spilling her wine on the fine white tablecloth, Henry laughed uproariously and slapped his knee. "Says a lot for the future of the estate, doesn't it? Can't hold his liquor."

He raised his glass to the sobbing child and drank deeply until it was empty. "Fill it again," he demanded of the footman standing in attendance behind him.

Leopold stood and waved the footman back. "I think you've had just about enough for one evening."

Henry leered at Mercy. "I think you should shut up. Are you sure she's a duchess? She's practically dancing in your lap."

Beth couldn't move. She sat in shocked horror as Leopold reached across the table, grabbed Henry by his cravat and hauled him toward the doorway. "How dare you?"

"Leopold, no," Mercy cried out.

"It's either him or me," Tobias promised, joining with his brother as they forced Henry from the room.

The sneer that crossed Henry's face made Beth shudder and she hurried to her son's side and asked him to leave with the servant escorting the young duke out of the room. He'd seen and heard far too much already. Heaven knew what Henry had whispered into George's ear during the meal.

Thankfully, her son was eager to comply with her wishes. When he was gone, she faced her brother-in-law. Had this ugly mood been simmering from the moment of his arrival?

While there was little difference on the surface, it was hard to ignore the curled fist at his side. Beth bravely stepped forward. "Come now, Henry. There's no need to argue like this."

He moved closer and the fumes of excessive drinking rolled over her. She gagged at the strong scent. Was Henry too drunk to be reasoned with? Tobias grabbed her arm suddenly and hauled her behind him.

"So that's the way it is, eh?" Henry nodded. "One or all, it doesn't make a damn bit of difference. You're all the same."

He pivoted and strode for the door, threw it wide, and stormed from the house. Beth stared after him in shocked silence. After a moment, embarrassment filled her. "I'm so very sorry about that. He was very drunk, I fear."

Tobias set his arm gently about her. "He was more than drunk, but you are blameless for any of that. You've not one thing to be sorry for, believe me."

Panic welled in her. "He's family."

Family that she'd have to live with. Her future did not look at all bright or lovely if she had to contend with a temper like that. Her husband had been far kinder than his sibling. She wondered how she had never known that before. Beth wrapped her arms about herself and trembled. She'd given her word to go to America, but she could not allow that man one more moment near her son. But how could she stay? What Henry wanted, he took. He'd been very clear about that. He'd cause more trouble for the Randalls than she ever wanted them to suffer.

"Good riddance to him," Mercy huffed as she and Blythe surrounded her. "You're not leaving with that man. I absolutely will not allow you to go."

"I agree," Leopold said firmly as he joined them. "William would turn in his grave if he could see how his brother just spoke to you. I could never be easy if you went with him. You and George will stay with us, for the rest of your life if you wish it. We'll convince him to return to America alone even if I have to pay the blackmail he hinted at three times over."

Beth shook as a sob lodged in her throat. She blubbered out

her thanks as she wept into her hands. The Randalls were such good and generous people to excuse her for bringing Henry into their midst. She didn't deserve their loyalty or support but she would take it for the sake of her son.

They led her back to the drawing room chairs, and after a time Henry was forgotten and talk turned to lighter matters and the wedding guests expected to come. After careful consideration, Mercy had whittled down her larger guest list to include only the very closest of friends. "I just cannot face a room of one hundred people asking the same question, 'where are the brother and sister now?'"

A sudden yearning filled Beth's heart. She wished Oliver were with them. He would know whether Henry would go away or not. She might not have always liked his bluntly worded truths, but she'd come to depend on them.

When the time came to say goodnight, Beth wearily trudged to her bedchamber.

George was awake and waiting for her. "Has he gone?" he asked immediately.

Beth nodded. "Yes, he took himself away an hour ago."

"Thank goodness," George muttered as he burrowed into her bed the way he had as a young boy. If he did that he was surely upset.

Beth sat next to him and caught up his hand. "We're not going. I'll tell your uncle tomorrow that you may choose to join him when you are older and of age."

"I won't go," George insisted, his hands slipping from hers. "Why does he say such horrible things about you?"

Beth's hands grew clammy and she rubbed them together anxiously. She drew a deep breath. "I think Uncle Henry hasn't had a very happy life. We've always had each other and he resents how close we are. You're his heir and he feels you should obey him without question."

George scowled. "Didn't like what he said about the duke. He's still a baby and shouldn't be laughed at like that."

Beth's heart overflowed with love for her son. "Yes, he is. But luckily he is too young to remember what has been said of him."

George met her gaze. "Will we leave Romsey now that you've not got a position? I remember you wanted one."

Beth shook her head. "The duchess insists we stay."

George launched up from the bed, wrapped his arms about her

neck, and hugged her tightly. "Then I will see my friend again."

Beth loosened his grip so she could breathe. "Which friend would that be?"

"Oliver Randall," he said, smiling from ear to ear.

A lump formed in her throat. "Dearest, he may not return for a very long time. He has lots of plans for his journey. I don't know when we will see him again."

George threw himself out of her bed. "But he will come back. There's something he has to do when the duke comes of age."

"Oh, George, that's a tremendously long time away."

"Doesn't matter, he promised to write to us. He wants to know that you are happy. I'll tell him everything in my letters. He'll be happy that we remained here."

When George bounced out of her room and his room grew dark, Beth followed to the door and peered into the shadows. If only she had George's faith in Oliver's return she could convince herself that one day she would be happy. She tucked him into bed, kissed his brow, and returned to her own room.

But sleep wouldn't come. She lay awake for hours, staring up at the canopy, willing herself not to cry. Frustrated, she flung off the bedclothes. She crept to her son's room to check he was deeply asleep and then padded down the hall to Oliver's bedchamber. She let herself in and shivered. Gone a day and the room was already so empty and cold, as if he'd been a figment of her imagination.

She entered his bedchamber and lay down on his pillows, drawing a deep breath of his lingering scent, her heart breaking with the loss all over again. At least here, she could cry all night without disturbing her son's rest. She'd get her tears from her system and face tomorrow's ugly confrontation with Henry with a calmer soul.

Chapter Twenty-Five

Seagulls squawked high overhead on ship mastheads, flightless because there was not enough wind even for them to soar away from England. "Sorry, sirs, but the wind and tide are against us this morning."

"Damnation." Oliver cursed as he stared out at the still waters of Portsmouth Harbor and beyond where nothing moved—no ship with a sail, at least. "How long?"

"There's no telling about the wind. P'raps it's better to wait a few hours." The captain scowled at the calm waters in disgust, lifted his eyes to an unmoving flag at the top of the *Jezebel's* mast, and muttered, "It's the devil's luck today. I can send word to your inn should you rather come aboard later."

Eamon nodded enthusiastically. "Will two in the afternoon be a fair time to return?"

The captain beamed. "That'll be grand, sirs. Now if you'll excuse me, I've a man to see about filling an empty corner of my hold. May as well take on what I can for the crossing."

He touched his cap and turned back the way he came.

Eamon started chuckling. "I don't think he's disappointed at all about the delay. The cargo hold was only half full I heard a seaman say."

Oliver ground his teeth at the weather's contrariness. All he wanted was to be onboard and headed for clear open water, but if there was no wind to move the ship along, that wish wouldn't be granted any time soon. He may as well stay on dry land until the weather changed.

He glanced at Eamon and noticed the direction of his gaze. "I suppose you want to visit the tavern while we wait."

Eamon grinned. "See, ten years kept apart and you can still read my mind."

Oliver looked about him. The docks were rather rough, even at this hour, and more than one fellow had sized them up as they'd stood near the duke's fine carriage. "Not here. We'll return to the inn and you can imbibe there until time to board."

"And the luggage?"

Oliver glanced up at the sailors idly leaning against the railings above. He didn't trust them not to sail away with their possessions stowed in the hold. "Our luggage will go back to the inn with us."

Eamon quickly gestured for the Romsey grooms to reload their belongings for the return trip to the inn. With one last look at the *Jezebel*, Oliver climbed into the carriage, disappointed by the unexpected delay to what should have been a fine morning. The carriage lurched forward and he kept his face to the window, soaking up the strangeness of the port town and the new faces he saw. He'd come to Portsmouth once before as a boy. The place had changed and grown considerably from what he remembered of it then.

"Perhaps it's a sign," Oliver muttered.

Eamon slued around to stare at him. "What was that?"

Oliver shrugged. "I considered sending you back to Romsey when we reached the inn last night but hesitated. However, given the lengths required to haul you from your bed and the wind being against us, I believe it right that we should part ways."

Eamon gaped. "Now see here a moment. If anyone was supposed to be a bad omen, it's certainly not me." He folded his arms over his chest. "The nerve of trying to be rid of me. You'd be bored without my scintillating company."

Oliver laughed suddenly, amused by Eamon's protests. "You spent the whole of yesterday's journey fast asleep."

Eamon shrugged. "Can I help it that I've seen that stretch of road a fair few times already? It's not new to me. I'm still going with you."

The carriage slowed and then shuddered to a stop. Above them, the Romsey coachman began swearing expansively at whatever it was that blocked their way. Oliver ignored the noise, staring out the window and down a narrow alley, reconsidering what it would take to convince Eamon to see sense. He was so wrapped up in his thoughts that it took a moment to register what his eyes were seeing. Henry Turner stood on the cobblestones of Portsmouth beside a grim dark inn, arguing with the proprietor.

That was impossible.

They shook hands and Turner reached into the carriage and dragged a small figure against his side. George. The boy struggled and although he watched intently, he did not see Elizabeth step from the carriage before it rolled away. Oliver's attempts at marshaling his patience ended.

He slammed his fist into the roof to signal he was getting out and threw the door open. "Excuse me," he said to Eamon.

He jumped from the carriage quickly, keeping his eye on the building George had been dragged into. Still no sign of Elizabeth and he couldn't believe she would willingly leave her son in Henry Turner's company, today of all days. How the devil had they got here so fast anyway? Surely they hadn't traveled at night?

"What the devil, Ollie? I thought we were going to be tucked up at the inn for the morning."

He glanced up at the coachman. "Wait for me here. I just saw George Turner go into that inn down there with his uncle and that associate of his."

The coachman nodded and ordered the grooms down to tend the horses.

Eamon peered down the laneway, but of course had missed seeing the boy. "That's impossible. They're not due to sail for two days."

"Impossible or not, I'm certain it's the boy. I must investigate."

Eamon caught his arm. "You knew they were leaving. What's the problem with an early departure?"

Oliver shook off his friend's grip. "Elizabeth wasn't with them, Eamon. I saw no sign of her luggage on the carriage, either."

"Hell's bells. They're in trouble, all right." Eamon patted at the bulge in his coat pocket where he'd stowed his pistol for when they'd been at the docks. "Ready."

Oliver had no time to argue that he didn't require company for this errand. He hurried up the lane and when the tavern came into view, he released the clip on the short blade strapped to his arm. Two bulky ruffians entered before them and he exchanged a long speaking glance with Eamon. "Watch your back."

Oliver pushed the door open, hearing the merry tinkle of bells over the noise of the patrons. He paused and scanned the room through thick drifts of pipe smoke. The patrons fell silent one by one, yet Oliver couldn't see or hear George anywhere. A man behind a slab of wood held up by two barrels squinted at them. "What can I get you, sir?"

"Information," Oliver answered, keeping one eye on those standing nearest. A low murmur filled the room as he approached the innkeeper. "I'm looking for a boy, about as high as my chest. Dark hair, blue eyed."

The innkeeper spat on the floor. "Ain't seen anyone of that description come in."

The murmurs returned at a louder pitch. "He's important to me," Oliver insisted.

The innkeeper leaned forward and grinned, showing off a toothless smile. "If he's so important, then how come he's not with you?"

"That is what I intend to find out." Oliver took a coin from his pocket and flicked it onto the battered table. "I've been away. He should be with his mother. She'll be distraught."

The innkeeper took the coin and examined it, his eyes brightening. "And if I should have seen him?"

"Then I'll pay for any damage caused in his retrieval."

Oliver sensed men closing behind him at the mention of payment. He turned, caught one man's wandering hand near his coat pocket, kicked another in the bollocks, and pressed the tip of his knife against the first fellow's right wrist. "You really shouldn't do that until you know where I've lived these past years. The things I've seen would make a depraved man beg for his mama's tit to nurse upon. Did you know it's possible to slice a man's john from his body and make him eat it before he draws his last breath? I can give everyone a demonstration of how it's done here and now if you'd like."

The innkeeper protested and the thief began to shake. The edge of the blade beaded with bright blood. Oliver eased back so he wouldn't inflict a deep cut that would hamper the man's criminal activities. The only man that deserved his anger was Henry Turner if he'd harmed one hair on Elizabeth's or George's head.

Eamon had taken a defensive stance behind him, pistols drawn and at the ready. "We just want the boy," Eamon said loudly.

The thief tipped his head toward the rear of the room. "He went in back."

Oliver released the would-be thief with a quick shove, but kept the blade ready in his hand. The injured fellow cradled his wrist but had the sense to remain at a distance.

The patrons shuffled out of the way, granting them access to the rear of the taproom. Not a soul made a sound. He glanced behind and nodded to Eamon.

He strode to the back room, pulse thundering in his ears, where a closed door greeted them. Oliver listened and heard Henry Turner speaking to someone beyond the wood. The words were indistinct, but he sounded well pleased with himself.

Oliver threw the door wide even as Eamon raised his pistol. As soon as they could see the whole of the room, George huddled in the far corner cowering in misery, they moved. Elizabeth wasn't present. Eamon dispatched Henry's associate to the far corner and held him there, leaving Oliver to deal with Turner. When he glimpsed the bruise forming on George's cheek, Oliver rushed Henry, caught him about the throat, lifted him, and slammed his back onto the table standing in the center of the room.

Oliver squeezed Henry's throat tightly as the man made crabbing motions to escape. "Do something, Fielding," Turner wheezed.

Oliver didn't dare look up. He'd trust that Eamon could hold his own until he got the answers he needed. "Where is Elizabeth?"

"Left the slut in the gutter where she belongs," Turner gasped out, wheezing the words around the constriction of Oliver's hand.

Turner clawed at Oliver, trying to break his grip or injure him enough to release him.

Oliver brought his blade up and laid it on Henry Turner's cheek, just below his eye, as anger bubbled over. "If Elizabeth has come to harm, I will gut you and throw your innards into the harbor for the fishes to consume."

Turner's eyes widened and his legs and arms struggled to get away from the blade about to pierce his skin. "She's at Romsey. I left her there. Unharmed."

Relief coursed through him. At least Elizabeth was safe. Oliver eased the blade back a touch, but kept a firm grip on Turner. "I'll be taking George with me when I leave. You will forget he exists from this moment on."

"He's my heir," Henry spluttered angrily. "My blood."

Oliver examined the face below him. Henry Turner was dying a slow death at his hands. If Oliver didn't relent, Turner would pass out before he suffocated. Oliver leaned close to Henry's ear, relaxing his grip a touch so he wouldn't lose consciousness. "He's my son," he growled. "My blood."

The lie tumbled easily from his mouth and pride filled him to say at long last what he'd unconsciously wished. George would be his son in truth as soon as he could convince Elizabeth to marry him.

Henry struggled. "That lying, unfaithful whore."

Oliver pressed the blade against the soft skin beneath Turner's eye until blood welled. He would not stand for this filth insulting the woman he loved. He watched the blood bead and swell and then fill every pockmark as it slid down Turner's ugly, pitted skin.

"Don't," George begged. "Don't hurt him too bad."

"Do you hear that? My boy is wiser than his years." Oliver dredged up every memory he had of the inmates of Skepington and allowed their rage to feed his expression. "If I killed you, it could be messy and I promise not one soul, not even Fielding, would recognize what was left after I was done with you."

Color leached from Henry's face and the scent of urine filled the room. "You're mad," he gasped, panting in fright.

Oliver straightened but kept his hand firmly about Turner's throat. "I've stared into the face of madness a thousand times but never seen my own. I'm a Randall. We look after our own, as I'm sure you've realized by now."

Out of the corner of his eye, he saw George move toward the doorway and the security offered by escape. He held up the blade and examined the bloody tip. "If you follow us, or even look twice at my son again, I'll hurt you so bad you'll beg me to slit your throat and end your miserable existence."

He wiped the blood across Turner's waistcoat, released his throat, and tossed a coin at Turner's associate, more money than he'd likely ever had. "For the inconvenience of working for a pitiful coward," Oliver told him.

Fielding nodded and pressed his back to the wall. "You'll have no trouble from me, I swear."

Eamon hurried George from the room as the patrons craned their necks to see what had happened, narrowing the path to freedom. Oliver followed along, judging the mood of the room with each step. The occupants were tense, held against the knife-edge, leaning toward action and spoiling for a good brawl. He reached for the bag of coins he carried beneath his coat, the bulk of his funds for the trip. He tossed it high, slashed at it with his short-bladed knife, letting the coins fall where they might. Money to buy them safe passage out of the inn and beyond.

The patrons and innkeeper scrambled for the coins on the floor instead of impeding him and he walked from the tavern without incident. Ahead, Eamon had forced George into the carriage and the boy waited with his face pressed to the glass. Oliver joined them, re-sheathing his short blade on his arm when he took his seat, quite content with his success.

When he looked up after tugging his coat sleeve back in place, Eamon and George were staring at him, wide-eyed.

"What?"

"Damnation, Oliver," Eamon whispered, his throat working as he swallowed. "Henry Turner wasn't the only one who could have soiled their trousers."

Oliver pursed his lips and then laughed to relieve the tension. "Sorry. I had no time to explain. I'm not mad and I've never done any of that before. I read something similar in a book once and thought terrifying threats would work best in such an environment."

George slumped back into his seat, his chest rising and falling frantically. "You lie very well, sir."

"I do." Oliver eased back on the seat and set his heels to the far side, next to the boy. "Have the carriage return to Romsey, Eamon. The boy will be wanting his mother and she him as soon as possible."

While Eamon shouted up directions to the surly driver, George looked at him oddly, curiosity burning in his eyes. "What you said? Was it *all* a lie?"

The boy had heard the lie that Oliver was his father. "Every word," he said. "Your mother is a faithful woman. However, one part could be true if I can convince her of the need. Would that bother you?"

"No, sir." The boy's eyes glowed with happiness. "I'd like that very much." When he grinned, he grabbed for his cheek, wincing at the pain.

"Coming or going," the coachman shouted back as he cracked the whip over the horses. "Make up your bloody mind."

Oliver drew the boy to the empty space beside him and examined the damage done to his face. A bruise had formed that caused pain even when touched lightly. "When did this happen?"

"Last night. Someone came into my room while I was sleeping. I called out, but mama never heard or came. I thought they must have had her too, but she wasn't there when they pushed me into the carriage. They drove all through the night."

Oliver brushed the boy's hair from his eyes, taking note of the rest of him. He was wearing mismatched clothes and his eyes were not clear or bright. "Have you slept or eaten since then?"

"A bit. But I'm not hungry. I don't think I could ever close my eyes again to sleep."

"You can and you will. You're safe now. Lie down over there. Eamon, move out of the way so the boy can stretch out," he instructed, warming to the task of taking care of another. "I'll wake you at the first inn we stop at once we are beyond Portsmouth's environs, George. I promise."

George glanced at Eamon nervously. "If you say I must."

Oliver removed his coat and covered George with it when he'd gotten comfortable. "Use that for warmth, lad, and get some rest. We'll be home again before you know it and your mother will want a full accounting of your disappearance. Better to be alert for her questions."

"Thank you, sir."

George nestled beneath his coat and after perhaps a bare mile he grew still as sleep claimed him. Oliver rubbed his tired eyes. He hadn't slept in several days now, himself, yet he wouldn't succumb until he had delivered the boy to Elizabeth. She would be frantic by this hour.

Eamon nudged him in the ribs, nodding to where George slept. "Now that, Ollie, was the smartest thing you've ever done, rescuing him from Turner. I'm proud of you."

"I'm not," Oliver replied. "I should have seen the danger and taken steps."

Eamon snorted. "You were there before it was too late, so why berate yourself."

"Elizabeth."

"She has your family about her for support. When they discover him missing, they'll likely be in pursuit. We may encounter them on the road back directly."

Oliver brightened. If Elizabeth pursued George, then her suffering would be lessened by the reduction of time. She could have her George back in her arms sooner than he could deliver him to Romsey. That thought made him smile.

"So, when are you to make an honest woman out of Beth Turner? I hear there are as many rules for dallying with a widow as there are for flirting with an upstairs maid."

Oliver looked at the boy across from him. "I'm not sure. She'll have had a fright at losing George. She won't think of anything but him when we see her."

Eamon settled himself more comfortably. "Well, don't leave it another dozen years or someone else will have her."

Anger curled inside Oliver at the idea of anyone touching his Elizabeth beyond a dance or rendering assistance to help her out of a carriage. He'd made enough mistakes already without missing what he should have seen before. He would wait a dozen years if he had to, but he was sure he wouldn't like it.

Eamon started to laugh. "Steady on, old man. Uncurl your fists. I've no interest in her beyond seeing the two of you leg-shackled."

Oliver eased his hands open, astounded by the sharp bite of

jealousy and possessiveness that had filled him. Is this what it was to be in love? Always anxious, always certain another man was lurking in wait for the woman you adored? After George's abduction, he was certain he could never let them out of his sight again. He shook his head at the confusion that filled him. He was going to botch any proposal, but he would convince her in the end, even if it took another twelve years of blundering.

Chapter Twenty-Six

A woman is only as foolish as the love that leads her astray. Beth sat up in Oliver's bed as sunlight streamed through the curtains, warning her that she'd slept well beyond her usual rising hour. What had she been thinking last night when, sleepless, she'd wandered the halls of the abbey and, instead of returning to her own room, had fallen into Oliver's just so she could breathe his scent?

She dived out of the bed, straightened it quickly so no one could tell it had been slept in, and hurried to put on her robe. If she wasn't careful, she'd be caught parading around the halls in her nightgown.

With one last look at Oliver's abandoned possessions, she crept as quietly as she could along the halls until she reached her own room. Once there, she let out a relieved breath and ran her fingers through her tangled hair. There was so much to do and decide. She had to be ready and prepared to face Henry and tell him they would not be traveling with him to America. She had to consider exactly what she would do with her life now that they would stay. Beth didn't want to be a burden on the Randalls. She would earn her way somehow.

She eased the door open and peered at the dimly lighted bed. The sheets were already turned back, signifying that her son was up. She moved to the window and flung the curtains wide. The morning was distinctly pretty, gardens waiting for the warmth of the day to bring out their best.

When she turned around, she gasped at the sight confronting her. Her son's room had been ransacked; his luggage was gone.

Beth checked everywhere and then checked her own room. Her bed was turned back, exactly as she'd left it last night, and nothing else had been disturbed that she could see. Yet when she took two steps forward, she discovered a grubby scrap of paper lying upon her sheets. Trembling, snatched it up and read.

I've no use for a slut who dishonors her family by spreading her legs for Oliver Randall. You'll never see the boy again.

Beth stared at the paper as her hand began to shake, blurring the words completely. Her breath came in short, painful gasps and she clutched the bedpost to support herself. How could Henry have come and taken her son without her permission? How dare he?

Sure that she had only just missed him, Beth strode across the room and wrenched her door open to begin a search, starting with the nearest chambers. At one room she encountered Leopold Randall, half-dressed for the day, the young duke playing at his feet. His eyes widened at her abrupt appearance. "Good God, woman. What the devil are you doing?"

Beth's tongue thickened. She couldn't speak the words out loud. She slammed the door shut on Leopold and the child and continued her search alone.

In an unoccupied chamber she saw signs that someone had used the bed, disturbing the coverlet and smearing mud upon the once pristine coverlet. She studied the marks. Whoever it had been had made quite a mess. They must have waited here for night to fall and the abbey to grow quiet before taking George. Had no one heard?

A sob tore from her throat as she retraced her steps, following the path of mud back to George's room. More mud was scattered on the floor rug beside the bed. From George's room she followed the small crumbs of dirt as far as she could. At the top of the staircase, the marks grew less apparent, as if they had only passed this way once.

Beth flew down the abbey staircase, checking the floor for signs as she went. At the long gallery there were more marks and a chill cut through her nightgown. She glanced down the deserted hallway and saw that a window had been left open. She couldn't believe such a mistake was possible after everything that had happened here these past months.

She reached for the window and lowered it, making sure to secure the latch properly. George couldn't be going to America without her. He was just hiding in the abbey. It was a terrible, cruel dream she would wake from soon. He was safely tucked up in bed with a book hidden beneath his pillow.

"Beth?"

Leopold Randall's voice cut through her dream like a hot knife through butter. She turned slowly, staring at him as panic rose. George could not be gone. He had to be here somewhere.

Leopold came closer. "What are you doing at the window?"

"George is gone."

He rushed to her side. "What do you mean George is gone?"

She gestured to the window behind her, noticing that she still held the proof of his abduction in her hand. "He's not here anymore. Henry's taken George away from me. I'll never see him again."

She stared at the note as her hand trembled. She'd brought this down on her own head by loving Oliver. She moaned as the room began to spin about her.

Leopold drew closer, but he too swam before her eyes. "Why the devil would he do that?"

Beth squeezed her eyes shut. Henry had warned her he'd be watching. He'd learned about Oliver somehow and was punishing her for her faithlessness to his family. That explained his anger last night. She crumpled into a heap on the hard floor and covered her face. She only had herself to blame.

The note disappeared from her lax fingers before she could prevent it as footsteps pounded toward her. Beth looked up helplessly as Leopold read Henry's words and learned her real character. He seemed to sway and then he looked down at her, pity in his eyes. "Is there any truth in this?"

Tobias moved into her line of sight. Shame filled her that the good people around her would find out this way, but she nodded. She wouldn't lie and pretend to be virtuous when she was anything but.

"Damn him," Leopold cursed. "You should have left him to burn, Tobias. That bloody bastard knew he was leaving and seduced Beth anyway."

Tobias rushed to her side and lifted her from the floor. "Here, lean on me while Leopold gets over the shock. I'm sure you need more comfort than this. He could be at it for a while."

Beth held tight to Tobias, her legs lacking the strength to stand unaided. "I deserve it and worse."

Tobias led her to the drawing room and eased her into a chair before the fire. He rubbed her hands briskly. "Shh, don't talk such nonsense. You're so cold, luv."

Without waiting for a reply, Tobias threw his coat about her shoulders and rubbed her arms. "Just blot out what my brother says for the moment and catch your breath."

Beth wrung her hands, trying to instill warmth into her fingers. She'd never felt this cold or empty before. She'd never *not* known where her son was. He should be in his bed, not on his way to America with her duplicitous brother-in-law.

Lighter footsteps drew to a halt some feet away. "Well, I'm not surprised entirely, so do shut up, Leopold," Blythe exclaimed with considerable heat. "Can't you see your timing is terrible? Forget about Oliver for the moment and think about Beth. She's in shock. Make yourself useful and pour a whiskey while we consider how to get George back."

Leopold stopped ranting long enough to complete the task and in the sudden silence, Beth sobbed. She'd lost everything she loved. Oliver was gone, George was gone, and there was nothing she could do about the loss of either of them.

A soft arm curled about her and a glass appeared before her eyes. "Sip this, slowly. mind," Blythe advised, rubbing her arms the way Tobias had done but more gently. Beth sipped the liquid. Her throat burned but the sensation was preferable to the cold that was consuming her. She didn't want to think. She didn't want to exist. She handed back the empty glass and requested another to blot out the pain. "He has a right to be angry. I've done a terrible thing."

"No more whiskey for you if that's what you're thinking," Blythe chided as she set the glass down. "You've done nothing but follow your heart. I think we can all agree that love makes us risk much when the reward can be so great."

Beth met her gaze. "I'm being punished for that very thing, my lady. For my foolishness and stupidity. Henry will never allow me to see George again. He's taken him away and I'll never find him now." She sobbed on the last and curled over as she cried.

Leopold took Blythe's place and eased her into a sitting position again. "Did you hear nothing during the night?"

"No," Beth gulped at the pain that engulfed her. "I wasn't in my room last night."

Leopold's gaze fell to the note in his hand, his frown growing.

Beth pressed her fingers to her temples at how stupid she had been. She'd known her brother-in-law was a harder man than most, but that he might abduct George to get his way had never occurred to her. She would never have let George out of her sight for even a minute if she had suspected. "I couldn't sleep for missing Oliver and I spent the night in his bed."

Leopold sat back, wiping his hand across his face. "How long have you been involved with my brother?"

Blythe shushed him. "That is no one's business but Beth's. Now, we need to get young George back where he belongs. He must be terrified to be stolen away in the dead of night."

Beth moaned at that image and Blythe tugged her to her feet. "Faith, now. We'll get him back. Why don't you come with me and get dressed? By the time we come down again, Leopold will have a plan prepared for pursuit."

Although she didn't want to move, she allowed herself to be led away. She put one foot before the other as she climbed the stairs with Blythe's aid, barely noticing that Mercy had joined them, and passed into her bedchamber. The emptiness of the next room brought more tears and Mercy quickly closed the door when she continued to stare into the wreckage that was once her son's neat room.

Numbness crept into her limbs as Blythe and Mercy undressed her from her night attire and redressed her in a warm day gown. She should have been appalled at such important women fussing over her, but she hadn't the will to protest. The two women dressed her hair, slid stockings up her legs and tied garters around her calves, slipped her feet into sturdy shoes suitable for travel, and a hundred other small kindnesses that barely penetrated her misery.

A few minutes later, or so it seemed to Beth, she jerked upright as the carriage wheel landed in a hole. Across from her, Tobias and Blythe were talking quietly, hands firmly holding each other's. Blythe leaned forward, peering into her eyes intently. "There you are. I was beginning to worry."

Beth scrambled to sit straighter, looking about her in alarm. "Where are we?"

"Some miles from Romsey by now," Tobias murmured.

Beth blinked and tried to adjust to the passage of time. How could she be here and not have noticed the change? She shook her head as her heartbeat quickened. George was gone. She longed for him and Oliver, too. She wanted them back in her arms where they belonged. "Where are we going?"

"Allen and his sons are leading the way on horseback. We're headed south, following the trail, or at least we hope we are."

Beside her, Leopold held out his hand. "I must apologize. It seems I'm the last to know everything about my brothers. I had no idea about Oliver. I was rude and I'm told rather hurtful in my speech to you. Forgive me."

Beth reluctantly set her hand in his and he squeezed her fingers tightly. "There is nothing to forgive," she whispered.

He smiled, a rueful expression that touched his eyes. "I've never understood my brother. I still cannot believe he abandoned you."

She lifted her chin, determined that there should be no misunderstandings about what had happened. "He never abandoned me. I knew he would leave." She'd gone into the affair with her eyes wide open and had only herself to blame for the loss of her reputation and her son. She'd caused Henry to take George away to protect him from her sins. "How am I to get George back even if we find where Henry has taken him?"

Tobias leaned forward and lifted a small chest from the floor. He shook it. "Money should work nicely. Turner made it very plain last night that he's a greedy sort."

Leopold sighed and raked a hand through his hair. "I thought I knew him. Seems he's much changed since we were young. I'm sorry, Beth. I invited him to call as often as he liked in order for you to become better acquainted. The servants report that windows have been found unlatched all over the abbey for days, like the one in the long gallery, but nothing has been stolen. Likely Turner's associate entered the abbey during dinner and waited for everyone to fall asleep before creeping into George's room."

Beth closed her eyes. "Henry has been very taken with the view from the long-gallery windows and others inside the abbey. He must have unlatched them when I wasn't looking."

Dread filled her. Had Henry been planning to leave her behind from the beginning? As the carriage rolled along, Beth tried to control her panic but she was sure her brother-in-law was already out of her reach. He might not even be heading in this direction. She stared out the window, trying to form a convincing argument to explain herself and get her son back. If Oliver was here, she could beg him to write one out for her to practice. He could be very convincing when he set his mind to it. Beth's arms ached as she wished for Oliver's calming presence to proclaim the odds of succeeding.

"Riders and a carriage approaching fast, Mr. Randall," the coachman called down. "Bloody hell, it's the other Romsey coach. Hold tight."

Beth braced herself and the coach rocked violently as they slowed and swerved to avoid the fast-approaching carriage. When they were almost at a complete stop, Leopold vaulted out the door to hurled abuse at the coachman. "Damnation. Are you trying to get us all killed?"

The other carriage's horses drew level with the window and the sweated beasts blew steam as they snorted in the cool air. She'd never known a Romsey groom to be so shoddy with the beasts. Charles Allen would be livid when he found out.

"Carrying important cargo, sir," the other coachman yelled back. "Thought it important to return to Romsey quick-smart."

Men on horseback circled the carriage and when she glanced up, Mr. Allen and his sons were grinning at her happily. They tipped their hats and kicked their horses toward Romsey, leaving them behind in their dust.

Tobias poked his head out the door and then began to chuckle to himself as he stepped out, too.

"Tobias, do share the joke," Blythe huffed.

After a moment, he held out his hand to Beth. "You're not going to believe your luck. Come and see what the important cargo is."

Chapter Twenty-Seven

———•———

Oliver's pulse settled to an easy rhythm as Beth emerged from the Romsey carriage with Tobias's assistance. She sobbed when she saw her son. George ran to her, wrapping himself tightly about her as if he'd never let her go. Oliver smiled as the happy pair clung to each other in joy. He would have been content to view their affection all day, but after a time he grew aware that Leopold was glaring at him.

"How did you come to have George Turner?" he demanded. "And why the hell are you not already on your ship?"

How indeed? He'd been mulling over that very circumstance on the return trip and was no closer to a logical answer. First the wind had prevented him from sailing that morning, turning him back the way he had come, and then their carriage had been stopped on the road. Maybe Eamon had been right. Maybe he was not meant to leave after all. "Fate showed me another path."

Leopold's eyes narrowed. "Fate did?"

"That, and an overturned cart blocking our way." Eamon grinned, rubbing his hands as he warmed to the tale. "Oliver's got damn sharp eyes and saw young George being pulled into a seedy tavern and his mother was not with him. Had a little chat with Beth's brother-in-law and came to a satisfactory agreement."

"Eamon," Leopold groaned, scolding for the implied outcome.

His friend held up his hands. "None of the negations were my doing."

"It was Oliver," George piped up. "He made Uncle Henry give me up."

Beth hugged George to her again and then knelt to examine his bruised face. Her brow creased in concern and Oliver wanted nothing more than to reassure her that there would be no lasting harm.

Leopold's frown grew. "How exactly did you do change his mind? Did you bribe him with your funds for the trip?"

Oliver had thought little of his lost funds or his trip since his first sighting of George being dragged into the inn. He really should have alerted the captain that they wouldn't be joining him for the trip, but getting the boy back to his mother was much more important than any travel plans. "The patrons of the inn where George was being held were very appreciative of my contribution," Oliver murmured eventually. "But Henry Turner will not show his face again."

When Leopold continued to stare, Eamon drew him aside but spoke loud enough to be heard by all. "If I can make a suggestion, sir, it's not in anyone's best interests to make him angry again. You won't like it. Trust me on this."

"Oliver." Leopold spun around, ignoring Eamon's warning. "What the devil did you do? You didn't murder Turner, did you?"

George started to giggle. "He made him soil his trousers in front of everyone."

"Oliver," Elizabeth chided. "That wasn't very nice."

Now that she had noticed him, Oliver strolled toward her. His hands itched to touch her skin and never let her go. "He wasn't a very nice man to begin with. Never did like him and even more so when I saw what he'd done to you and George. We returned as fast as we could."

"Thank you. I'm forever in your debt for rescuing my son."

He touched her cheek gently. "There is no debt between us to be repaid. It was my pleasure."

Elizabeth's frown grew as she drew back. "Your trip?"

"Will still be there when I want to go." He gestured to his carriage, hoping she would travel with him so they might talk privately. "Shall we return to Romsey?"

"You're coming home with us?" Beth appeared shocked. "Surely there is another ship that might take you another day.

There's money in our carriage should you require reimbursement. I'm sure your brother will repay you for the inconvenience we've caused and I can repay him later when I can."

"There's no inconvenience involved." He smiled, a little puzzled that she did not appear keen to have him go home with them. "It's not money I need."

Her skin pinked and she took a further step back, increasing the distance so he'd either have to shout or follow. "Thank you for returning George to me."

George squawked a protest as he was pulled away to the other carriage. Oliver followed Elizabeth's retreat in confusion. What had he said wrong this time?

Eamon clapped him on the shoulder. "Remember what you said you'd do before. Let her go for now."

Although he didn't want to, he had little choice but to return to his carriage without the two people that mattered most to him. He sat in glum silence as the carriage got underway. Because they faced the right direction, their carriage went first, but he called out to the driver to wait and allow the other to lead the way. At least this way he would know exactly where they were and occasionally catch sight of their carriage at any curve in the road.

They rattled through Romsey's gates hours later and drew up before the house, which was cloaked in darkness. Oliver was quick to get out but was too late. Elizabeth had already disappeared inside the abbey, taking with George with her.

Leopold stepped up to his side. "I'd like a word with you in private."

"It can wait." He stepped away but Leopold's hand clamped onto his arm and held him back.

"I don't believe it can. Now. In the study."

Tobias drew closer and frowned at their elder brother. "It really is none of our business, Leopold."

"You stay out of it." Leopold gestured for Oliver to precede him and, sensing the inevitability of the discussion, Oliver walked toward the duke's study, disappointment clouding his mind. He'd deal with whatever was on Leopold's agenda and then find Elizabeth and George and make plans for them all.

He moved into the quiet room and stood waiting.

Leopold wasted no time. "You seduced her and left her. How

dare you, sir! I brought her here—my friend's widow—to make her life better, not to become your plaything. Have you no conscience, no sense of duty to her or your family? Imagine my surprise to learn that you've been sniffing round her skirts while my back was turned."

"It would have been far more disrespectful to Elizabeth to have made love to her where you could see," he pointed out.

"So you do not deny that you seduced her."

A smile tugged at Oliver's lips. "You make it sound as if I imposed on her."

Leopold deflated quickly. "Well, didn't you?"

"Of course not. We discussed the matter in detail beforehand and she was well aware of my plans to leave. I was careful not to get her with child. Not that this is any of your concern. If I remember correctly, you bedded a married woman and got a child on her and didn't even know her name. Elizabeth is a widow. Our affair hurt no one."

"It hurt her."

Oliver frowned. "In light of my reception today, I think you may be exaggerating. It is clear that she's not happy to see me again. Perhaps I should resume my journey without delay after all."

"No, you won't," Tobias's voice cut in from the doorway. "You didn't see her face yesterday after you left. A sorrier sight I've never seen. She missed you terribly and you've only been gone a day."

Hope filled him slowly and he met his younger brother's stare directly. "Then I'll stay and try to convince her."

"To do what?" Leopold cut in. "To lose what little is left of her pride after you abandoned her? There is not one servant in this house that doesn't know by now that she was your lover."

"The gossip will die down in time without additional reason to flourish." Oliver nodded as he rearranged his plans for the future to accommodate Elizabeth's understandably troubled emotional state. "Eamon reminded me that she might need time after the scare of George's abduction and I'll give her that."

Leopold's fists clenched at his sides. "So you are not going to be a gentleman and march upstairs and propose a marriage between you to restore her reputation?"

Oliver imagined such a request voiced at this point and saw the likely conclusion wasn't in his favor. "No," he said firmly. When Leopold's face grew red he added, "Not yet."

Leopold shook his head. "I will never understand you. Don't you care about her even a little?"

"I care about her enough to put her first. She will want to spend time with George and until she is calm again and secure in the knowledge that Henry will not return to steal him away, she will never leave George's side long enough for me to voice a proper proposal."

Leopold snorted, a grudging agreement that his assessment wasn't wrong.

Oliver rubbed his eyes as weariness tugged at his senses. "I will behave as I have always done and attend to George's lessons. He has much to learn of languages before we travel to the continent."

"You're still going?"

Oliver nodded. "The boy has already expressed a wish to go and I am not against the idea. Elizabeth will warm to my ideas eventually."

"It could take a while," Tobias cautioned with a laugh.

Oliver shrugged. "The coliseum isn't going anywhere. And while I wait for Elizabeth to be at ease, I can begin to write a history of Romsey. The boy is pestering me to write one and I've decided it's a good idea."

Leopold's eyes narrowed. "Will you include the location of the sanctuary and the true entrance to it?"

Oliver smiled tightly. "What's to tell? It doesn't exist anymore."

The door swung wide and the duchess flew into the room. "I just heard the news." She pulled Oliver into a tight embrace and hugged him. "Thank God for you, Oliver. I've been so worried. We could have lost George forever to that dreadful man."

Oliver greeted her and then glanced over her head, disappointed to see she was alone. "Where is he now?"

"He's with my son. Beth is there, too, if that is what you're really asking. Would you care to join us?"

He shook his head. "They'll both enjoy the young duke's company far more without me. I'll see them again later, perhaps."

He would see them only if Elizabeth wanted them to see him.

For all he knew, she might very well remain behind locked doors forever. He sighed, wishing her chambers were closer to his. If she was truly worried, the east wing had excellent locks now they had been repaired.

The duchess peered up at him. "How long are you staying? At least until the wedding?"

The eager expression on her face made him laugh out loud. "Perhaps a bit longer than that."

She beamed. "We're going to have a grand family dinner shortly to honor your timely rescue of George. As the guest of honor, you are expected to attend and not be at all tardy."

He grinned down at the woman determined to remake the pattern for all future duchesses of Romsey. "I'll be early if you like."

She spread her fingers over her chest as if in shock, grinned, and then swept from the room with a happy giggle. Oliver shook his head. Who'd have thought he'd find the antics of the Duchess of Romsey amusing?

Tobias approached and set his hands to Oliver's back, giving him a none-too-gentle shove toward the door. "The dining room, if you've forgotten, is this way. Move along, I'm starving."

As soon as Elizabeth stepped into the dining room, he became aware of her tension. She wouldn't look at him and, determined not to make her uncomfortable, he tried to avoid her as well. But it was difficult to be indifferent. The duchess placed him directly across the table where he could see but not touch the woman he wanted.

When Elizabeth spoke softly to her son, he listened, blocking out everything else being said until Eamon, whom the duchess insisted joined them before he resumed his duties tomorrow, began to speak of the rescue. Eamon had those gathered hanging on his every word. "Our Ollie was like the hand of God in his vengeance. A poor pickpocket almost had his hand severed for standing in his way."

"Hardly pricked his skin," Oliver corrected.

Eamon ignored his interruption and continued, embellishing expansively until they'd faced a whole roomful of cutthroats instead of just Henry Turner and one associate. Only he and George exchanged speaking glances that told of their amusement at the scale of the story. The only good that came from Eamon's was that Oliver was spared the need to talk. He never liked to boast and Eamon was enjoying the task immensely.

Without the pressure to be agreeable for the present, he spent his time considering what his new future might entail. More of this, certainly. Elizabeth enjoyed dinner conversation. He would do his best to make her happy and be on time for meals.

Eamon emptied his glass and leaned his elbow onto the table. "Of course, what set Oliver into a rage were the slights Turner made against Beth. Turner almost lost an eye. I've never seen anyone as angry as Oliver was then."

When Elizabeth looked embarrassed, Oliver intervened. "Eamon, that's enough."

"It's what you whispered to Turner that really saved the day."

The duchess, who'd been goading Eamon to divulge his wild tales, sat forward. "What did he say next?"

Oliver met Eamon's gaze and shook his head. That remark had to remain private and unsaid. Eamon merely grinned but Oliver picked up his butter knife and twisted it so Eamon couldn't misunderstand him.

"I forget the whole of it now," he mumbled and then he raised his glass high. "To George Turner, a fellow with a bright future ahead of him, right here in England."

"To George," they all intoned and then started chatting animatedly once more.

Oliver looked across the table to where Elizabeth and George sat, his chest tightening with familiar longing. Rather than remain where Elizabeth would be made nervous by his presence, he excused himself as soon as he could politely do so and returned to his apartment. A cheery fire greeted him, his trunks emptied and gone.

He collapsed onto the couch, set his hands behind his head, and stared up at the molded ceiling. The duchess's wedding was set for next week. The house would be besieged days before then. He'd have to wait at least that long before he could approach Elizabeth or even have her in his bed again.

He closed his eyes, contentment filling him. He was a patient man and Elizabeth was surely worth the boredom of any wait.

Chapter Twenty-Eight

A few days later...

Beth folded her day gown across a chair and let out a sigh. The whispers and twitters as she passed were slowly abating and life was settling down to normal. Mercy had refused to return her to the position of housekeeper as the upstairs maid Annie had been advanced and was thriving in the position. The abbey was running as smoothly as it could before a wedding and she wasn't needed for much beyond offering a little help for that.

She'd spent the last few days with Blythe and had let down her guard and told her about Oliver. Much to her surprise, Blythe wasn't concerned by her lack of virtue, claiming that she understood completely the allure of the Randall men. They'd also talked of their children, the ones lost to illness, and the countess had confessed she was terrified of losing another child. Beth had done her best to comfort her and had urged her to confide her fears to Tobias. She understood her feelings on the matter very well. Beth still ached for her daughter and lost son.

But she still had George to coddle and protect, which was why she had requested all the keys to her son's room be left with her. She didn't feel confident yet that Henry wouldn't return, although Oliver promised he was long gone. George was still Henry's heir. At night, she had very little to do beside read before the fire and try not to jump at every little sound.

"Are you going to bed soon?" George asked from the doorway to his room, book clutched in his hand as one often was.

Beth drew her robe tighter about her shoulders, took her customary place before the fire, and patted the cushion next to her. "I thought I would read first like you. Come sit with me."

Instead of coming closer, George inched toward the door. "It's too difficult. I need help with it."

Beth frowned and glanced at the small mantel clock. It was too late for him to be roaming the halls in his nightshirt. "Then read something else."

George shuffled to her bedroom door, hand fiddling with the latch. "I'll ask Oliver."

The next instant he was out the door before she could say not to go. Beth called out and rushed to the doorway, but only caught a fleeting glimpse of him as he disappeared around a corner. Cursing under her breath, she hesitated to follow. He hadn't liked the restrictions she'd placed on his movements. He was not to be alone and he was to go to bed well before she turned in. She had also asked him not to spend all his time with Oliver.

Since Oliver's return, she'd been avoiding him except at mealtimes when she couldn't and she retired early most nights, taking George with her. They had not spoken since the day he returned her son. She had not gone to him at night and he had stayed away from her bed too.

The truth was, she was waiting for him to announce he was leaving again and desperately hoping her heart wouldn't break when he did. Essential to her happiness was not to think kindly toward him at all. He didn't want her beyond the thrill of sex. They had no future together besides scandalizing the district. It was better not to take up where they had left off.

When she judged enough time had passed to get his answers and George hadn't returned of his own accord, she started to worry. Had he run into trouble and needed her? Should she make sure he had reached Oliver's rooms, after all?

She drew a deep breath, swiftly redressed into a day gown, and then hurried along the now-darkened passageways until she came to the open door of Oliver's apartment. Heart racing, she eased closer, listening to the low rumble of conversation as Oliver patiently explained the essentials of flower propagation to her son.

"Come in, Elizabeth," Oliver called. "We'll be done in a moment."

When she stepped into the room, she gasped at the mess Oliver had made of the fine chamber. It wasn't necessary to have this many books open at once. It looked as if he'd done nothing but read since his return a week ago. When she lifted her gaze, her heart tumbled erratically. Oliver was watching her, his lips turned up, his eyes alight with pleasure. She rubbed her damp palms over her dress. "Have the maids been here at all since you've come back?"

Oliver shrugged, lowering his gaze as his lips turned down. "They come to the doorway and take away the dirty dishes, but they cannot clean without moving things. It's intolerable and I sent them away."

Elizabeth scowled at him. "Terrifying the servants again?"

He ruffled George's hair before he turned to the fire and took a seat close to it. He sprawled in a chair and studied her. "Eamon's wild recounting of events in Portsmouth has made them even more skittish. It cannot be helped, so I choose to stay here, out of the way."

Beth glanced at her son. He appeared to be engrossed in his book, but then he snuck a peek at her as if he was listening to every word they spoke. She moved toward Oliver. "Is none of it true then?"

Oliver's lips pursed as if he was deciding how much to reveal. She would rather have the whole of it now and from him than Eamon's gross exaggerations. She sat across from him and leaned forward. "The truth, if you please."

"I would have killed him if harm had come to you." A brief grimace flickered across his face. "I had my hands about his throat, a short blade below his eye, and if I had not believed you safe I would have gutted him on that table."

Beth rocked back in her chair, astonished by the heat in his words. He was usually the most temperate of men. He never raged in anger. He never leaped about when excited by new events. Anger was not part of his usual dispassionate nature.

"You forgot to mention leaving his body for the fishes in the harbor," George called out. Oliver's eyes never faltered as he watched her. Given his lack of response to George, he had in fact threatened that very thing.

Beth was struck by his calmness, as if he'd been expecting her to come to him. She licked her lips and his gaze wavered slightly, a small smile lifting the corner of his mouth as his eyes dipped a fraction. When he smiled, he became another person entirely. Someone Beth wanted very much to be near, but they were not alone. She looked away to George as heat filled her cheeks. But George had disappeared. She stood and looked about for him.

"He's taken his book into the other room so we might talk privately," Oliver said softly. "What else do you want to know?"

Beth's heart began to thud. The hints that Eamon had made that there was a definite reason Henry wouldn't return pricked her mind. She licked her lips, suddenly nervous of what argument Oliver could have made. But she had wanted the truth and Oliver would give it to her if she asked. "You say Henry won't be back and your threats of causing him physical harm did sound convincing, but at dinner Eamon hinted something else. A conversation you don't want anyone else to know about. What was it that convinced Henry to give George to you?"

"You are correct. It wasn't what I threatened," he said softly. "I told Turner that George was my son. That's why he won't be back. He would never let his money fall to a child who was not of his blood."

When Elizabeth raised a hand to her mouth, utterly shocked by his confession, Oliver worried even more for his plans for the future. He wasn't the least bit ashamed of himself for doing what he judged as necessary. There had been no other way to convince the man.

Her hand lowered, revealing trembling lips he longed to kiss. "But that's a lie. How could you say such a thing? How could he believe you?"

"Because my anger, coupled with George's bookish nature, gave him all the proof he required to believe me." Oliver shook his head. "It's done. There's only a slim chance George will not be cut off from inheriting Turner's property when he dies, but it seemed the best and only acceptable outcome."

When Elizabeth pressed her hands to her face, Oliver shifted to her side. She had suffered because of their affair and wouldn't thank him at first for his decision. At the time, there hadn't been any other options available to him that would guarantee Henry Turner's immediate compliance. He'd had to let Turner believe the worst or he wouldn't have gone away. Any bribe would be followed by another demand when the money ran out.

Instead of giving Elizabeth space to rally her thoughts and become angry with him, Oliver picked up her hand. "It's for the best, really," he said quickly. "George has little interest in America and you didn't want to go there, either."

Her gaze dipped to their joined hands as she slipped free of his grip. "That's not for you to say."

As conversations went, this was not turning out the way he hoped. He edged closer. "I missed you."

Elizabeth stilled. "You were gone but a day and a night."

"An eternity." He swallowed as nervousness, a rare feeling for him, rushed through him unabated. "But I have also missed speaking to you these past few days, too. You're angry and avoiding me. I've heard the whispers about us."

"Hardly whispers when your brother practically shouted it loud enough to be heard in London. But I'm angry with myself, not you." She drew in a deep, weary breath. "I knew the risks to my reputation and behaved foolishly."

Oliver quickly recaptured her hand. "Not so foolishly when you consider the circumstances."

She faced him at last, her eyes narrowing. "What circumstances do you think excuses such a lapse in judgment?"

"I have noticed that when one is in love, there is nothing one won't do to be near that person."

She drew back as if he'd insulted her. "You make me out to have no willpower?"

"I wasn't speaking of you." He turned her hand over and traced the faint lines on her palm. Then he drew the ribbon he carried from his pocket and returned it to her keeping. "You dropped this."

She frowned at it. "This isn't mine."

"Yes, it is." Oliver closed her slack fingers over the ribbon. "But it took me twelve years to deliver it back and I apologize for my tardiness."

Her eyes widened.

"Elizabeth, before another moment passes there is something I should confess." He lifted her hand and kissed it. "I love you. I have admired you for a very long time and never understood how deeply. I was young and foolish and thought I had all the time in the world. When Turner began to court you and you accepted his offer of marriage, I thought I had misunderstood what love was. I turned to my studies and then the duke sent me away."

Her hand turned in his, their fingers linking together tightly, the ribbon pressed against his skin again. "I was so afraid for you," she whispered. "No one dared ask where you all were."

He covered her hand with his. "When I was locked away, I consoled myself that fate had chosen a safer path for you. If you had become my wife and not married Turner, you could have been harmed in the duke's quest to wipe my family from the face of the earth. I prayed the duke would overlook that you'd been a friend of my sister and mother and that as Turner's wife you would remain free."

Her other hand covered his as tears spilled down her cheeks. Oliver quickly wiped them away, his heart full of love for her and her precious emotions. "I've been alone all my life, Elizabeth, either by design or the absence of choice. I don't wish to remain in one place forever, but I don't wish to be without you. The world is a very large place and I cannot bear to be so far away from you ever again."

Her eyes closed, blocking his view of her expression.

"I think you ought to marry me and when George is a little older we should travel the world together."

Her throat moved as she swallowed. "And if I do not wish to travel beyond England?"

He had always believed that he was alone in his desire for adventure. If she didn't want to share in his dreams then there could be strife between them in the future. He didn't want that. He couldn't bear to lose now what he'd searched his whole life to find. "Then loving you will be the greatest adventure of my life. Do you think you could put up with me that long? I will likely say and do all the wrong things and make you angry. I'm blunt and the niceties of social discourse quite often bore me.

"I offer myself to you, Elizabeth. To be your husband and

friend, though little good it will do you. Let me love you all the days of my life and protect and treasure every one of your scowls."

"Well, it certainly will be an adventure." Her gaze grew flinty. "Did you really frighten Henry enough to soil himself in a public tavern?"

"Not one of my finer moments, but I had quite enough experience with madmen to pull it off convincingly." He dug into his pocket and pulled out the other matter that he wanted to discuss with her. "While I have you alone, I need your advice. Do you recognize this?"

He opened his hand to reveal the jade brooch once belonging to his sister.

"Oh no." Elizabeth took the brooch from his palm and held it, her thumbs sliding over the glossy, deep green stones. "This belonged to Rosemary. Where did you find it?"

"In the duke's sanctuary," he admitted without a shred of hesitation at revealing the truth. A weight came off his shoulders with his confession. If he truly loved her, then there shouldn't be secrets between them. "Should I tell my brothers I found it and where?"

Elizabeth leaned against him. "This isn't proof that she's dead. Only that she was being held for a time. Rose was strong and the most devious young woman I knew. Don't tell them. Let them hope a little longer that she'll be found safe and sound."

Oliver took the piece back and tucked it out of sight in his pocket. He would do what Elizabeth suggested. He would continue as caretaker of the secrets of Romsey Abbey, guarding the spoils until the young duke came of age.

He gathered Elizabeth in his arms and held her tightly, ready and willing to do so for the rest of his life. "I'm trying to be patient but I fear our time alone is short and that George will return to us soon. What must I do to convince you?"

Elizabeth looked up at him, hand rising to cup his face. "I'm already convinced."

Oliver lowered his head and brushed his lips against Elizabeth's, his heart beating faster with each tender kiss. With George in the other room, he couldn't become carried away, so he kept his kisses light rather than show the hunger she caused to burn in him. Eventually he released her, content to simply be by her side. He had found exactly where he belonged and never doubted for a moment that he would enjoy the adventure of love.

A movement beyond her shoulder drew his attention and he turned his head slightly to see his accomplice. Elizabeth's son danced a merry jig, smiled widely, and then ducked back inside his new bedchamber before his mother could realize George had played a large part in bringing her here tonight so Oliver could propose.

Epilogue

Beth fitted a diamond choker around Blythe's throat and stepped back to see the full effect of her wedding attire. "Perfection. Tobias is the luckiest man today."

Mercy, seated across the room at a similar dressing table, cleared her throat loudly.

Beth rushed to the other side of the room and set her hands to the duchess's shoulders. "So is Leopold, I promise." She giggled at the expression on Mercy's face and checked that the diamond-tipped pins in the duchess's dark hair were secure still. "They are both very fortunate to have such lovely women agree to put up with them."

Mercy caught her hand and squeezed. "Can you believe I'm nervous?"

"I am too," Blythe agreed as she joined them.

Beth glanced between them. "What is there to be nervous about? It's obvious they love you and would do anything you ask of them."

Someone tapped at the door and Beth hurried to intercept the messenger, only opening the door a small amount. "Is it time?"

"The vicar is waiting, the guests are gathered in the drawing room, drinking anything that's given them," Murphy warned with a wink as he passed two bunches of freshly cut flowers through the gap. "The brides' grooms are no worse for the drink consumed last night in celebration and are practically a wreck of nerves and impatience. In short, there's much to laugh over today."

"You're enjoying their discomfort far too much, Mr. Murphy," Beth said, but was delighted by the events of the day. She juggled the flowers into one arm and wagged her finger at him. "If you are not careful to hide it, they will get their revenge when it's your turn."

He peered over her head, trying to see the ladies waiting behind her. Beth quickly set her foot behind the door to keep his curiosity from being satisfied. Murphy's expression grew sly and then he laughed. "You first. When Her Grace and the countess are ready we await them downstairs."

He departed and Beth faced her friends. "It's time."

The sisters exchanged nervous glances and then together they each took a bunch of flowers. Beth followed behind her friends as they strolled down the deserted hallways of Romsey Abbey toward their wedding, happy as never before. She had always loved attending weddings and this one was special because she'd been allowed to share in the preparations.

At the foot of the stairs, Beth left them to enter the drawing room alone and took a place to the left of the vicar. She scanned the heads before her and saw no strangers in their midst. Disappointment filled her that the duchess's and countess's brother had not arrived at the last minute.

Beth slid into the vacant space beside George and waited for the ceremony to begin. Mercy and Blythe appeared at the doorway and paced into the room at a leisurely speed, attention fixed on the two Randall men waiting for them.

As the service got underway, her glance was drawn to Oliver. He had not pushed her to set a date or even announce that they would marry. In the days after his proposal, she'd been grateful because this wedding had consumed her every spare moment. Yet now that Leopold would have Mercy and Tobias would marry Blythe, impatience to be with Oliver surfaced. They couldn't marry until the banns were called and that would mean four more weeks of separation.

At long last the brides were married to their grooms and the guests began to crowd the newlyweds and chatter between themselves. George excused himself from her side as she waited her turn to congratulate each new couple, smiling happy tears at their joy. "You kept your title in the end, Your Grace."

Mercy shook her head. "I didn't want to, but as you know my husband is stubborn and insisted it should be kept for Edwin's benefit. Any correspondence I send will be cumbersome."

Leopold laughed. "It will be worth it, Your Grace. Trust me."

"Oh, I do trust you." Mercy's hand cupped her new husband's face. "From the moment we met I have known exactly how true your heart was."

They stared into each other's eyes and Beth quickly decided to leave them to their own devices. She excused herself and turned to the other newly married couple and embraced Blythe. "Mrs. Randall, so pleased to meet you."

The former countess grinned impishly as she hung on her husband's arm. "Thank you, Beth. I'm so happy."

Her eyes filled with tears and Beth dug for a lacy handkerchief to offer the lady before she ruined her complexion.

Her husband leaned forward. "How long do we have to mingle?"

"As long as your wife requires," Beth teased. Tobias hadn't been too comfortable around most of the exalted guests invited for the wedding in the past few days, but for Blythe's sake he'd kept his boredom from showing until now. "You have the wedding breakfast and toasts to sit through next and then..."

Beth left the rest unsaid. Once the newly married couples had departed the breakfast, the guests would amuse themselves until their departure. Careful planning meant that everything was arranged in advance and Beth had nothing further to do today.

She scanned the room and then heaved a sigh when she couldn't find the man she wanted. Oliver had been even less inclined to talk to the guests than Tobias and had already disappeared. At least she knew where he'd probably be. He'll have taken George to the library to continue his study of languages.

Oliver hurried George into Romsey's long gallery where the wedding breakfast was being held. He slid into his place beside Elizabeth as George took the other, just in time to hear a guest propose a toast to the couples' happiness and contentment.

Judging by the dreamy smile that played over the duchess's

face that contentment would only increase in the next few months' time when she announced that she carried Leopold's child.

When Elizabeth put her glass down, she turned to him. "Where were you?"

"It's a surprise for later," Oliver said with a wink. It had taken him and George little time to make their preparations for their first adventure. After careful consideration, he wasn't giving Elizabeth a chance to change her mind.

He suffered through the small talk expected when dining with strangers, keeping one eye on the brides and grooms. First Tobias and Blythe disappeared from sight and then Leopold, on seeing their younger brother had already absconded with his bride, grabbed the duchess's hand and lured her away from her friends.

Oliver bowed his head as he laughed at his brothers' hurry to get their brides alone. He was feeling a similar inclination for privacy with Elizabeth, although he had to wait some hours for that likelihood. When Beth appeared restless, he helped her stand and gave the signal, a nod to George, for him to leave via the side door.

When Elizabeth looked about for her son a little anxiously, Oliver held out his arm. "He's this way, my angel."

A pretty blush swept over her cheeks and she allowed him to draw her to the entrance hall. Eamon waited with his and Elizabeth's cloaks draped over his arm. "Carriage is ready and waiting, sir."

"Excellent." Oliver slipped into his topcoat. "You know what to do?"

"Of course." Eamon snapped out the cloak and covered Elizabeth's shoulders. "Best slip this on, Mrs. Turner. A light snow is falling and we don't want you catching a chill."

"Oliver?" Her eyes narrowed dangerously. "What are you up to?"

Oliver caught her hand in his and squeezed. "Leopold and Mercy are likely to be in each other's pockets as soon as the guests have departed tomorrow. Tobias and Blythe will be at Harrowdale and will hardly want anyone. I thought you and I might undertake our first adventure together. A trip to Scotland, if you agree, to be married as soon as we cross the border."

A deep frown line appeared between her brows. "I don't know. I couldn't leave George behind with a pair of distracted newlyweds. What if you're wrong and Henry comes back?"

Oliver smiled down at her. "Can you not guess what plans I've made?"

She looked about them quickly. "Where's George?"

He tipped his head toward the front doors as Eamon opened them. "Outside. Waiting in the carriage for his mother to hurry up and elope. He's very keen to visit Scotland and I couldn't deprive him of the chance to see his fondest wish for us to be married come true. He's not always a patient boy, apparently. He seems to want to call me papa very much and cannot wait for the banns to be called."

"He'll be as old as us if you two don't get a move on," Eamon grumbled as he held the door open despite the draft.

Oliver glanced out to the carriage and spotted George's face pressed to the glass. Her son gestured for them to hurry up, practically bouncing on the padded benches in his eagerness to be underway.

Beth caught his arm. "I can't leave without saying goodbye."

"Yes, you can. I already told my brothers what I was planning last night and received their full blessing. Now, come along, my angel. The housekeeper has packed everything you could possibly need and we've many days till we reach the border. George suggested a detour into Wales on the return trip, but it depends on you and the weather not being against us."

"You've convinced my son to conspire against me," she said as he handed her into the carriage. "You know I always feared your influence over him and it seems I was right to be wary."

Her words sounded aggrieved, but when he poked his head through the doorway her blue eyes were bright with amusement. She leaned out again to touch his face.

Oliver caught her hand and kissed it. "I have to say, his help has been most appreciated. You should know it was his idea that we elope, not mine."

George rolled his eyes. "He would have waited forever."

When Elizabeth launched herself at her son, tickling him for his part in their conspiracy, Oliver drew back, rather pleased with her easy acceptance of their plans. There'd always been a chance she'd refuse and want to wait for the banns to be called, but bringing George along on the trip to Scotland had eased her mind. Having the boy along was hardly an inconvenience. After all, her child was part of his fate.

He checked the carriage was properly loaded and turned to Romsey's butler. "Should be back in three weeks, four at the outside if the weather is against us." He shook Eamon's hand and then glanced up at the façade of the abbey. The stone work was really quite breathtaking. He should make a note of it in the history he was writing.

Eamon pushed Oliver into the carriage roughly. "Take your time. Enjoy your adventure, Ollie."

Eamon shut the door, stowed the step away, and then called out, "Take 'em away."

"Oh, no," Elizabeth called out. "I have an idea. Wait here."

She scrambled from the carriage without waiting for the step to be lowered again and flew into the abbey, disappearing from sight very quickly. Eamon followed, but when five minutes had passed, Oliver began to be alarmed. As he and George stepped from the carriage again to determine whether they would go or not, Elizabeth emerged, passing a note to Eamon as she came. "Have Leopold send this to the Times and any paper he considers a possibility."

Oliver assisted her into the carriage, puzzled by her smug expression.

Her brow rose. "I realized exactly what we needed to say to bring Rosemary home. I've asked for Leopold to place an announcement of our marriage into the papers. She won't be able to resist returning to discover the truth. It was her fondest wish."

Oliver caught her hand in his. "And mine."

The carriage lurched and George's questions began. They talked and planned and discussed and exclaimed over the sights moving past their window. As he'd predicted, this journey was a lot livelier than his previous trip to Portsmouth with Eamon. Elizabeth joined in on occasion and after a time, he detected her interest in the adventure was growing. He would make sure she was comfortable every step of the way.

A smile pulled at his lips as he held Elizabeth's hand. He and George had agreed that they would behave as a family from the moment they left Romsey. At every stop on the way to Scotland, Oliver planned to introduce Elizabeth as his wife so she would be spared the discomfort of speculation and potential embarrassment at their elopement.

He made himself comfortable for the journey and listened to his new family talk of the wedding that had just occurred and the adventure they were on now. For all his impatience for adventure beyond England's shores, he treasured this moment, a gift he'd waited his whole life to experience. It was good to be traveling in the right direction with the two people he needed most in his life. The spoils of love and friendship seated before him were beyond precious and were his to guard till his dying breath.

Take a peek at the final Wild Randalls novel.

Hunting the Hero

Prologue

The devil chased away the daylight as Constantine urged his horse to take him far from his responsibilities and into the arms of willing debauchery. He thundered down the lane, running away from his guilt and toward the distant manor house outlined by the falling sun.

His heart pounded as it always did when he rode, keeping time with his mount's hooves upon the earthen road beneath them. But it was more than just the thrill of being free that filled him with anticipation. Today he had made a decision. Tonight he hoped to forget. Constantine crested the rise and slowed his horse to a trot as the remote manor house loomed before him. The place had no name but was widely known for its warm welcome. What else could you expect from a bawdy house perched high on a hill?

He swung off his mount as two liveried footman hurried toward him, one intent on his horse, the other upon him. "Your name, sir?"

Constantine experienced a pang of uncertainty, then brushed it aside. "Lord Grayling."

The bewigged footman bowed deferentially. "Welcome to the House, my lord. If you'd be so kind as to come this way, Mrs. Cohen will be only too happy to accommodate your every need this evening."

It wasn't Mrs. Cohen's accommodation Constantine required, but one of the younger courtesans in her employ. Perhaps they could banish the memory of his late wife from his mind, along with his part in her death.

Once inside, the footman took his riding crop, hat, gloves, and caped coat away, leaving him free to stroll about the elegantly appointed lower hall unimpeded. Spartan but elegant. So far the rumors were true. Mrs. Cohen had been much sought after in

London during her youth, but as age had lessened her appeal, she'd retired to the countryside to groom others for men's pleasures. He'd never met her, but the stories of her establishment were legend. They said a man could buy any pleasure for the right price.

Before he'd gone too many steps, an older woman long past the first blush of youth, but still lovely, appeared. "Mrs. Cohen?"

"My Lord Grayling. What an unexpected surprise. Welcome to the House."

Constantine was well prepared for this adventure. He reached into his coat pocket and handed over the expected funds. "A token of my appreciation."

The madam's expression eased into extreme friendliness and another footman appeared with a glass of wine balanced upon a gleaming silver tray. "You must be thirsty from your long ride. I trust your journey was uneventful."

"It was," he assured her, unsurprised that she knew he'd traveled some distance to arrive here. He wouldn't be shocked to learn the woman knew the location of every gentleman of consequence within a fifty-mile radius of her establishment, as well as the state of their pocketbook and their love life. She was in the business of providing a service where it was most needed.

Constantine took the glass and sipped. A remarkably fine vintage filled his mouth and he nodded. "Perfect."

The madam sent the footman away and gestured to an adjacent room. "I think you will find exactly what you require in this direction. Dark or pale, full-figured or slim. The House prides itself on ensuring a gentleman's pleasure."

Constantine nodded. He was tired of spending his nights alone with only his guilt for company. He was weary of mourning the life he had lost.

At the threshold of the saloon—a room soaked in red velvet and supple limbs—he saw the ladies of the night reclined in shimmering, half-undone gowns as they listened to the strains of Bach adequately played by another of their number. A few gentlemen, some with vaguely familiar faces, graced the room, all engaged with willing women perched upon their laps.

The scene was one he had viewed before his marriage but found little pleasure in now. He wasn't one for public spectacles.

Private pleasures were all he desired tonight. It was simply a matter of choosing a face with an appealing body and then losing himself in desire.

He scanned the room, searching for a face and form that would inspire him and satisfy his hunger. A leggy blonde sat alone and unoccupied for the moment. The madam noticed the direction of his gaze and provided her name. "Solange."

A rare jewel. Constantine doubted names held any accuracy in this place. With any luck she'd be willing, pliant, and easy on the senses of a man who'd come for distraction. He'd begin his quest there.

He strolled forward and limpid eyes flowed over him, caressing without touching. A prelude to intimacy to come. Her lips lifted into a smile as she rose to her feet, gliding toward him with smooth steps. When she held out her gloved hand, he kissed the back as if she were a dear friend.

"Welcome," she said, her voice soft and easy on the ears.

Constantine smiled in response. "Grayling."

Her hands touched his arm in a gentle caress, luring him toward her body, attempting to beguile, subtly at first. The smallest whisper of anticipation coursed through him. Perhaps a rare jewel would be enough? Perhaps Solange could provide the pleasure he sought. Yet even as he formed that thought, another filled him. Solange was lovely, but would she provide him with the challenge he craved?

Would she bend to his will completely, allow him to satisfy his needs even if it left her wanting? Would she dare to complain about his selfishness? There was no way to predict the outcome.

What Constantine missed most was the chase of love and passion. The hunt and claiming of victory. He'd had that once, so he knew what he missed and wanted tonight. A woman whose passionate nature could keep pace with his.

Solange leaned close to whisper in his ear. "Shall we sit and listen for a while, my lord?"

Constantine didn't particularly care for the music, but the performance would give him time to consider whether Solange would suit. "Of course."

She grabbed his hand and guided him toward an empty corner settee. Constantine followed her and after he'd sat, allowed her to press another glass of wine into his hand. While he sipped, Solange's nimble fingers stroked the top of his thigh. But the soft touches failed to arouse. That whisper of desire he'd felt at first sight had vanished as if it had never been. Constantine cursed under his breath.

After a short period, Solange turned her attention from the pianist and caught his eye. Her hands glided up his inner thigh to tease him with the promise of later pleasures. As she leaned close to nuzzle his neck above his cravat, he realized nothing had changed. He was no more aroused by her touch than he had been when he'd set off for the brothel that evening. Even when her fingers skimmed his chest and then tangled in his hair, he had no reaction whatsoever. The gentle kisses she bestowed to his jaw were persistent, but not enough to arouse. If he got her to the bedchamber, he feared neither one of them would be happy.

Constantine concentrated on everything else but what she did. Solange's ministrations had not banished his wife far enough into the past to allow him to lose himself in the moment. He wanted to forget he'd loved his wife. He wanted to banish the guilt that haunted him.

He glanced beyond Solange's shoulder to see who else lingered in the room. He'd choose another. Someone he hoped had enough mastery to cure him of his longing for the perfect life he'd lost.

There were three other unattached women in the room, but as he inspected them, they failed to stir him any more than Solange had. Perhaps he should have gone to London when Rothwell had suggested it. A few weeks of debauchery in the company of a trusted friend might have been better than the pleasures afforded by this private country house. It was just his luck that his situation prevented him from visiting the capital just now.

A flutter of pale skirts caught his attention as a slight woman paused in the doorway of the saloon. A slim figure appeared, deep black hair carelessly tumbling around her head as if she'd stumbled from bed and could just as easily return to it. She claimed his complete attention and he couldn't look away from her whiskey-brown eyes. Their eyes held as the plunking of the pianoforte dimmed.

Small limbs, perfect skin, and a smile that wasn't the least sincere.

For a moment he couldn't breathe. Whoever she was, she made no attempt to join them, no attempt to tempt him or any other man in the room. But she had done the impossible with one haughty glance. She had made his pulse riot.

When she moved on, Constantine continued to stare at the vacant space where she'd stood, waiting for her to come back into view. He'd never been so mesmerized by a woman before. The shock of being instantly aroused to the point of pain took a moment to sink in. She was just a slip of a girl really. Barely grown enough to be in a place like this, let alone have that effect on him.

Yet with one glance, an invisible hand had closed around his privates and urged him to follow.

Constantine extricated himself from Solange's clinging grasp, ignoring her huff and pout as he handed her his wine glass and excused himself to get a second, longer look at the dark-haired girl.

The hallway was empty, and as he looked down the hall trying to decide where she might have disappeared to, he cursed his foolishness for chasing after a light-skirt who'd made no effort to attract his attention.

As he took a few steps away from the pianoforte's tapping, he detected voices speaking urgently not too far away. Mrs. Cohen's voice he clearly heard coming from a nearby room, followed by a quieter response from someone else. A door stood ajar and he eased closer to it.

As he neared the doorway, Mrs. Cohen burst out angrily, "What do you mean you're not needed? Tonight is always our busiest night."

Constantine peeked through the gap, noting the dark-haired girl was indeed tiny when compared with the madam of the bawdy house. But she had the courage to stand up against a madam who could very likely throw her out into the cold Wiltshire winter without a moment's hesitation or regret.

The madam glanced over her shoulder and he ducked back out of sight before he was seen. He might be impatient for an introduction so he could dismiss his curiosity soon after, but he was interested in their argument too. It was not every day a man overheard an honest conversation in a place like this.

"I refuse to listen to Mallory's dull playing for one more night," the dark-haired girl muttered in a smooth, sultry voice that belied her tiny appearance. "She hasn't the talent to entertain the whole room and your busiest night is always filled with the same faces."

"Lord Grayling has come and needs to be entertained," Mrs. Cohen answered in a shocked tone.

On hearing his name, Constantine eased close to the door and peeked through the crack again. The dark-haired nymph stood with her back to the fire, rubbing her hands together as if she was chilled through. Judging by the sheer drifts of muslin wrapped about her that revealed the slim curves of her hips, she very well might be.

"If Solange is the sort to tempt him, then I'm sure he will be well satisfied," she said, her tone dripping with contempt. Her shoulder lifted a touch as she dismissed him out of hand. "Lord Squires is always expected at ten. He usually asks for me."

Mrs. Cohen drew closer. "Squires would be nothing compared to Grayling in your bed. If you would but listen to what was said of him you would not be so dismissive. How can you not accept the challenge of stealing him away from Solange?"

The slim woman turned, eyes narrowing in suspicion. "Gossip is seldom accurate and for a madam who should want peaceful relations between her employees, you certainly are stirring the pot of late. Why would you want me to captivate Lord Grayling so well that he sets aside that insipid creature? It's hardly a fair challenge."

Constantine choked. They were discussing him as if he were a prime piece of beef. He clamped his lips together and fought to remain silent.

The madam shrugged. "Solange is getting above herself."

A deep throaty laugh left the smaller woman's throat, forcing Constantine to revise his initial estimate of her as someone young and inexperienced. "And that shall never do," she purred. "Very well. I shall do what I can to lure the handsome lord into my bed just so you may prove your point and give Solange the setdown she deserves." She studied her fingertips by firelight. "I think as a reward I should have another trinket, one for my fingers this time."

"You and your gemstones." Mrs. Cohen wagged an excessively bejeweled finger at the tiny woman. "Only if you succeed, Calista. Only if he is sated and comes back for you another night, then I'll give you half his fee too."

A devilishly wicked smile twisted the dark-haired girl's lips, turning a formerly remarkable face into the most arousing sight he had ever beheld. Those lips and whiskey-brown eyes were so damn expressive. What would she look like as they made love? He adjusted his trousers. Damn woman could even affect him through the crack of the door. Her sudden throaty laugh sent chills racing down his spine. "Oh, I'm sure Lord Grayling's seduction is well in hand. Trust me on this."

"What would I do without you?" Mrs. Cohen murmured, genuine affection softening her voice. "These are powerful men and must be looked after as if they were made of glass."

"Not glass, Linnie. Something much, much warmer." Calista's gaze shifted to the doorway where he hid. Her lips lifted into a cunning smile as if she knew he was there, listening while they planned his seduction. "I've been at this for a long time now and I know what men want. Trust me."

The challenge was boldly made. All men wanted the same thing from a woman, didn't they? No demands but on their body, no conversation save for what they expected in bed. There was no doubt her experiences had made Calista overconfident, too. But his curiosity was roused and he was determined to find out more about her.

Constantine moved until he stood openly in the doorway, nudging the opening wider so he could view the entire room. Before him, Mrs. Cohen towered over the woman called Calista who didn't reach higher than his chest. Constantine was drawn to the stubborn, smug glint in Calista's eyes. They sparkled with the thrill of her dare.

Her gaze dropped to his groin and her lips curved into a satisfied smile. Damn woman. She thought she'd won already. However, he'd show her he could hold his own when it came to pleasure. There was no point pretending he was unaware of her game.

He moved into the room and cleared his throat. "An

introduction, Mrs. Cohen?"

Mrs. Cohen spun about quickly, her manner changing to one of deference. "Lord Grayling. I did not... I was led to believe you were otherwise occupied."

Cohen sent Calista a furious glance. Was the girl in trouble with her employer for failing to inform her that a guest was listening to every word they said? He hoped the punishment would not be too severe. "So I overheard." Constantine smiled winningly at the madam. "However, I believe there is a trinket to be won for a successful seduction. Do you place wagers involving all your patrons? The gentlemen who recommended your establishment will be interested in that tidbit."

Mrs. Cohen pressed her hand to her brow. "No, never."

Calista strutted forward, hands on her hips, haughty glint firmly in place. God, she had nerve. The bold move placed her between him and the bawd as if the larger woman might need her protection. "This was a private conversation, my lord."

"About me."

She shrugged as if the matter were of no importance. "Wagers are placed in any number of places and at any time about many things. Do you take offence to each and every one?"

"I never said I was offended. I just doubt your ability to do as you claim."

Calista's lips pressed together as if she was annoyed by his skepticism regarding her prowess in the bedroom. A wild impulse to laugh at her vexation rose in his chest. This woman did not like her claims to be challenged. That made him all the more determined to spend the night in her bed purely to see the lengths she would go to win her pretty bauble from the madam.

Her eyes narrowed to slits. She might be tiny but perhaps she wasn't as delicate as he'd first thought. Calista was no young miss but a mature woman, one who might have extensive experience in dealing with demanding men. Would she enjoy the challenge of her work, too?

She stepped forward and held out her bare, ringless hand to him. "Calista, my lord."

He took her hand, noting the coldness of her slim fingers as he kissed the back of them. "A pleasure."

He released her hand even while imagining that cold grip

wrapped around his limbs and other parts. How long would it take to warm her until her skin glistened by firelight? He knew several ways to build a heat quickly, and a romp in between the sheets was certainly the most appealing.

"A pleasure, certainly." Calista circled him, her hand sweeping over his bottom in a fleeting caress. He withheld a groan, determined not to betray how deeply she affected him. "Not yet, but soon," she said.

The dark-haired woman raised a brow, as if daring him to disagree with her. For reasons he couldn't fathom, he accepted her silent challenge. It wouldn't be him to cry for mercy at the end of the night. She would be the one asking him for pleasure to cease. He held out his hand. "Very soon."

Amusement twinkled in her eyes and after a moment Calista placed her cold, slender hand in his. "Do you really believe you can handle me, my lord?"

He gripped her tightly, feeling the bones of her hand shift within his. He relaxed his grip but didn't dare let her go. "Oh, yes. I do."

About Heather Boyd

Determined to escape the Aussie sun on a scorching camping holiday, Heather picked up a pen and notebook from a corner store and started writing her very first novel—Chills. Eight years later, she is the author of over thirty romances and publisher of several anthologies too. Addicted to all things tech (never again will Heather write a novel longhand) and fascinated by English society of the early 1800's, Heather spends her days getting her characters in and out of trouble and into bed together (if they make it that far). She lives on the edge of beautiful Lake Macquarie, Australia with her trio of mischievous rogues (husband and two sons) along with one rescued cat whose only interest in her career is that it provides him with food on demand.

You can find details of her work and writing at
www.Heather-Boyd.com